Monster Allergy 3

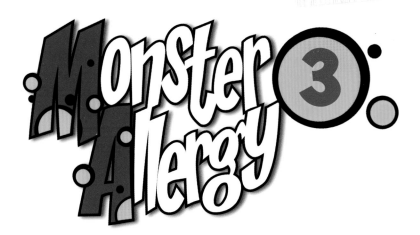

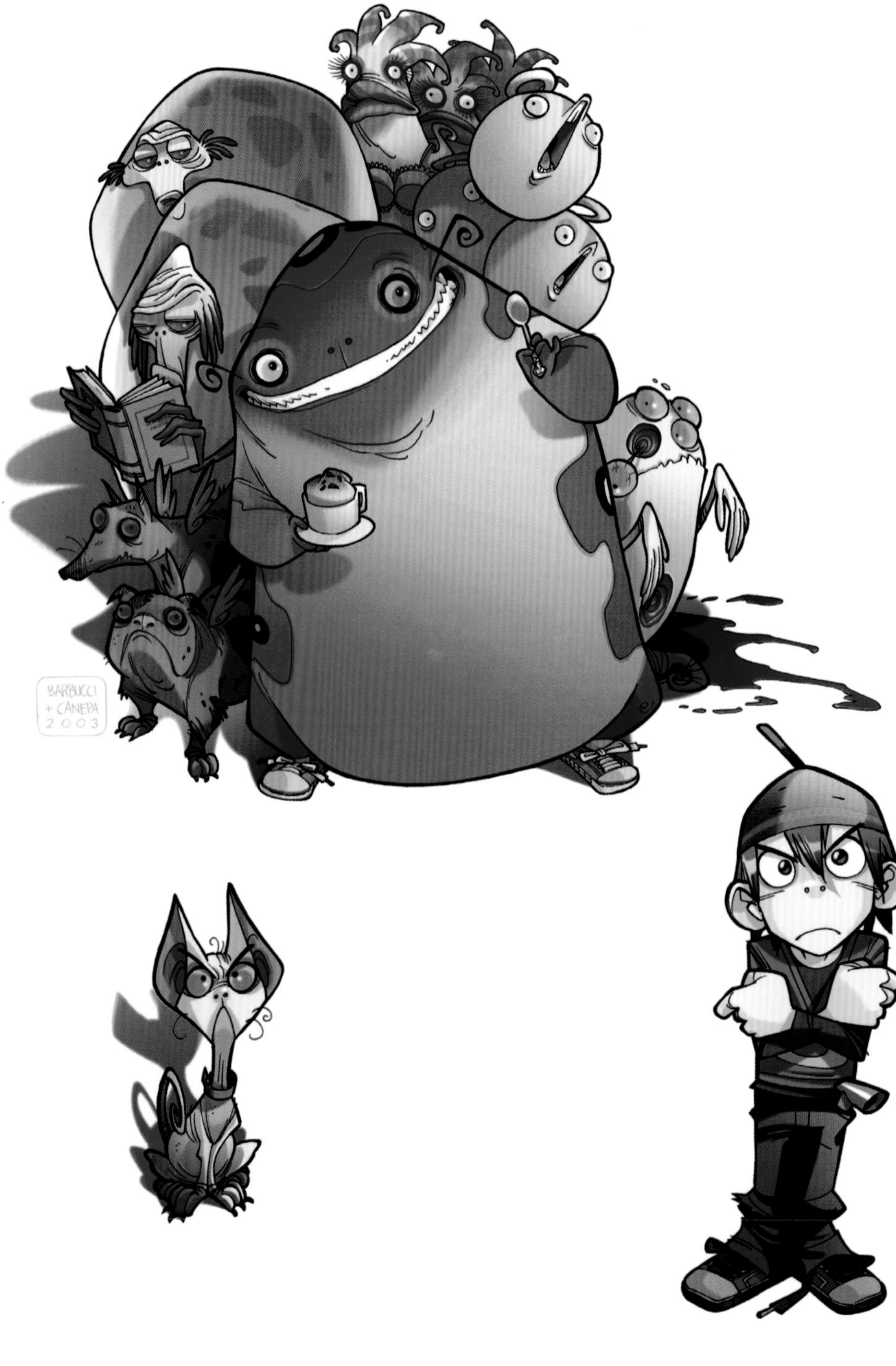
BARBUCCI
+ CANEPA
2003

Monster Allergy 3

The Stellar Tutor

INSIGHT COMICS

San Rafael • Los Angeles • London

PART 1 THE STELLAR TUTOR

Plot: Katja Centomo
Script: Bruno Enna
Script Supervisor: Francesco Artibani
Pencils: Antonello Dalena
Inks: Cristina Giorgilli and Raffaella Seccia
Design Supervisor: Alessandro Barbucci
Colors: Cecilia Giumento
Color Supervisor: Barbara Canepa

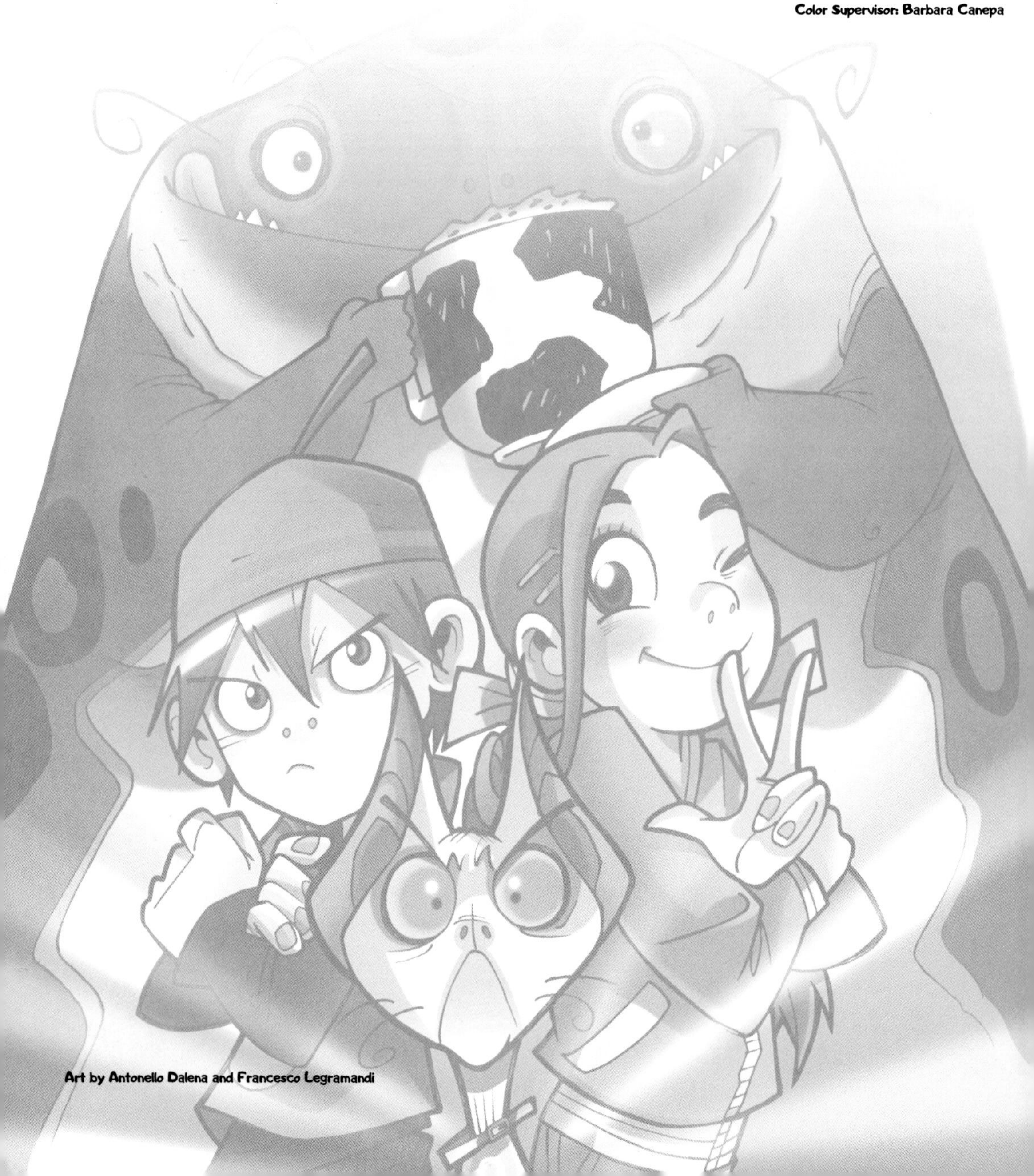

Art by Antonello Dalena and Francesco Legramandi

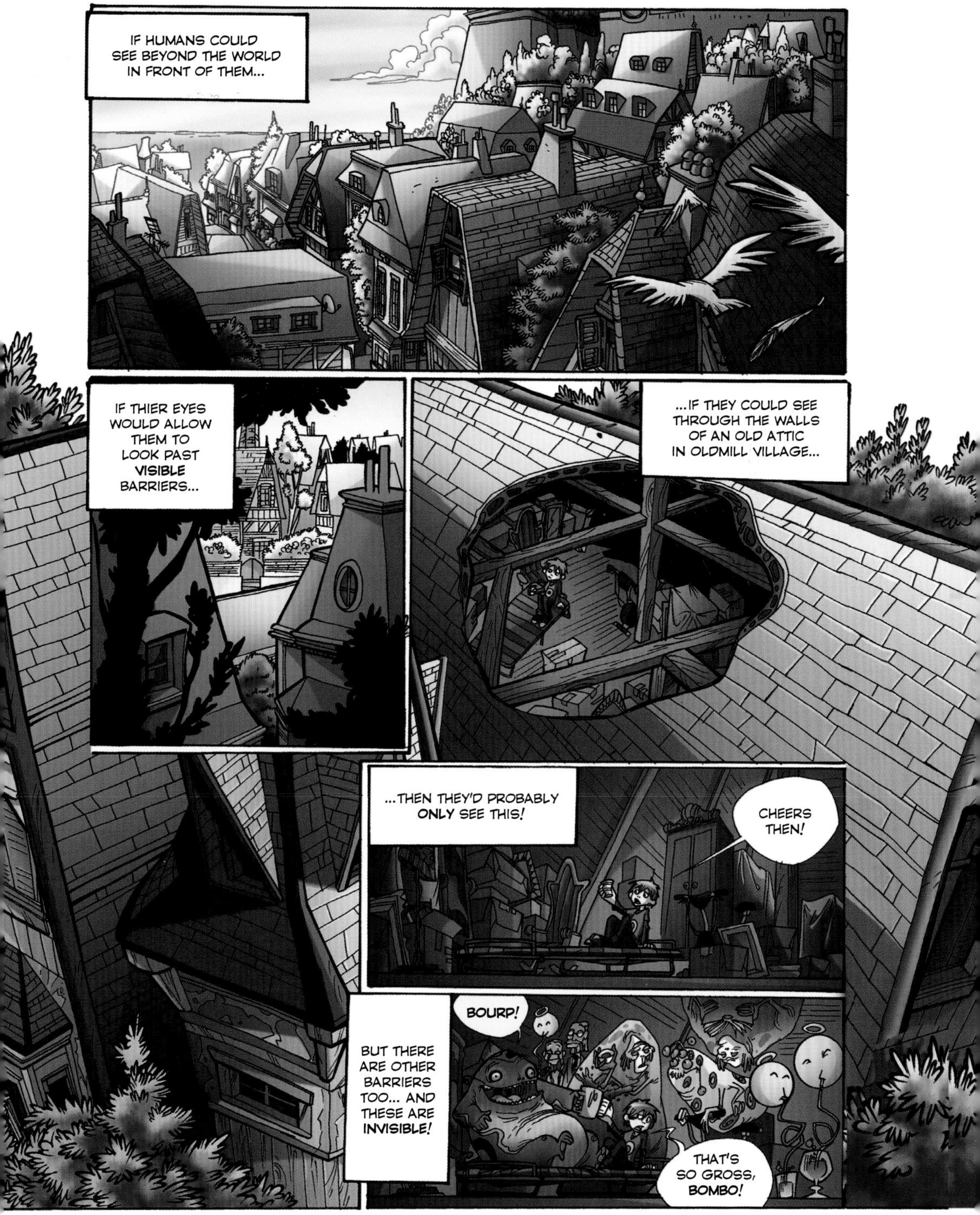
IF HUMANS COULD SEE BEYOND THE WORLD IN FRONT OF THEM...
IF THIER EYES WOULD ALLOW THEM TO LOOK PAST **VISIBLE** BARRIERS...
...IF THEY COULD SEE THROUGH THE WALLS OF AN OLD ATTIC IN OLDMILL VILLAGE...
...THEN THEY'D PROBABLY **ONLY** SEE THIS!
CHEERS THEN!
BUT THERE ARE OTHER BARRIERS TOO... AND THESE ARE **INVISIBLE**!
BOURP!
THAT'S SO GROSS, **BOMBO**!

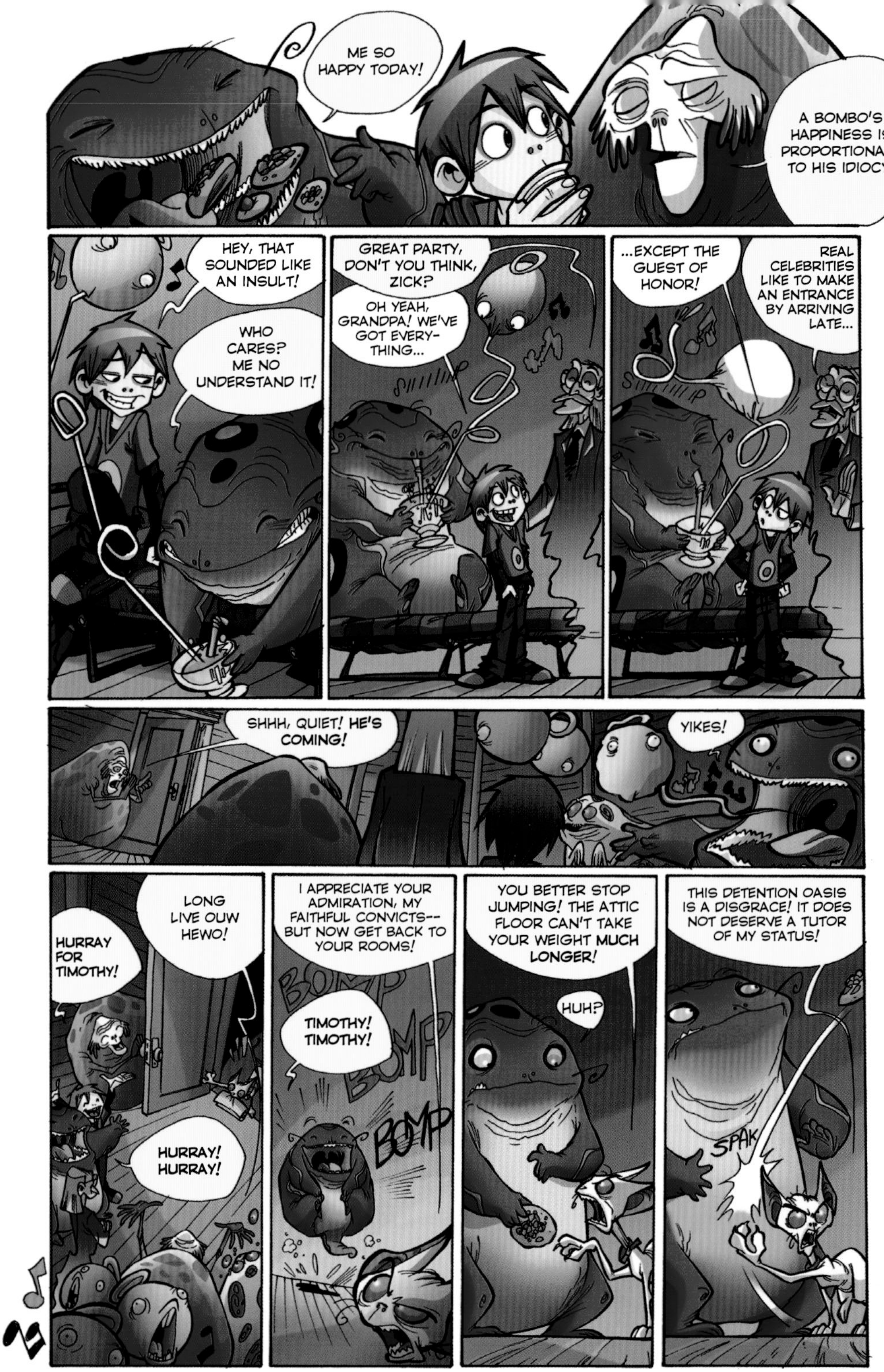
ME SO HAPPY TODAY!
A BOMBO'S HAPPINESS IS PROPORTIONATE TO HIS IDIOCY.
HEY, THAT SOUNDED LIKE AN INSULT!
WHO CARES? ME NO UNDERSTAND IT!
GREAT PARTY, DON'T YOU THINK, ZICK?
OH YEAH, GRANDPA! WE'VE GOT EVERY-THING...
...EXCEPT THE GUEST OF HONOR!
REAL CELEBRITIES LIKE TO MAKE AN ENTRANCE BY ARRIVING LATE...
SHHH, QUIET! HE'S COMING!
YIKES!
HURRAY FOR TIMOTHY!
LONG LIVE OUW HEWO!
HURRAY! HURRAY!
I APPRECIATE YOUR ADMIRATION, MY FAITHFUL CONVICTS-- BUT NOW GET BACK TO YOUR ROOMS!
BOMP
BOMP
BOMP
TIMOTHY! TIMOTHY!
BOMP
YOU BETTER STOP JUMPING! THE ATTIC FLOOR CAN'T TAKE YOUR WEIGHT MUCH LONGER!
HUH?
THIS DETENTION OASIS IS A DISGRACE! IT DOES NOT DESERVE A TUTOR OF MY STATUS!
SPAK

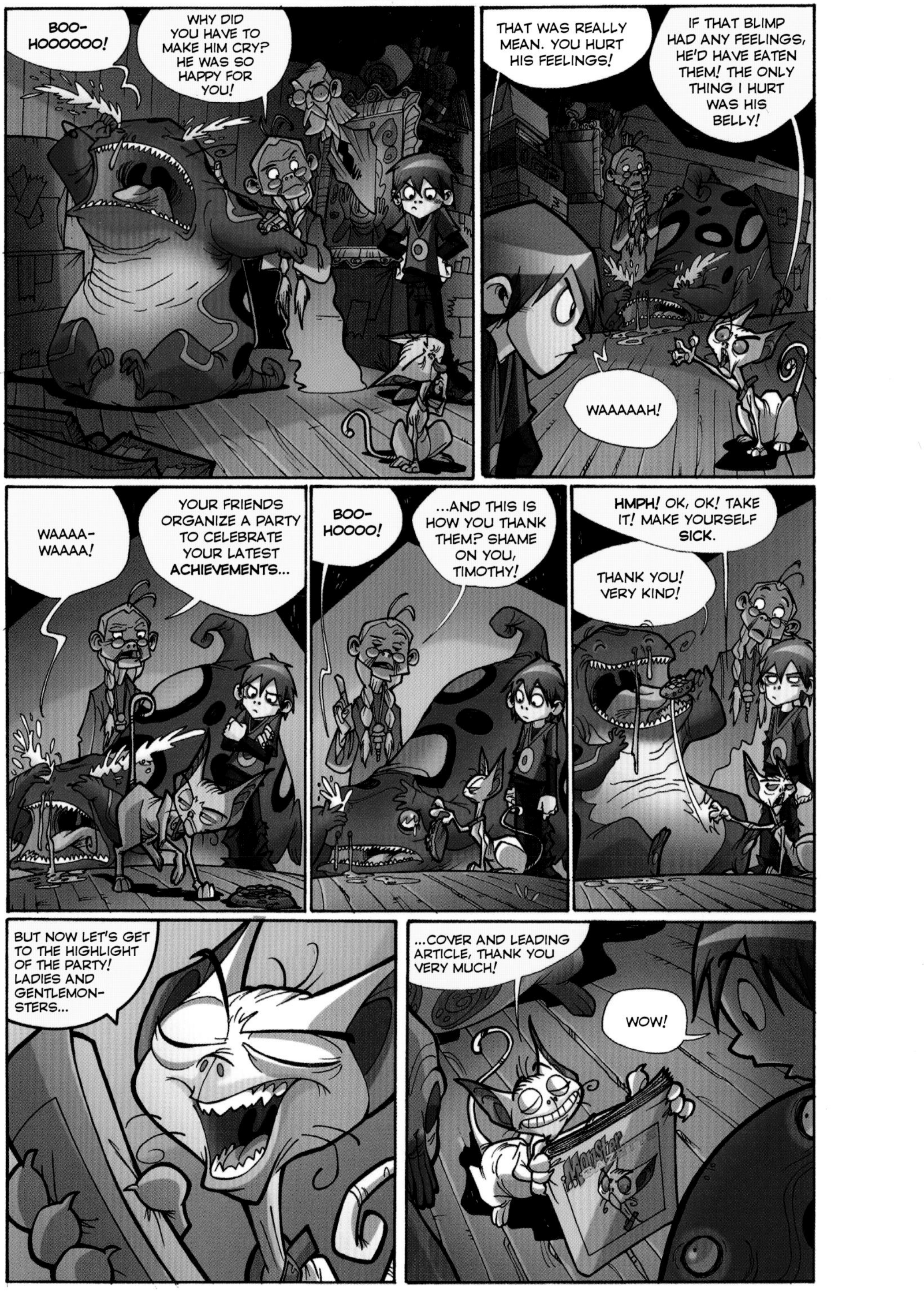
BOO-HOOOOOO!
WHY DID YOU HAVE TO MAKE HIM CRY? HE WAS SO HAPPY FOR YOU!
THAT WAS REALLY MEAN. YOU HURT HIS FEELINGS!
IF THAT BLIMP HAD ANY FEELINGS, HE'D HAVE EATEN THEM! THE ONLY THING I HURT WAS HIS BELLY!
WAAAAAH!
WAAAA-WAAAA!
YOUR FRIENDS ORGANIZE A PARTY TO CELEBRATE YOUR LATEST ACHIEVEMENTS...
BOO-HOOOO!
...AND THIS IS HOW YOU THANK THEM? SHAME ON YOU, TIMOTHY!
HMPH! OK, OK! TAKE IT! MAKE YOURSELF SICK.
THANK YOU! VERY KIND!
BUT NOW LET'S GET TO THE HIGHLIGHT OF THE PARTY! LADIES AND GENTLEMON-STERS...
...COVER AND LEADING ARTICLE, THANK YOU VERY MUCH!
WOW!

THE TUTOR TIMOTHY-MOTH...

...IN A DARING AND DANGEROUS MISSION...

...THAT WOULD BE ME...

...LIKE ALL THE OPERATIONS I'M INVOLVED WITH...

IF YOU INTERRUPT ME AGAIN, I'LL STOP READING!

DEAL! JUST TURN THE PAGES, I'LL DO THE REST!

SO... THE TUTOR BLAH BLAH BLAH... AFTER SINGLE-HANDEDLY DEFEATING THE NOTORIOUS MAGNACAT...*

*SEE MONSTER ALLERGY, VOL. 2

SINGLE-HANDEDLY? DON'T I GET ANY CREDIT? I WAS THERE TOO!

A MINOR DETAIL!

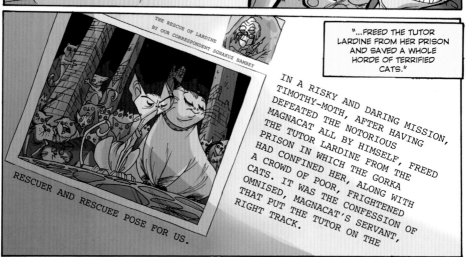

THE RESCUE OF LARDINE BY OUR CORRESPONDENT SGNAKUZ BAMBEY

RESCUER AND RESCUEE POSE FOR US.

"...FREED THE TUTOR LARDINE FROM HER PRISON AND SAVED A WHOLE HORDE OF TERRIFIED CATS."

IN A RISKY AND DARING MISSION, TIMOTHY-MOTH, AFTER HAVING DEFEATED THE NOTORIOUS MAGNACAT ALL BY HIMSELF, FREED THE TUTOR LARDINE FROM THE PRISON IN WHICH THE GORKA HAD CONFINED HER, ALONG WITH A CROWD OF POOR, FRIGHTENED CATS. IT WAS THE CONFESSION OF OMNISED, MAGNACAT'S SERVANT, THAT PUT THE TUTOR ON THE RIGHT TRACK.

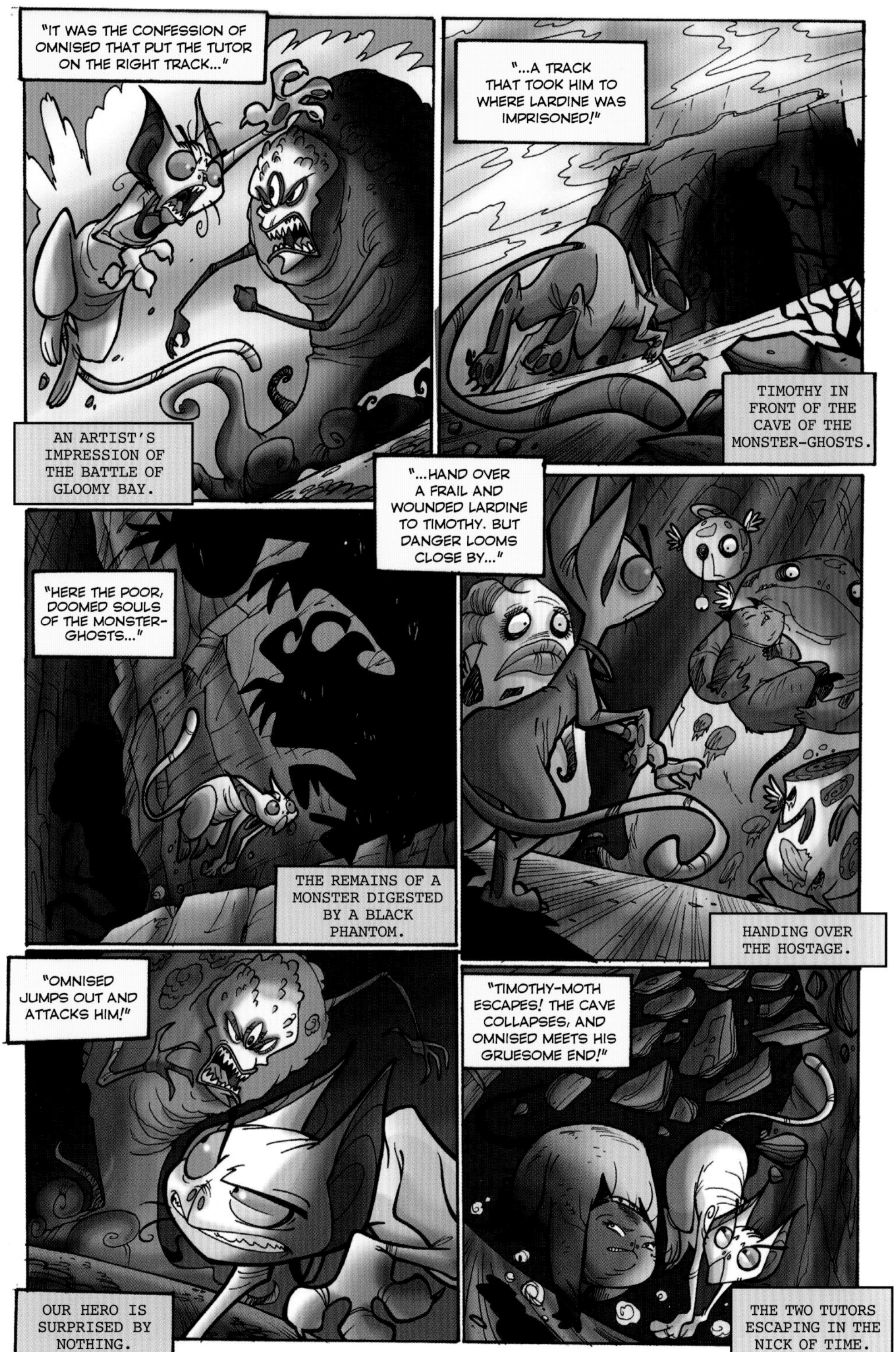
"IT WAS THE CONFESSION OF OMNISED THAT PUT THE TUTOR ON THE RIGHT TRACK..."
AN ARTIST'S IMPRESSION OF THE BATTLE OF GLOOMY BAY.
"...A TRACK THAT TOOK HIM TO WHERE LARDINE WAS IMPRISONED!"
TIMOTHY IN FRONT OF THE CAVE OF THE MONSTER-GHOSTS.
"HERE THE POOR, DOOMED SOULS OF THE MONSTER-GHOSTS..."
THE REMAINS OF A MONSTER DIGESTED BY A BLACK PHANTOM.
"...HAND OVER A FRAIL AND WOUNDED LARDINE TO TIMOTHY. BUT DANGER LOOMS CLOSE BY..."
HANDING OVER THE HOSTAGE.
"OMNISED JUMPS OUT AND ATTACKS HIM!"
OUR HERO IS SURPRISED BY NOTHING.
"TIMOTHY-MOTH ESCAPES! THE CAVE COLLAPSES, AND OMNISED MEETS HIS GRUESOME END!"
THE TWO TUTORS ESCAPING IN THE NICK OF TIME.

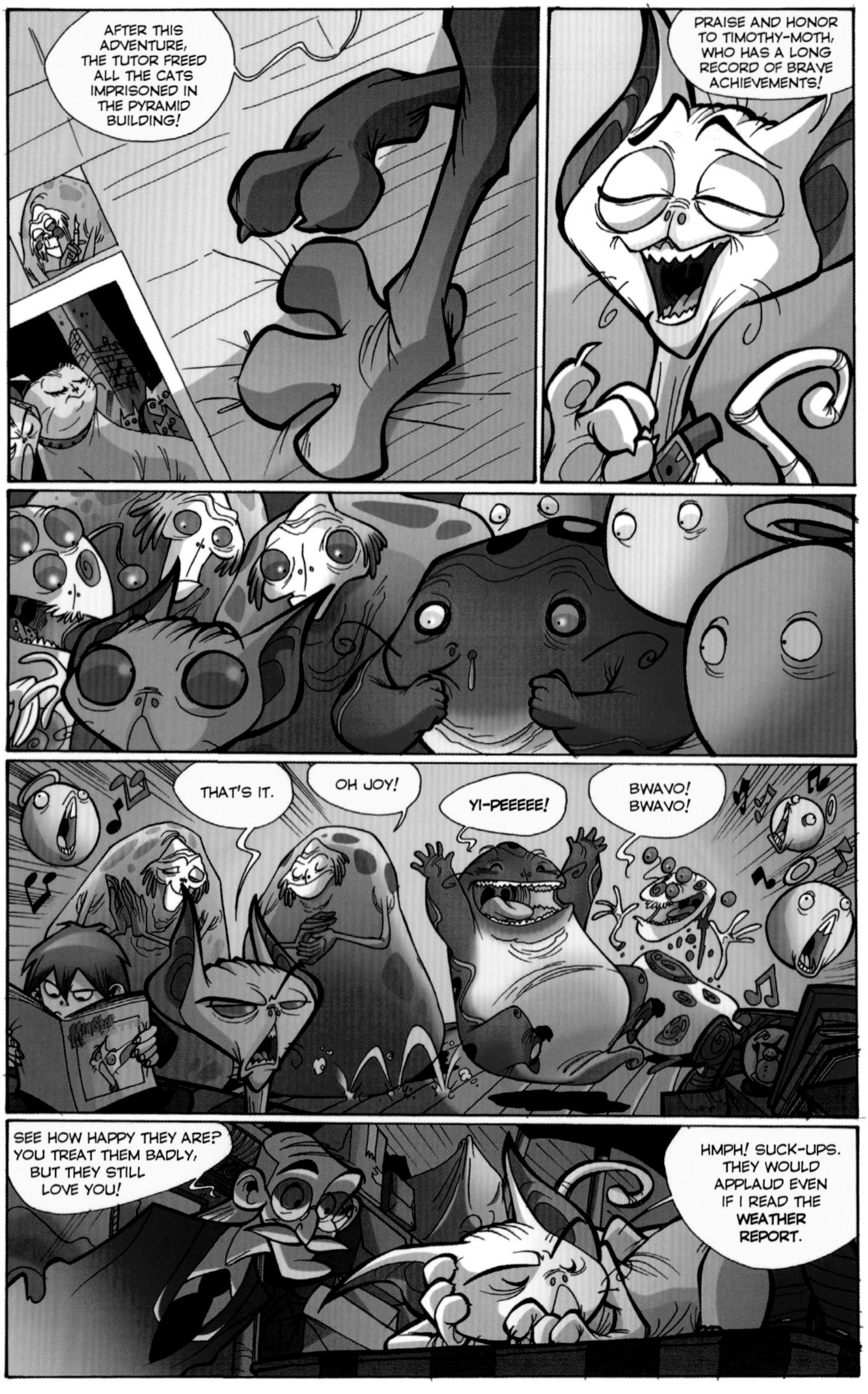
AFTER THIS ADVENTURE, THE TUTOR FREED ALL THE CATS IMPRISONED IN THE PYRAMID BUILDING!
PRAISE AND HONOR TO TIMOTHY-MOTH, WHO HAS A LONG RECORD OF BRAVE ACHIEVEMENTS!
THAT'S IT.
OH JOY!
YI-PEEEEE!
BWAVO! BWAVO!
SEE HOW HAPPY THEY ARE? YOU TREAT THEM BADLY, BUT THEY STILL LOVE YOU!
HMPH! SUCK-UPS. THEY WOULD APPLAUD EVEN IF I READ THE WEATHER REPORT.

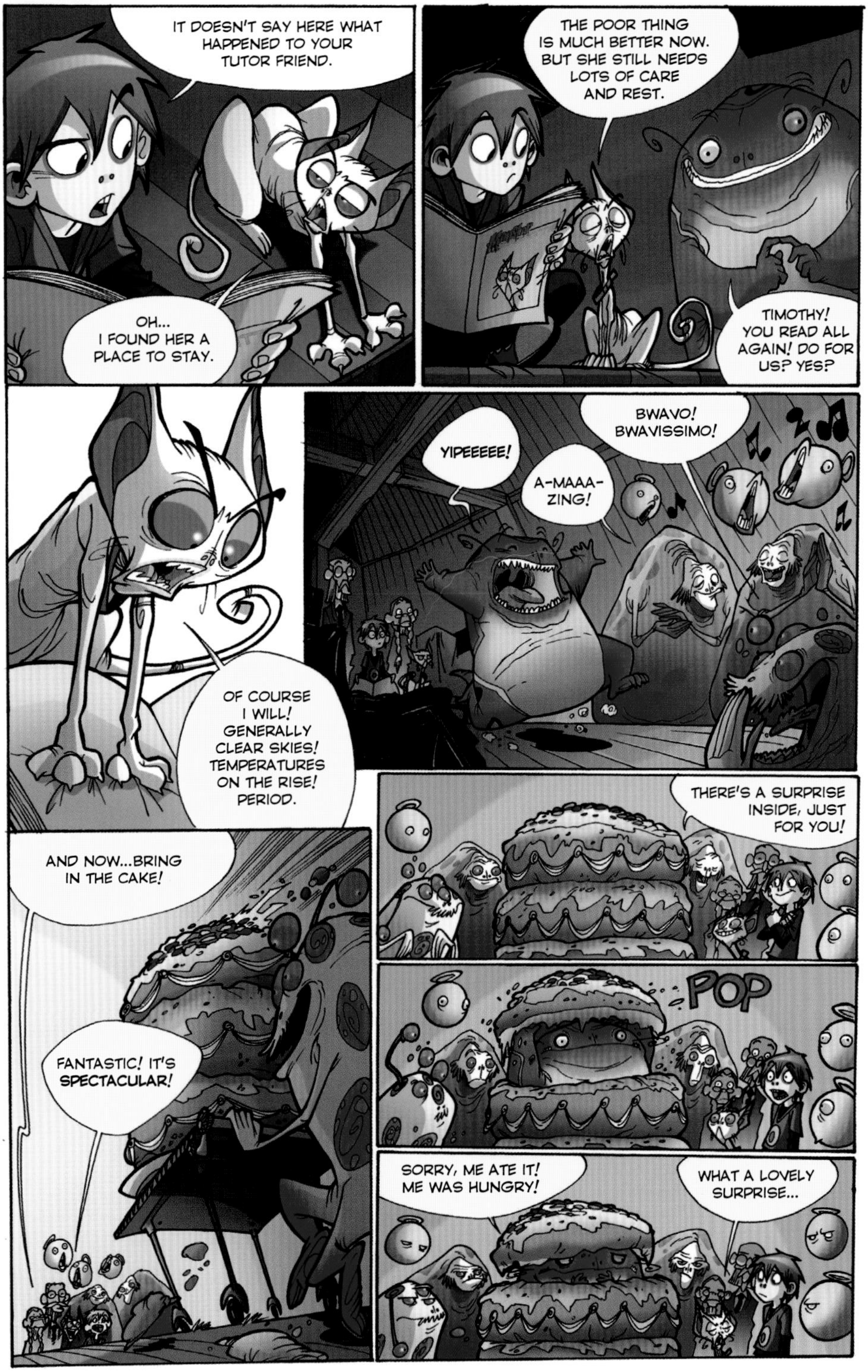
IT DOESN'T SAY HERE WHAT HAPPENED TO YOUR TUTOR FRIEND.
OH... I FOUND HER A PLACE TO STAY.
THE POOR THING IS MUCH BETTER NOW. BUT SHE STILL NEEDS LOTS OF CARE AND REST.
TIMOTHY! YOU READ ALL AGAIN! DO FOR US? YES?
OF COURSE I WILL! GENERALLY CLEAR SKIES! TEMPERATURES ON THE RISE! PERIOD.
YIPEEEEE!
A-MAAA-ZING!
BWAVO! BWAVISSIMO!
AND NOW...BRING IN THE CAKE!
FANTASTIC! IT'S SPECTACULAR!
THERE'S A SURPRISE INSIDE, JUST FOR YOU!
POP
SORRY, ME ATE IT! ME WAS HUNGRY!
WHAT A LOVELY SURPRISE...

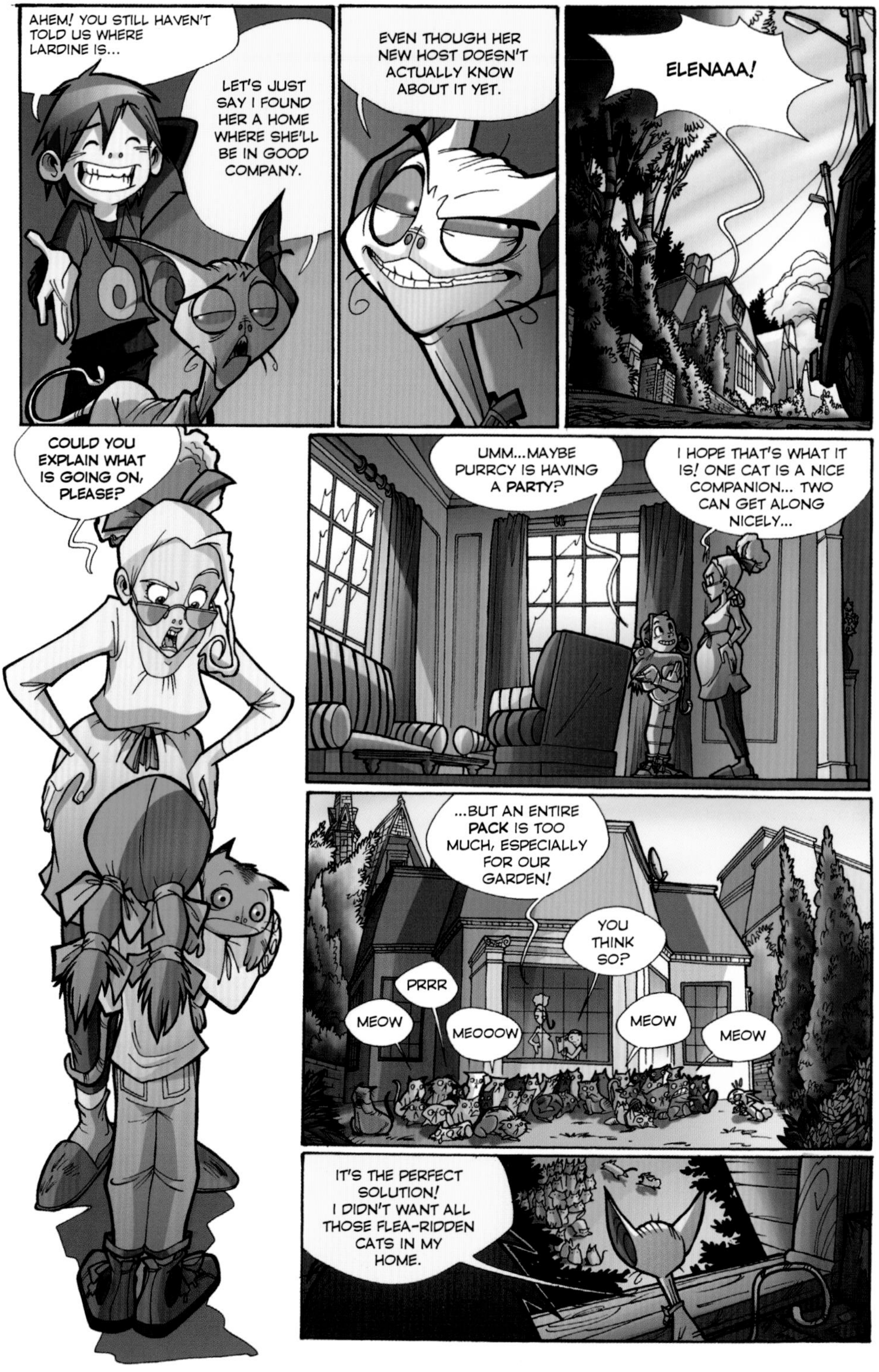

AHEM! YOU STILL HAVEN'T TOLD US WHERE LARDINE IS...
LET'S JUST SAY I FOUND HER A HOME WHERE SHE'LL BE IN GOOD COMPANY.
EVEN THOUGH HER NEW HOST DOESN'T ACTUALLY KNOW ABOUT IT YET.
ELENAAA!
COULD YOU EXPLAIN WHAT IS GOING ON, PLEASE?
UMM...MAYBE PURRCY IS HAVING A PARTY?
I HOPE THAT'S WHAT IT IS! ONE CAT IS A NICE COMPANION... TWO CAN GET ALONG NICELY...
...BUT AN ENTIRE PACK IS TOO MUCH, ESPECIALLY FOR OUR GARDEN!
YOU THINK SO?
PRRR
MEOW
MEOOOW
MEOW
MEOW
IT'S THE PERFECT SOLUTION! I DIDN'T WANT ALL THOSE FLEA-RIDDEN CATS IN MY HOME.

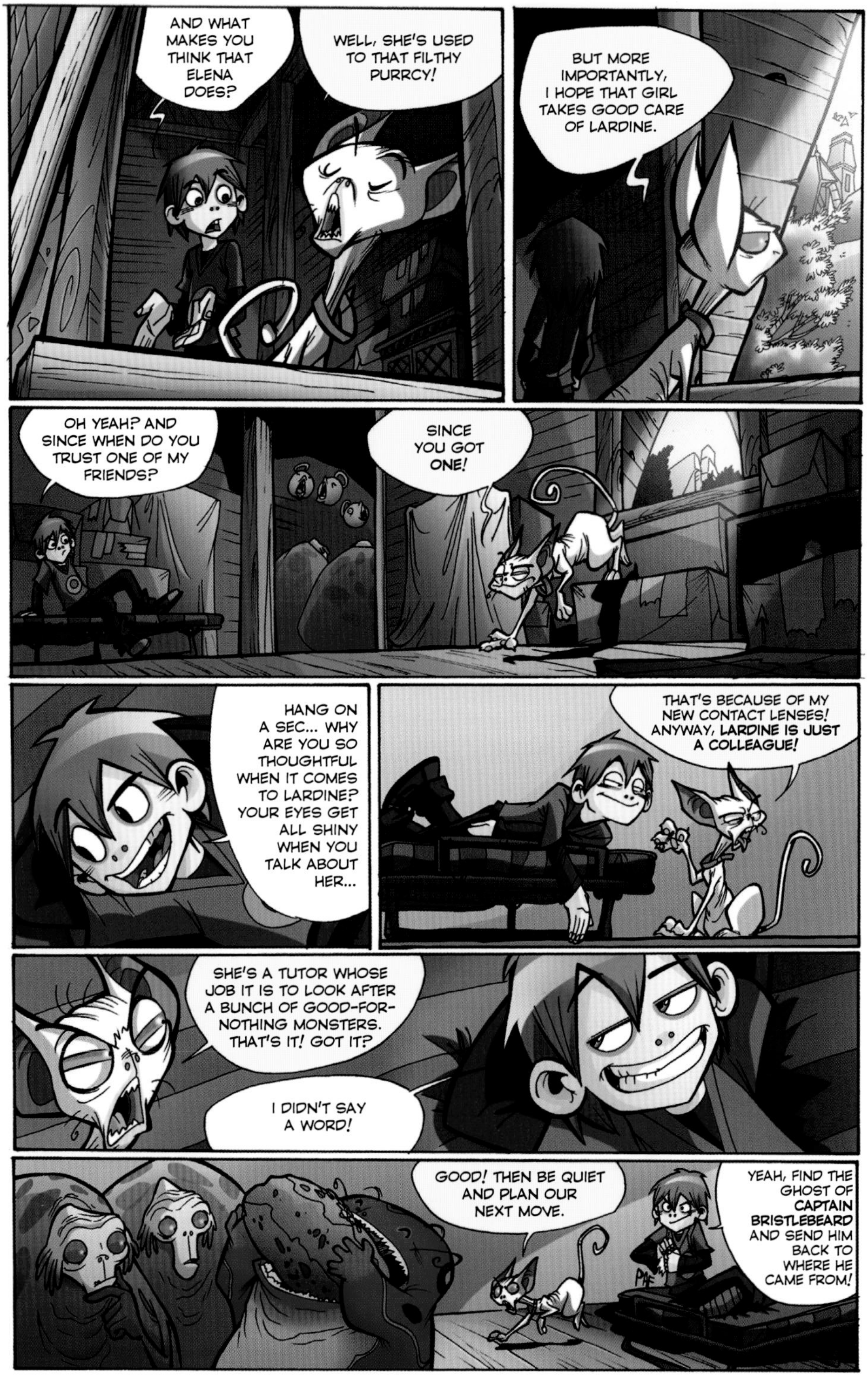
AND WHAT MAKES YOU THINK THAT ELENA DOES?
WELL, SHE'S USED TO THAT FILTHY PURRCY!
BUT MORE IMPORTANTLY, I HOPE THAT GIRL TAKES GOOD CARE OF LARDINE.
OH YEAH? AND SINCE WHEN DO YOU TRUST ONE OF MY FRIENDS?
SINCE YOU GOT ONE!
HANG ON A SEC... WHY ARE YOU SO THOUGHTFUL WHEN IT COMES TO LARDINE? YOUR EYES GET ALL SHINY WHEN YOU TALK ABOUT HER...
THAT'S BECAUSE OF MY NEW CONTACT LENSES! ANYWAY, LARDINE IS JUST A COLLEAGUE!
SHE'S A TUTOR WHOSE JOB IT IS TO LOOK AFTER A BUNCH OF GOOD-FOR-NOTHING MONSTERS. THAT'S IT! GOT IT?
I DIDN'T SAY A WORD!
GOOD! THEN BE QUIET AND PLAN OUR NEXT MOVE.
YEAH, FIND THE GHOST OF CAPTAIN BRISTLEBEARD AND SEND HIM BACK TO WHERE HE CAME FROM!

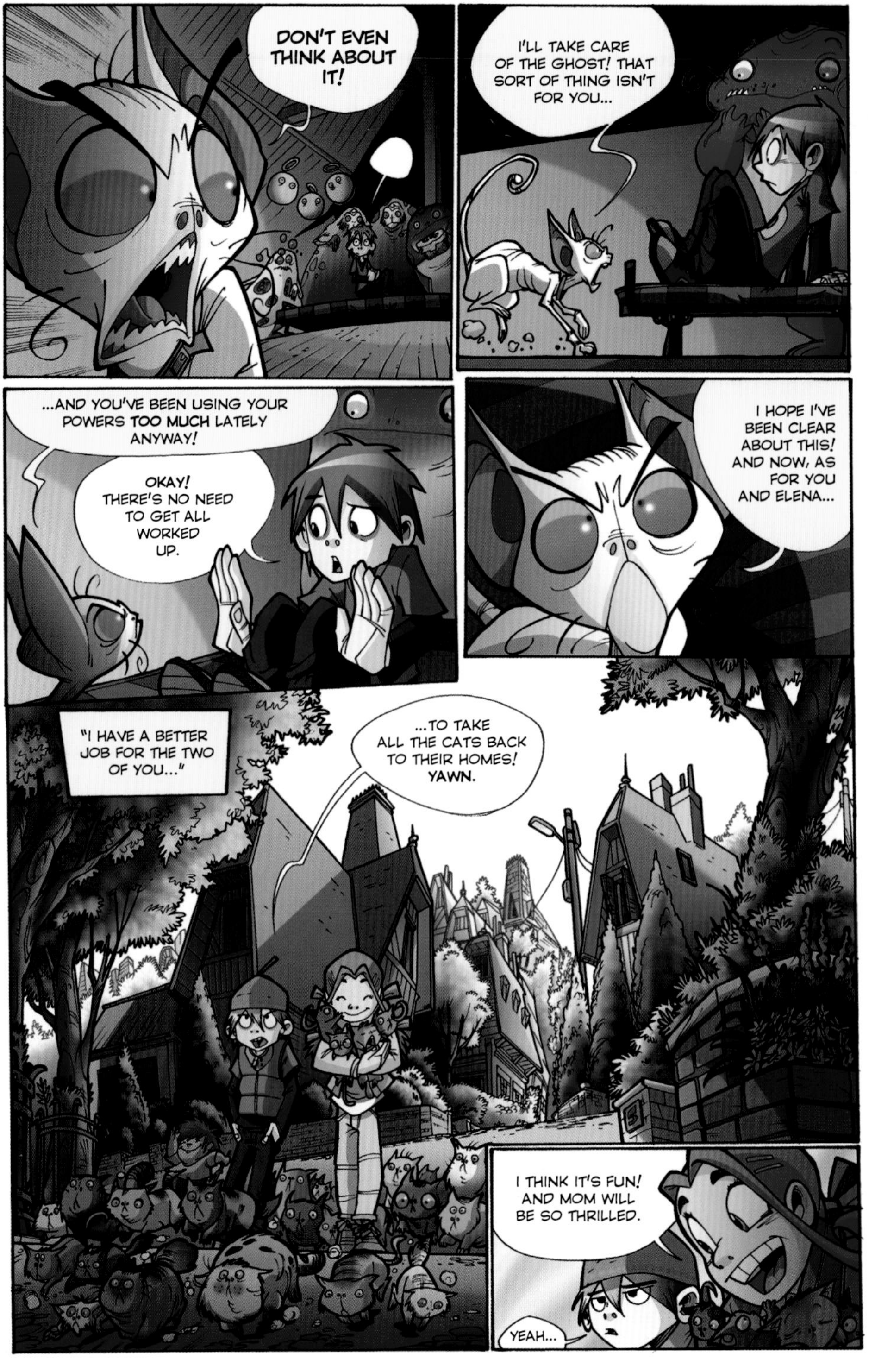
DON'T EVEN THINK ABOUT IT!
I'LL TAKE CARE OF THE GHOST! THAT SORT OF THING ISN'T FOR YOU...
...AND YOU'VE BEEN USING YOUR POWERS TOO MUCH LATELY ANYWAY!
OKAY! THERE'S NO NEED TO GET ALL WORKED UP.
I HOPE I'VE BEEN CLEAR ABOUT THIS! AND NOW, AS FOR YOU AND ELENA...
"I HAVE A BETTER JOB FOR THE TWO OF YOU..."
...TO TAKE ALL THE CATS BACK TO THEIR HOMES! YAWN.
I THINK IT'S FUN! AND MOM WILL BE SO THRILLED.
YEAH...

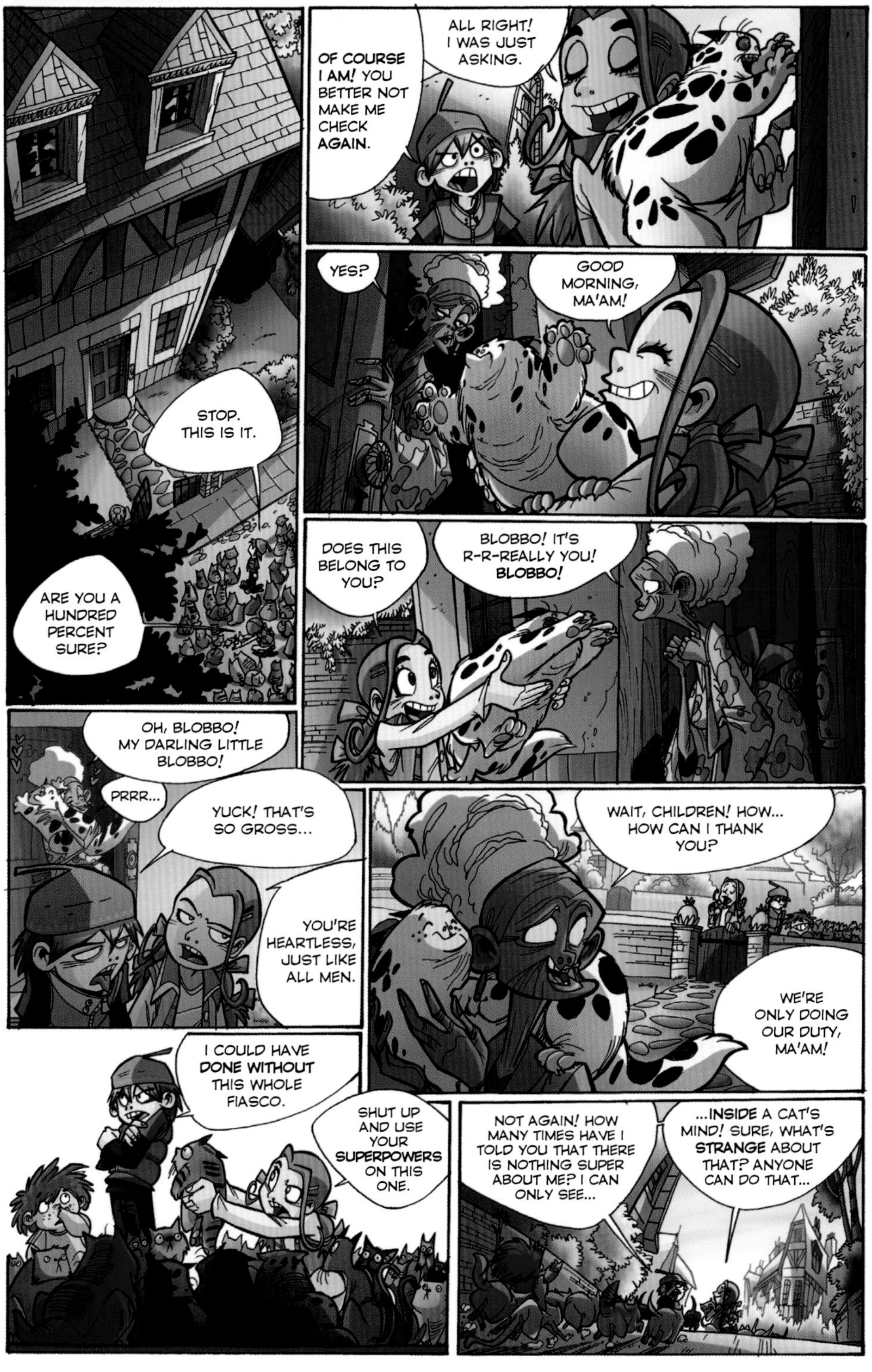
STOP. THIS IS IT.
ARE YOU A HUNDRED PERCENT SURE?
OF COURSE I AM! YOU BETTER NOT MAKE ME CHECK AGAIN.
ALL RIGHT! I WAS JUST ASKING.
YES?
GOOD MORNING, MA'AM!
DOES THIS BELONG TO YOU?
BLOBBO! IT'S R-R-REALLY YOU! BLOBBO!
OH, BLOBBO! MY DARLING LITTLE BLOBBO!
PRRR...
YUCK! THAT'S SO GROSS...
YOU'RE HEARTLESS, JUST LIKE ALL MEN.
WAIT, CHILDREN! HOW... HOW CAN I THANK YOU?
WE'RE ONLY DOING OUR DUTY, MA'AM!
I COULD HAVE DONE WITHOUT THIS WHOLE FIASCO.
SHUT UP AND USE YOUR SUPERPOWERS ON THIS ONE.
NOT AGAIN! HOW MANY TIMES HAVE I TOLD YOU THAT THERE IS NOTHING SUPER ABOUT ME? I CAN ONLY SEE...
...INSIDE A CAT'S MIND! SURE, WHAT'S STRANGE ABOUT THAT? ANYONE CAN DO THAT...

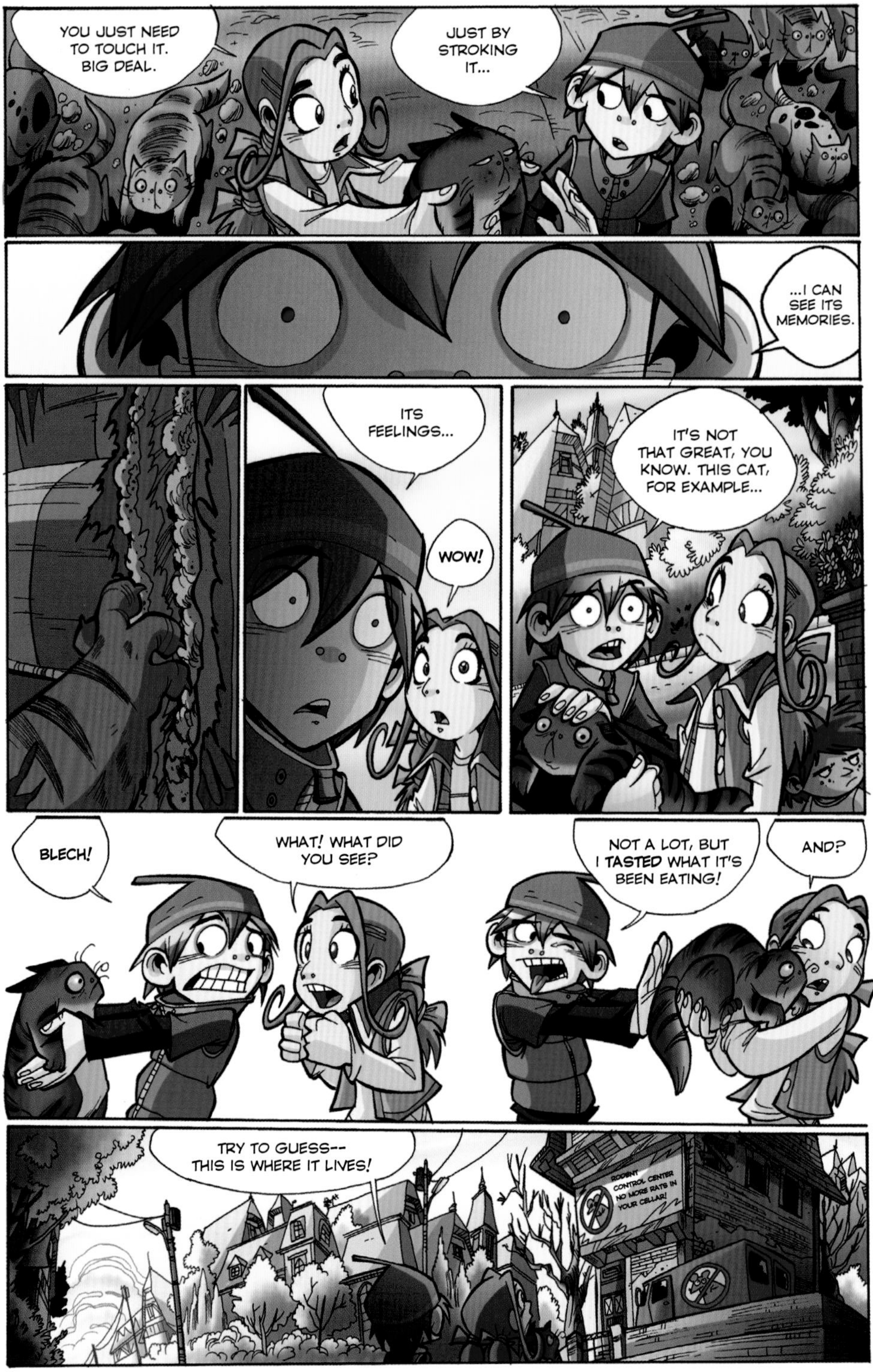
YOU JUST NEED TO TOUCH IT. BIG DEAL.
JUST BY STROKING IT...
...I CAN SEE ITS MEMORIES.
ITS FEELINGS...
WOW!
IT'S NOT THAT GREAT, YOU KNOW. THIS CAT, FOR EXAMPLE...
BLECH!
WHAT! WHAT DID YOU SEE?
NOT A LOT, BUT I TASTED WHAT IT'S BEEN EATING!
AND?
TRY TO GUESS-- THIS IS WHERE IT LIVES!
RODENT CONTROL CENTER
NO MORE RATS IN YOUR CELLAR!

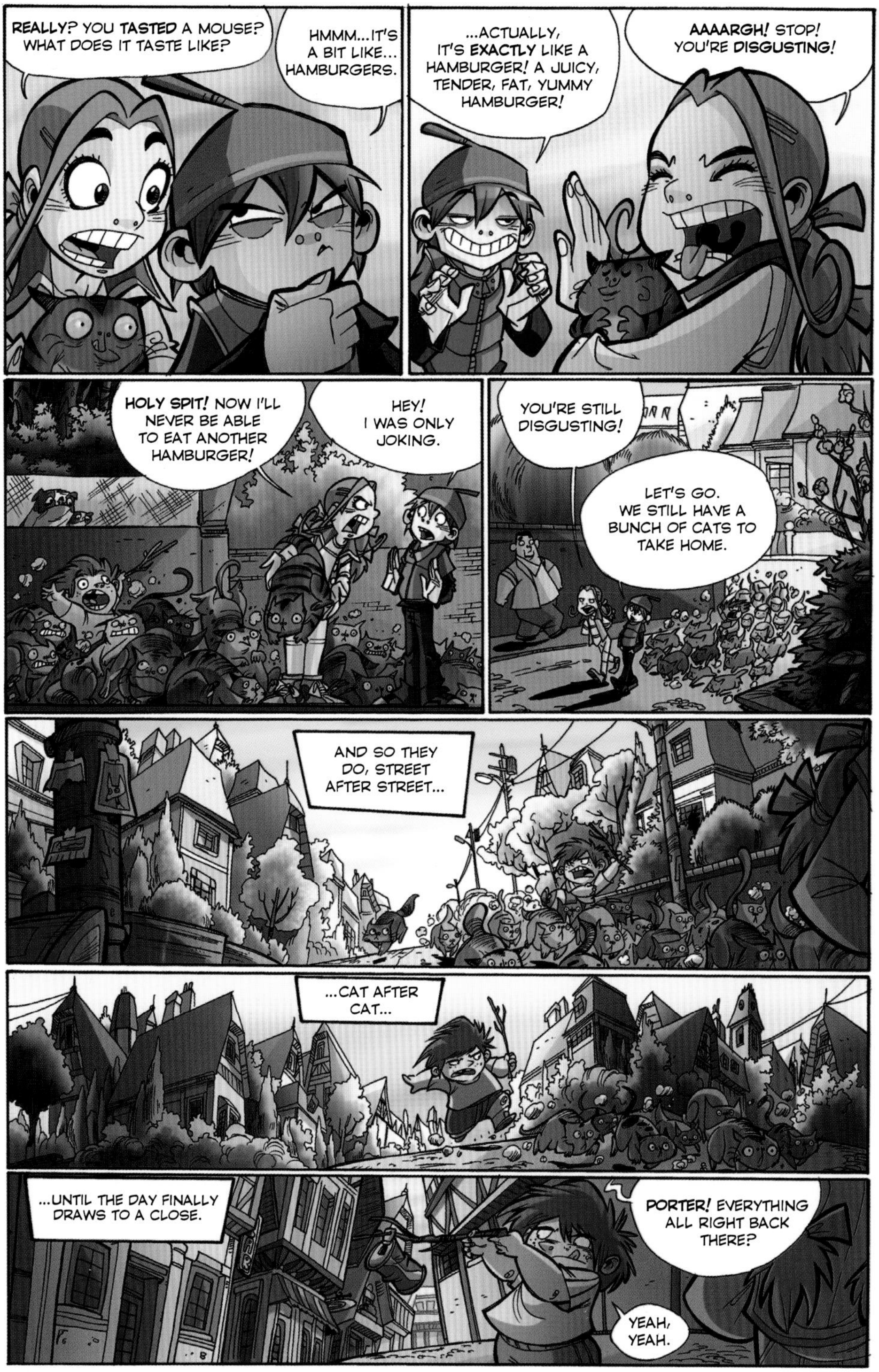
REALLY? YOU TASTED A MOUSE? WHAT DOES IT TASTE LIKE?
HMMM...IT'S A BIT LIKE... HAMBURGERS.
...ACTUALLY, IT'S EXACTLY LIKE A HAMBURGER! A JUICY, TENDER, FAT, YUMMY HAMBURGER!
AAAARGH! STOP! YOU'RE DISGUSTING!
HOLY SPIT! NOW I'LL NEVER BE ABLE TO EAT ANOTHER HAMBURGER!
HEY! I WAS ONLY JOKING.
YOU'RE STILL DISGUSTING!
LET'S GO. WE STILL HAVE A BUNCH OF CATS TO TAKE HOME.
AND SO THEY DO, STREET AFTER STREET...
...CAT AFTER CAT...
...UNTIL THE DAY FINALLY DRAWS TO A CLOSE.
PORTER! EVERYTHING ALL RIGHT BACK THERE?
YEAH, YEAH.

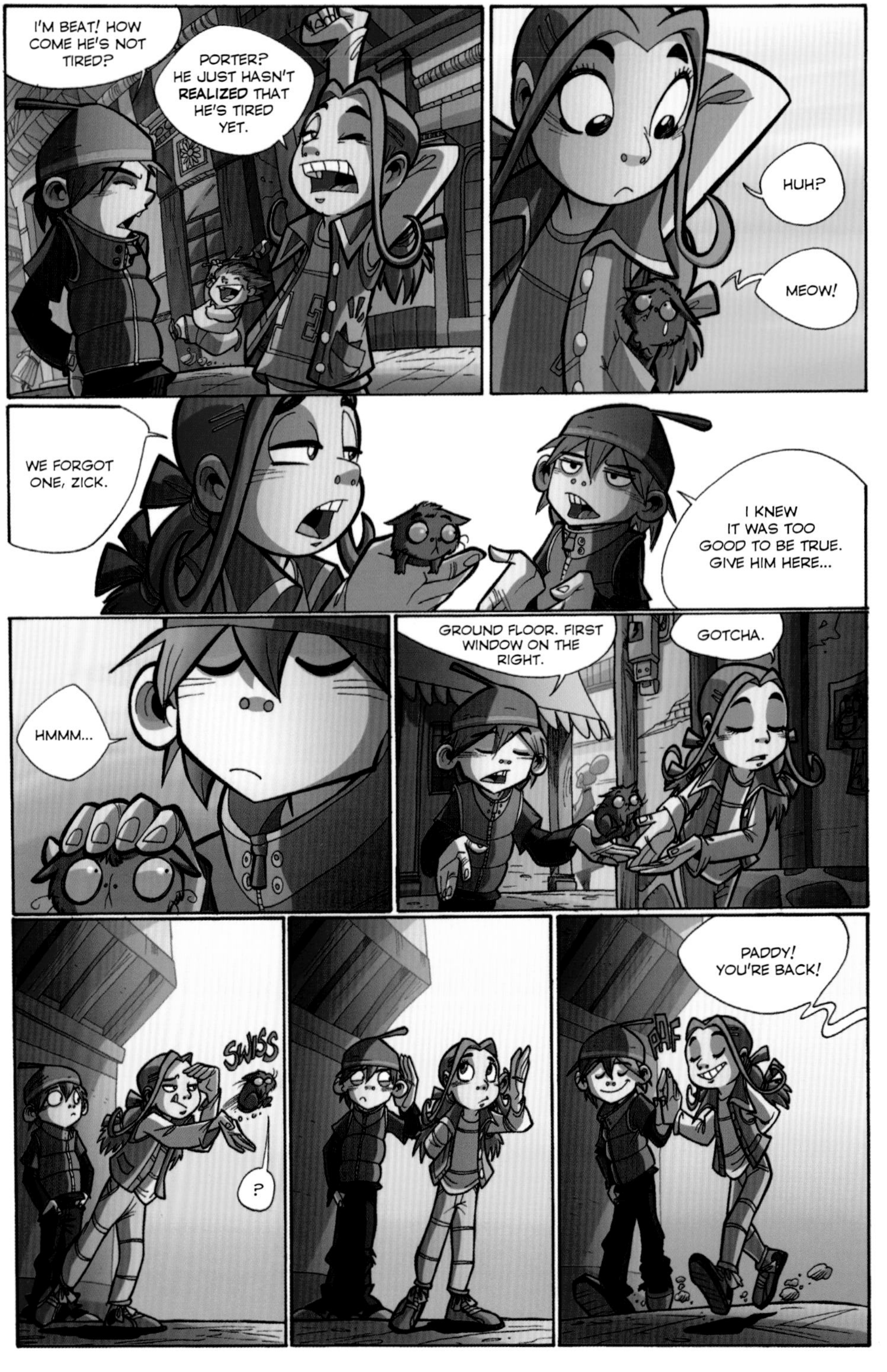

I'M BEAT! HOW COME HE'S NOT TIRED?
PORTER? HE JUST HASN'T **REALIZED** THAT HE'S TIRED YET.
HUH?
MEOW!
WE FORGOT ONE, ZICK.
I KNEW IT WAS TOO GOOD TO BE TRUE. GIVE HIM HERE...
HMMM...
GROUND FLOOR. FIRST WINDOW ON THE RIGHT.
GOTCHA.
SWISS
?
PADDY! YOU'RE BACK!
PAF

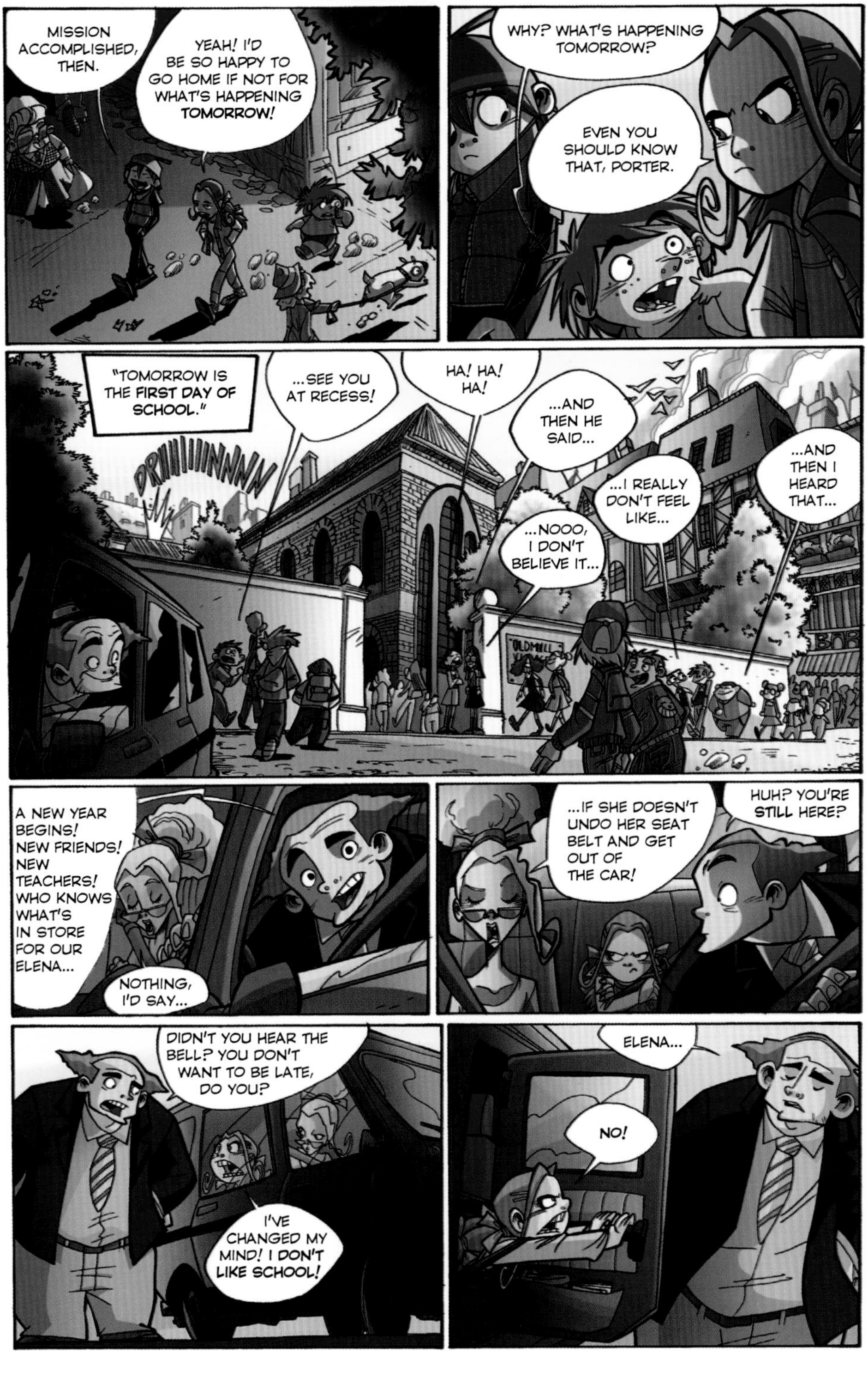
MISSION ACCOMPLISHED, THEN.
YEAH! I'D BE SO HAPPY TO GO HOME IF NOT FOR WHAT'S HAPPENING TOMORROW!
WHY? WHAT'S HAPPENING TOMORROW?
EVEN YOU SHOULD KNOW THAT, PORTER.
"TOMORROW IS THE FIRST DAY OF SCHOOL."
DRNIIIIIINNNN
...SEE YOU AT RECESS!
HA! HA! HA!
...AND THEN HE SAID...
...I REALLY DON'T FEEL LIKE...
...NOOO, I DON'T BELIEVE IT...
...AND THEN I HEARD THAT...
A NEW YEAR BEGINS! NEW FRIENDS! NEW TEACHERS! WHO KNOWS WHAT'S IN STORE FOR OUR ELENA...
NOTHING, I'D SAY...
...IF SHE DOESN'T UNDO HER SEAT BELT AND GET OUT OF THE CAR!
HUH? YOU'RE STILL HERE?
DIDN'T YOU HEAR THE BELL? YOU DON'T WANT TO BE LATE, DO YOU?
I'VE CHANGED MY MIND! I DON'T LIKE SCHOOL!
ELENA...
NO!

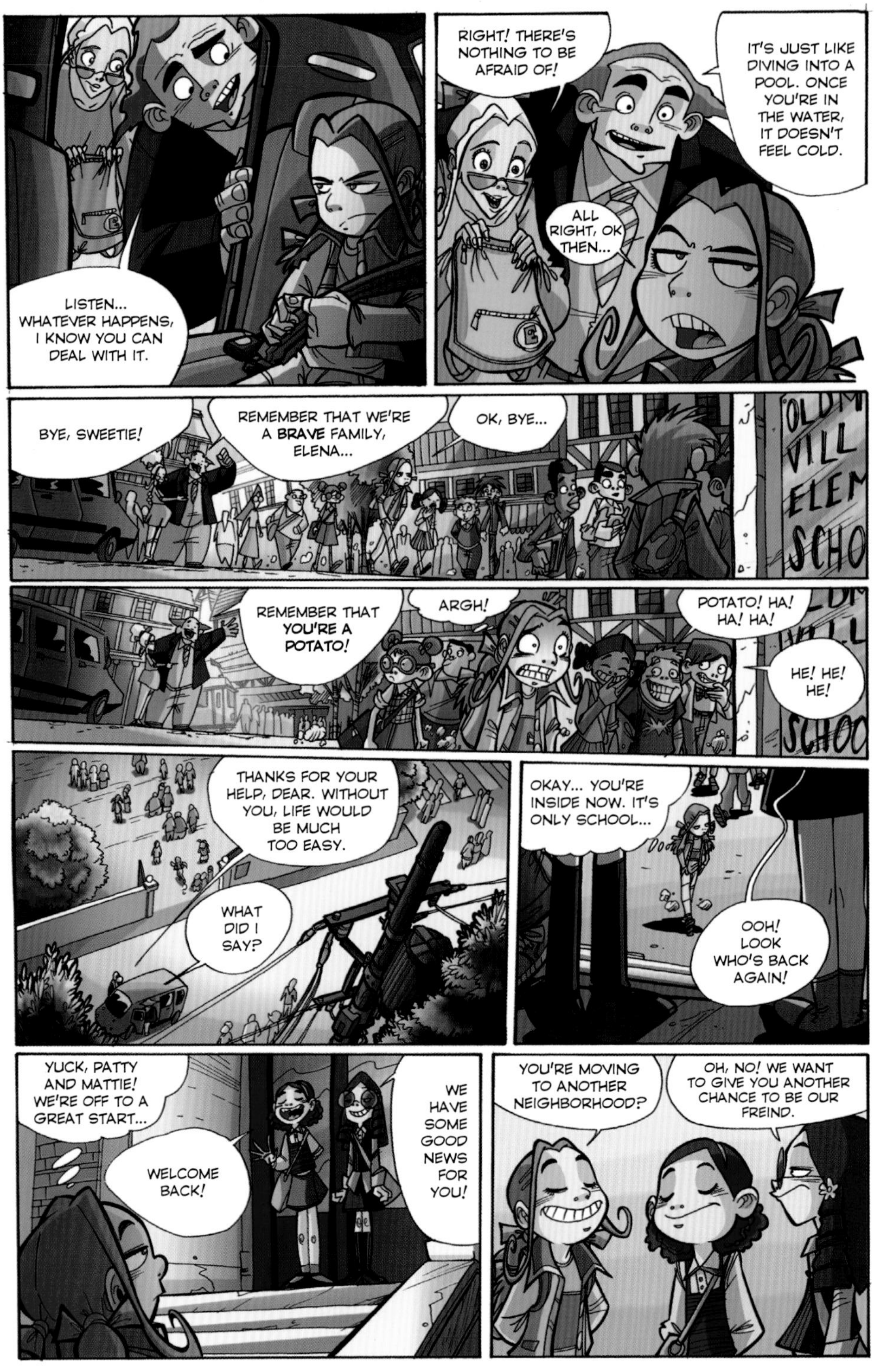
LISTEN... WHATEVER HAPPENS, I KNOW YOU CAN DEAL WITH IT.
RIGHT! THERE'S NOTHING TO BE AFRAID OF!
IT'S JUST LIKE DIVING INTO A POOL. ONCE YOU'RE IN THE WATER, IT DOESN'T FEEL COLD.
ALL RIGHT, OK THEN...
BYE, SWEETIE!
REMEMBER THAT WE'RE A **BRAVE** FAMILY, ELENA...
OK, BYE...
REMEMBER THAT **YOU'RE A POTATO!**
ARGH!
POTATO! HA! HA! HA!
HE! HE! HE!
THANKS FOR YOUR HELP, DEAR. WITHOUT YOU, LIFE WOULD BE MUCH TOO EASY.
WHAT DID I SAY?
OKAY... YOU'RE INSIDE NOW. IT'S ONLY SCHOOL...
OOH! LOOK WHO'S BACK AGAIN!
YUCK, PATTY AND MATTIE! WE'RE OFF TO A GREAT START...
WELCOME BACK!
WE HAVE SOME GOOD NEWS FOR YOU!
YOU'RE MOVING TO ANOTHER NEIGHBORHOOD?
OH, NO! WE WANT TO GIVE YOU ANOTHER CHANCE TO BE OUR FREIND.

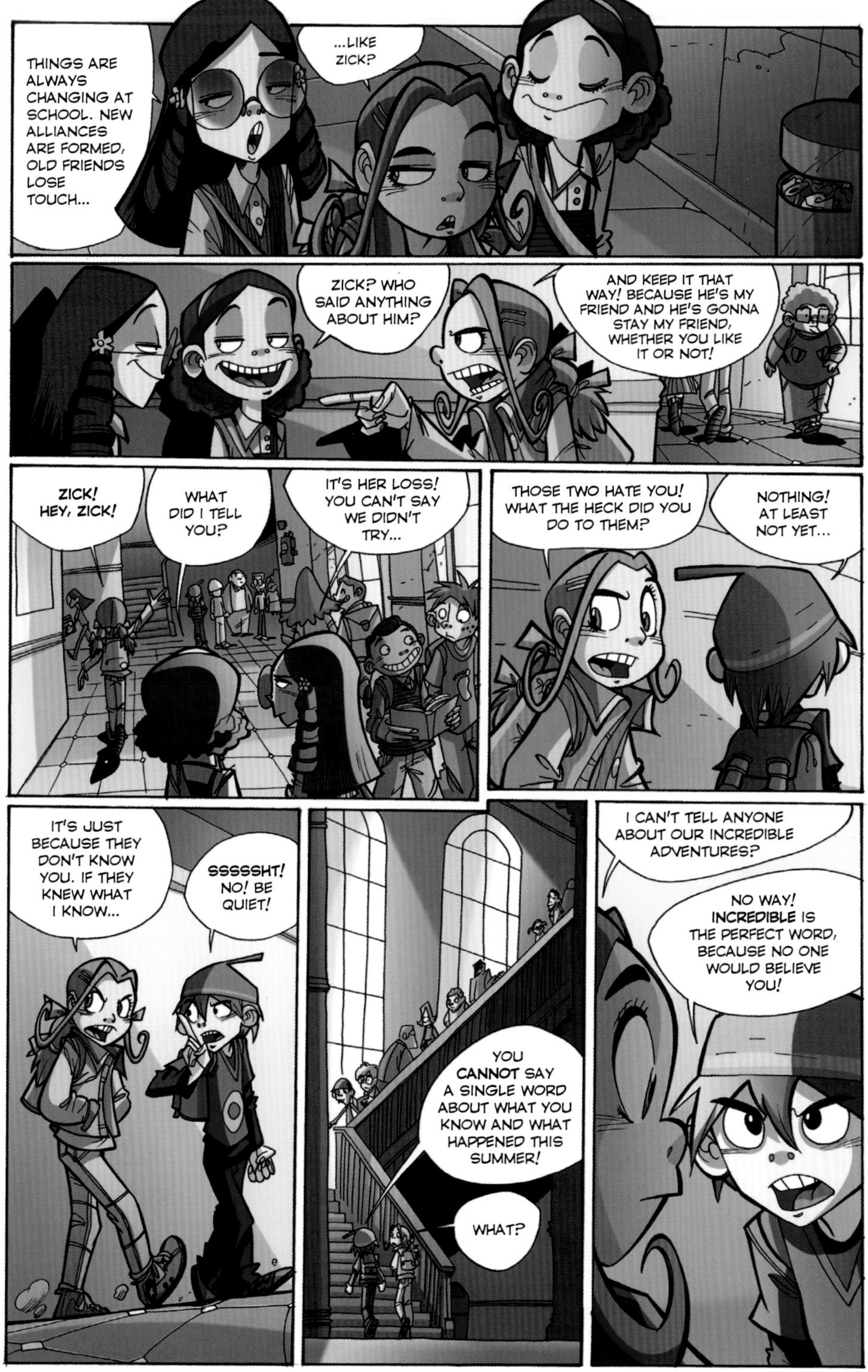
THINGS ARE ALWAYS CHANGING AT SCHOOL. NEW ALLIANCES ARE FORMED, OLD FRIENDS LOSE TOUCH...
...LIKE ZICK?
ZICK? WHO SAID ANYTHING ABOUT HIM?
AND KEEP IT THAT WAY! BECAUSE HE'S MY FRIEND AND HE'S GONNA STAY MY FRIEND, WHETHER YOU LIKE IT OR NOT!
ZICK! HEY, ZICK!
WHAT DID I TELL YOU?
IT'S HER LOSS! YOU CAN'T SAY WE DIDN'T TRY...
THOSE TWO HATE YOU! WHAT THE HECK DID YOU DO TO THEM?
NOTHING! AT LEAST NOT YET...
IT'S JUST BECAUSE THEY DON'T KNOW YOU. IF THEY KNEW WHAT I KNOW...
SSSSSHT! NO! BE QUIET!
YOU CANNOT SAY A SINGLE WORD ABOUT WHAT YOU KNOW AND WHAT HAPPENED THIS SUMMER!
WHAT?
I CAN'T TELL ANYONE ABOUT OUR INCREDIBLE ADVENTURES?
NO WAY! INCREDIBLE IS THE PERFECT WORD, BECAUSE NO ONE WOULD BELIEVE YOU!

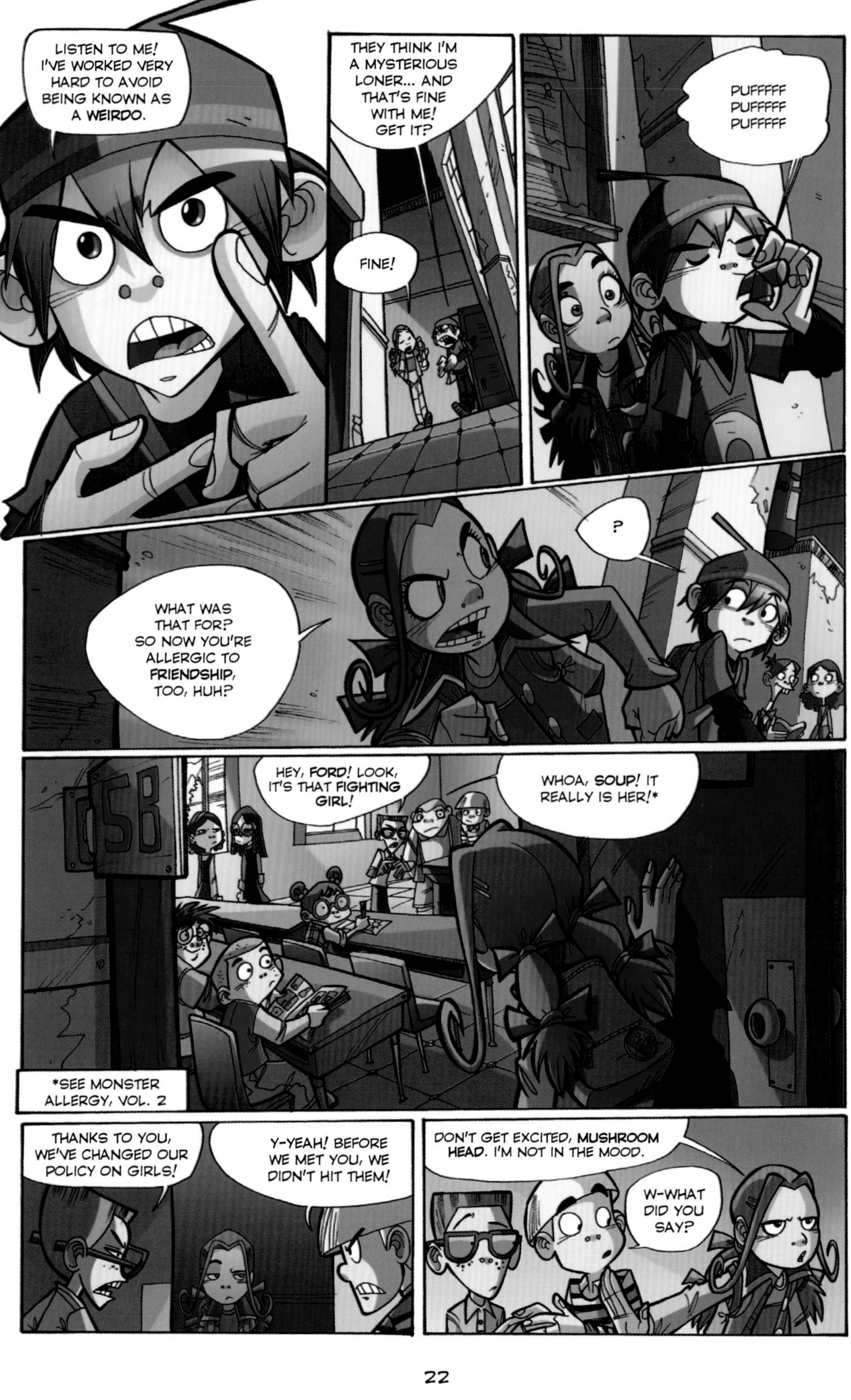
LISTEN TO ME! I'VE WORKED VERY HARD TO AVOID BEING KNOWN AS A WEIRDO.
THEY THINK I'M A MYSTERIOUS LONER... AND THAT'S FINE WITH ME! GET IT?
FINE!
PUFFFFF PUFFFFF PUFFFFF
?
WHAT WAS THAT FOR? SO NOW YOU'RE ALLERGIC TO FRIENDSHIP, TOO, HUH?
HEY, FORD! LOOK, IT'S THAT FIGHTING GIRL!
WHOA, SOUP! IT REALLY IS HER!*
5B
*SEE MONSTER ALLERGY, VOL. 2
THANKS TO YOU, WE'VE CHANGED OUR POLICY ON GIRLS!
Y-YEAH! BEFORE WE MET YOU, WE DIDN'T HIT THEM!
DON'T GET EXCITED, MUSHROOM HEAD. I'M NOT IN THE MOOD.
W-WHAT DID YOU SAY?

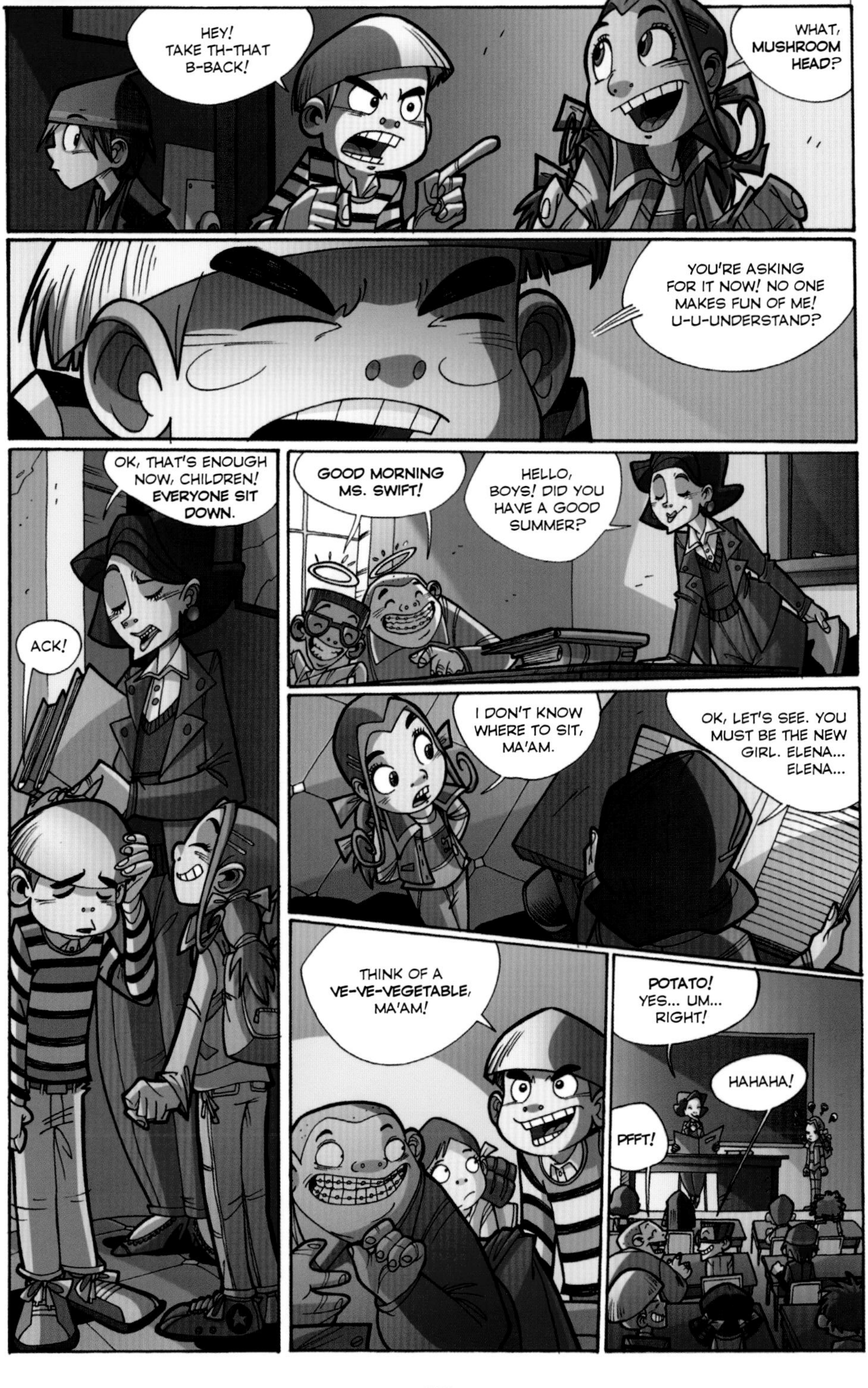
HEY! TAKE TH-THAT B-BACK!
WHAT, MUSHROOM HEAD?
YOU'RE ASKING FOR IT NOW! NO ONE MAKES FUN OF ME! U-U-UNDERSTAND?
OK, THAT'S ENOUGH NOW, CHILDREN! EVERYONE SIT DOWN.
ACK!
GOOD MORNING MS. SWIFT!
HELLO, BOYS! DID YOU HAVE A GOOD SUMMER?
I DON'T KNOW WHERE TO SIT, MA'AM.
OK, LET'S SEE. YOU MUST BE THE NEW GIRL. ELENA... ELENA...
THINK OF A VE-VE-VEGETABLE, MA'AM!
POTATO! YES... UM... RIGHT!
HAHAHA!
PFFT!

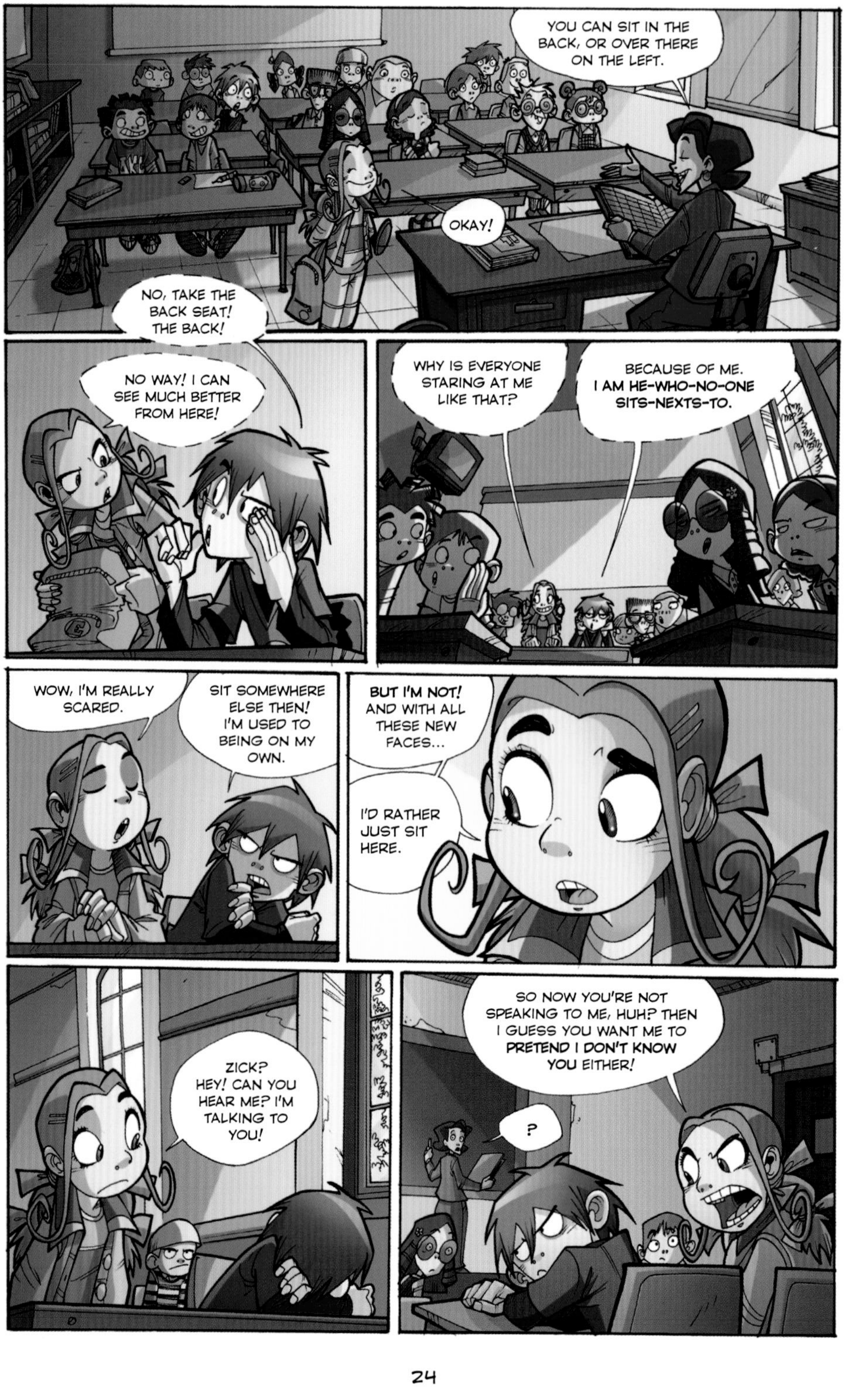
YOU CAN SIT IN THE BACK, OR OVER THERE ON THE LEFT.
OKAY!
NO, TAKE THE BACK SEAT! THE BACK!
NO WAY! I CAN SEE MUCH BETTER FROM HERE!
WHY IS EVERYONE STARING AT ME LIKE THAT?
BECAUSE OF ME. I AM HE-WHO-NO-ONE SITS-NEXTS-TO.
WOW, I'M REALLY SCARED.
SIT SOMEWHERE ELSE THEN! I'M USED TO BEING ON MY OWN.
BUT I'M NOT! AND WITH ALL THESE NEW FACES...
I'D RATHER JUST SIT HERE.
ZICK? HEY! CAN YOU HEAR ME? I'M TALKING TO YOU!
SO NOW YOU'RE NOT SPEAKING TO ME, HUH? THEN I GUESS YOU WANT ME TO PRETEND I DON'T KNOW YOU EITHER!
?

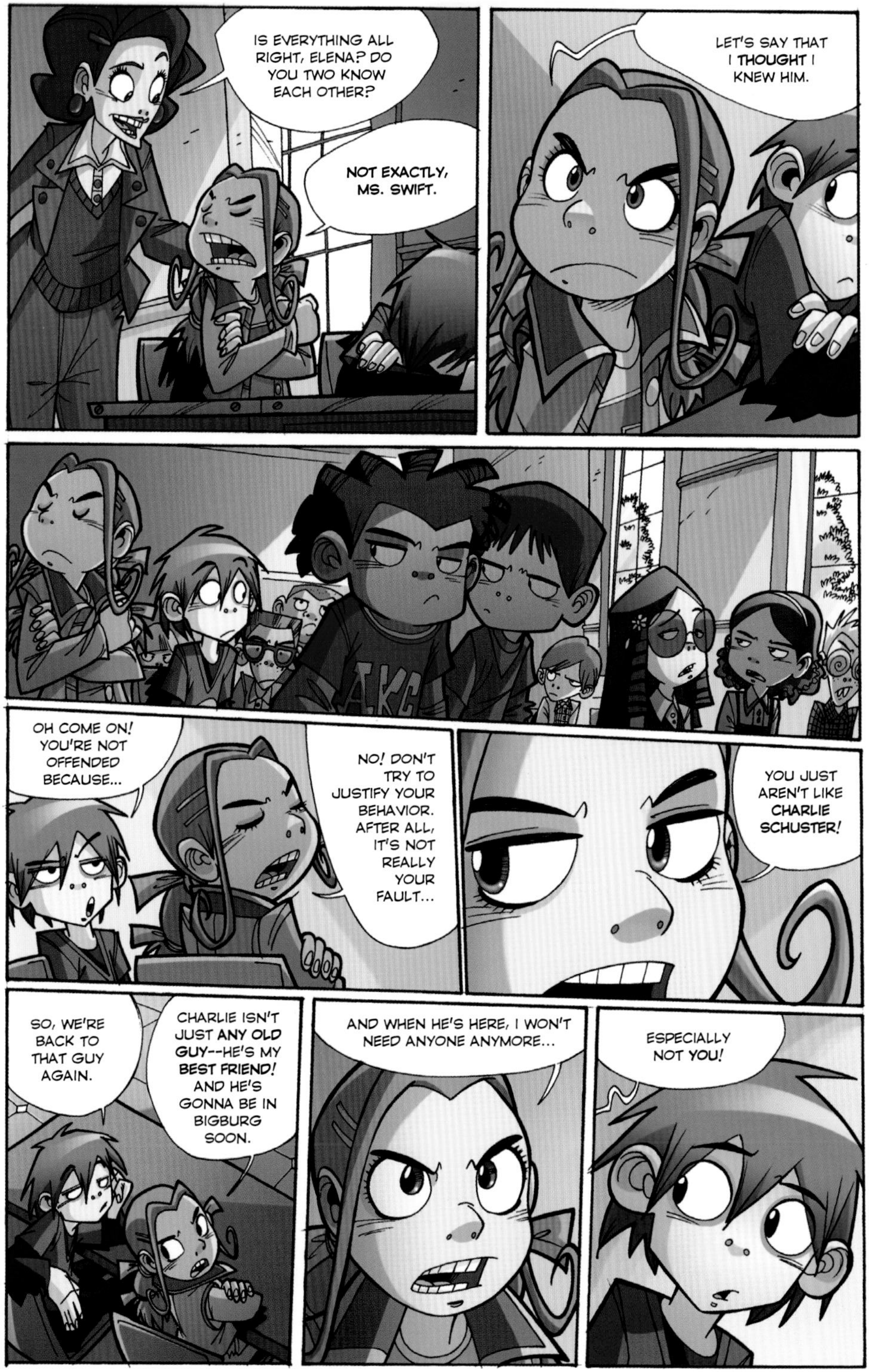
IS EVERYTHING ALL RIGHT, ELENA? DO YOU TWO KNOW EACH OTHER?
NOT EXACTLY, MS. SWIFT.
LET'S SAY THAT I **THOUGHT** I KNEW HIM.
OH COME ON! YOU'RE NOT OFFENDED BECAUSE...
NO! DON'T TRY TO JUSTIFY YOUR BEHAVIOR. AFTER ALL, IT'S NOT REALLY YOUR FAULT...
YOU JUST AREN'T LIKE **CHARLIE SCHUSTER!**
SO, WE'RE BACK TO THAT GUY AGAIN.
CHARLIE ISN'T JUST **ANY OLD GUY**--HE'S MY **BEST FRIEND!** AND HE'S GONNA BE IN BIGBURG SOON.
AND WHEN HE'S HERE, I WON'T NEED ANYONE ANYMORE...
ESPECIALLY NOT **YOU!**

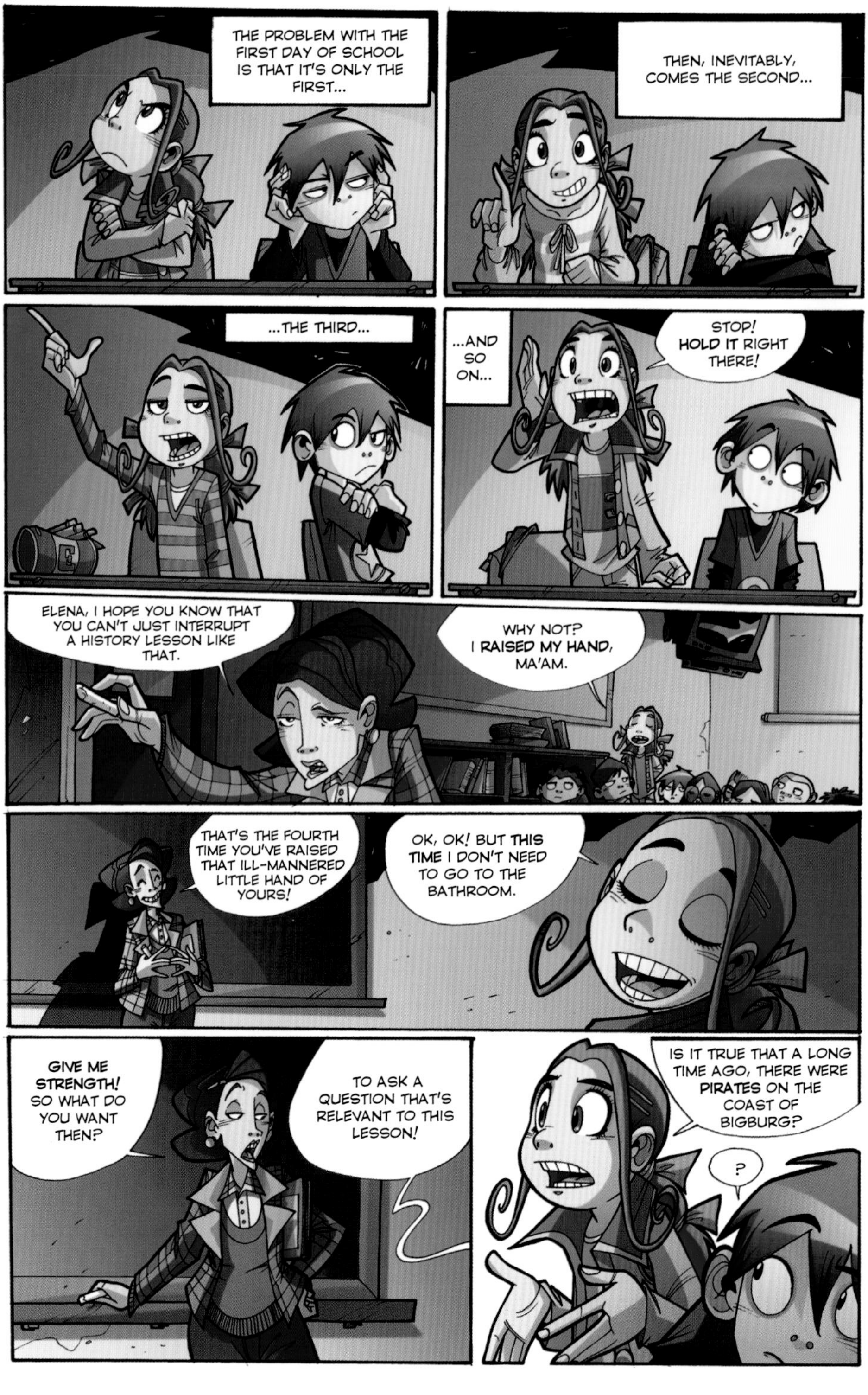
THE PROBLEM WITH THE FIRST DAY OF SCHOOL IS THAT IT'S ONLY THE FIRST...
THEN, INEVITABLY, COMES THE SECOND...
...THE THIRD...
...AND SO ON...
STOP! HOLD IT RIGHT THERE!
ELENA, I HOPE YOU KNOW THAT YOU CAN'T JUST INTERRUPT A HISTORY LESSON LIKE THAT.
WHY NOT? I RAISED MY HAND, MA'AM.
THAT'S THE FOURTH TIME YOU'VE RAISED THAT ILL-MANNERED LITTLE HAND OF YOURS!
OK, OK! BUT THIS TIME I DON'T NEED TO GO TO THE BATHROOM.
GIVE ME STRENGTH! SO WHAT DO YOU WANT THEN?
TO ASK A QUESTION THAT'S RELEVANT TO THIS LESSON!
IS IT TRUE THAT A LONG TIME AGO, THERE WERE PIRATES ON THE COAST OF BIGBURG?
?

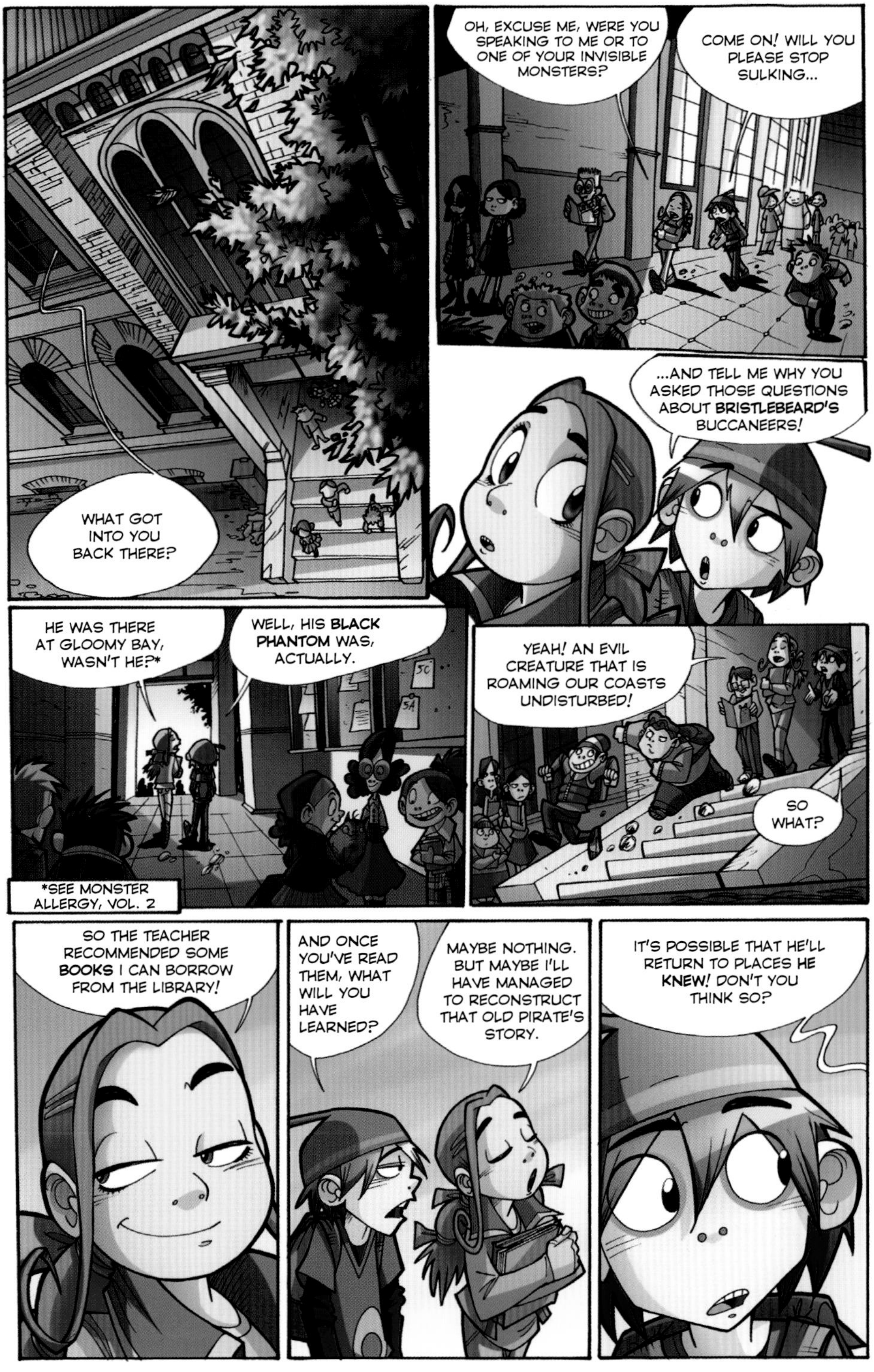
WHAT GOT INTO YOU BACK THERE?
OH, EXCUSE ME, WERE YOU SPEAKING TO ME OR TO ONE OF YOUR INVISIBLE MONSTERS?
COME ON! WILL YOU PLEASE STOP SULKING...
...AND TELL ME WHY YOU ASKED THOSE QUESTIONS ABOUT **BRISTLEBEARD'S** BUCCANEERS!
HE WAS THERE AT GLOOMY BAY, WASN'T HE?*
WELL, HIS **BLACK PHANTOM** WAS, ACTUALLY.
*SEE MONSTER ALLERGY, VOL. 2
YEAH! AN EVIL CREATURE THAT IS ROAMING OUR COASTS UNDISTURBED!
SO WHAT?
SO THE TEACHER RECOMMENDED SOME **BOOKS** I CAN BORROW FROM THE LIBRARY!
AND ONCE YOU'VE READ THEM, WHAT WILL YOU HAVE LEARNED?
MAYBE NOTHING. BUT MAYBE I'LL HAVE MANAGED TO RECONSTRUCT THAT OLD PIRATE'S STORY.
IT'S POSSIBLE THAT HE'LL RETURN TO PLACES **HE KNEW**! DON'T YOU THINK SO?

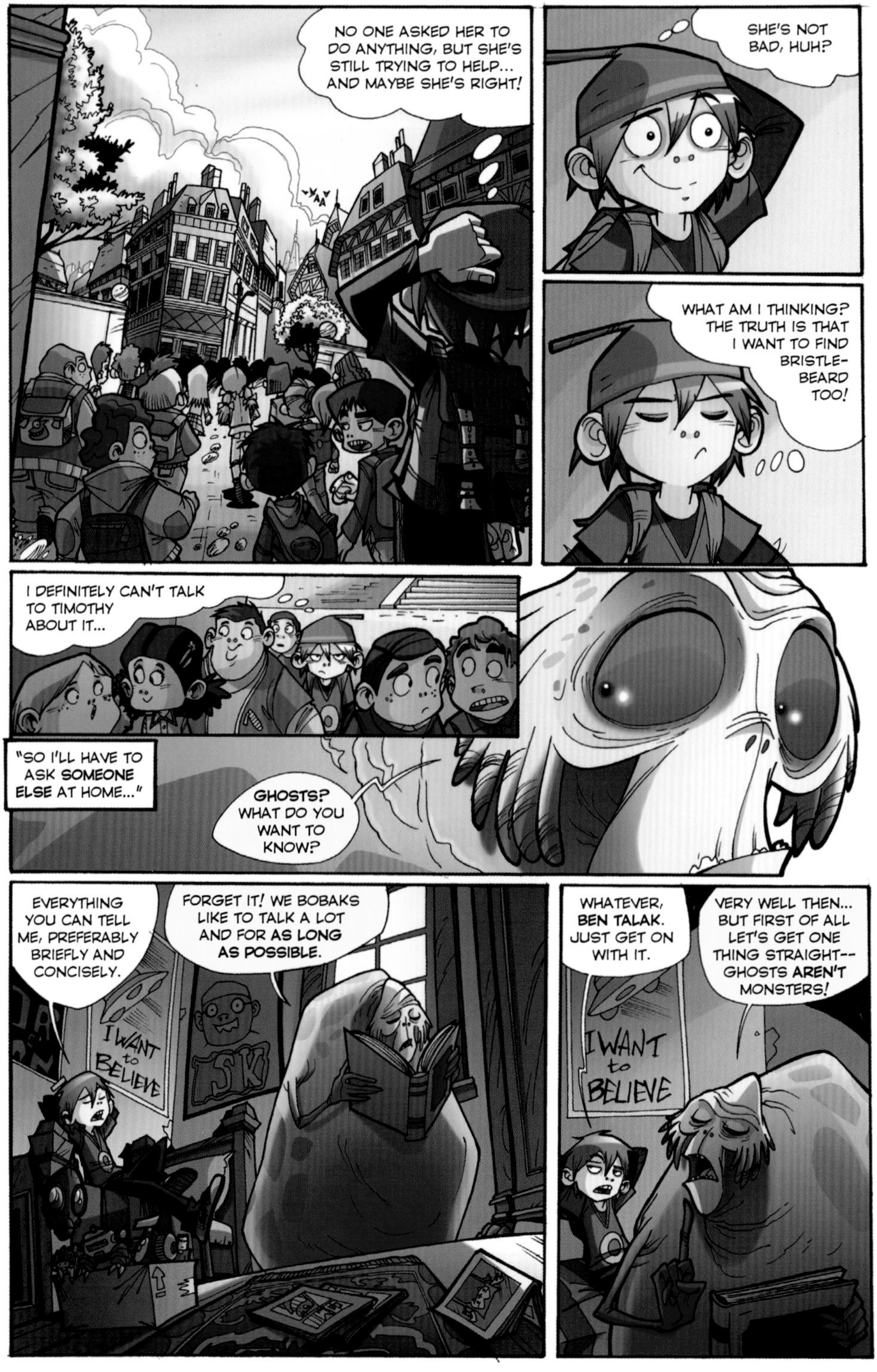
NO ONE ASKED HER TO DO ANYTHING, BUT SHE'S STILL TRYING TO HELP... AND MAYBE SHE'S RIGHT!
SHE'S NOT BAD, HUH?
WHAT AM I THINKING? THE TRUTH IS THAT I WANT TO FIND BRISTLE-BEARD TOO!
I DEFINITELY CAN'T TALK TO TIMOTHY ABOUT IT...
"SO I'LL HAVE TO ASK SOMEONE ELSE AT HOME..."
GHOSTS? WHAT DO YOU WANT TO KNOW?
EVERYTHING YOU CAN TELL ME, PREFERABLY BRIEFLY AND CONCISELY.
FORGET IT! WE BOBAKS LIKE TO TALK A LOT AND FOR AS LONG AS POSSIBLE.
I WANT to BELIEVE
WHATEVER, BEN TALAK. JUST GET ON WITH IT.
VERY WELL THEN... BUT FIRST OF ALL LET'S GET ONE THING STRAIGHT-- GHOSTS AREN'T MONSTERS!
I WANT to BELIEVE

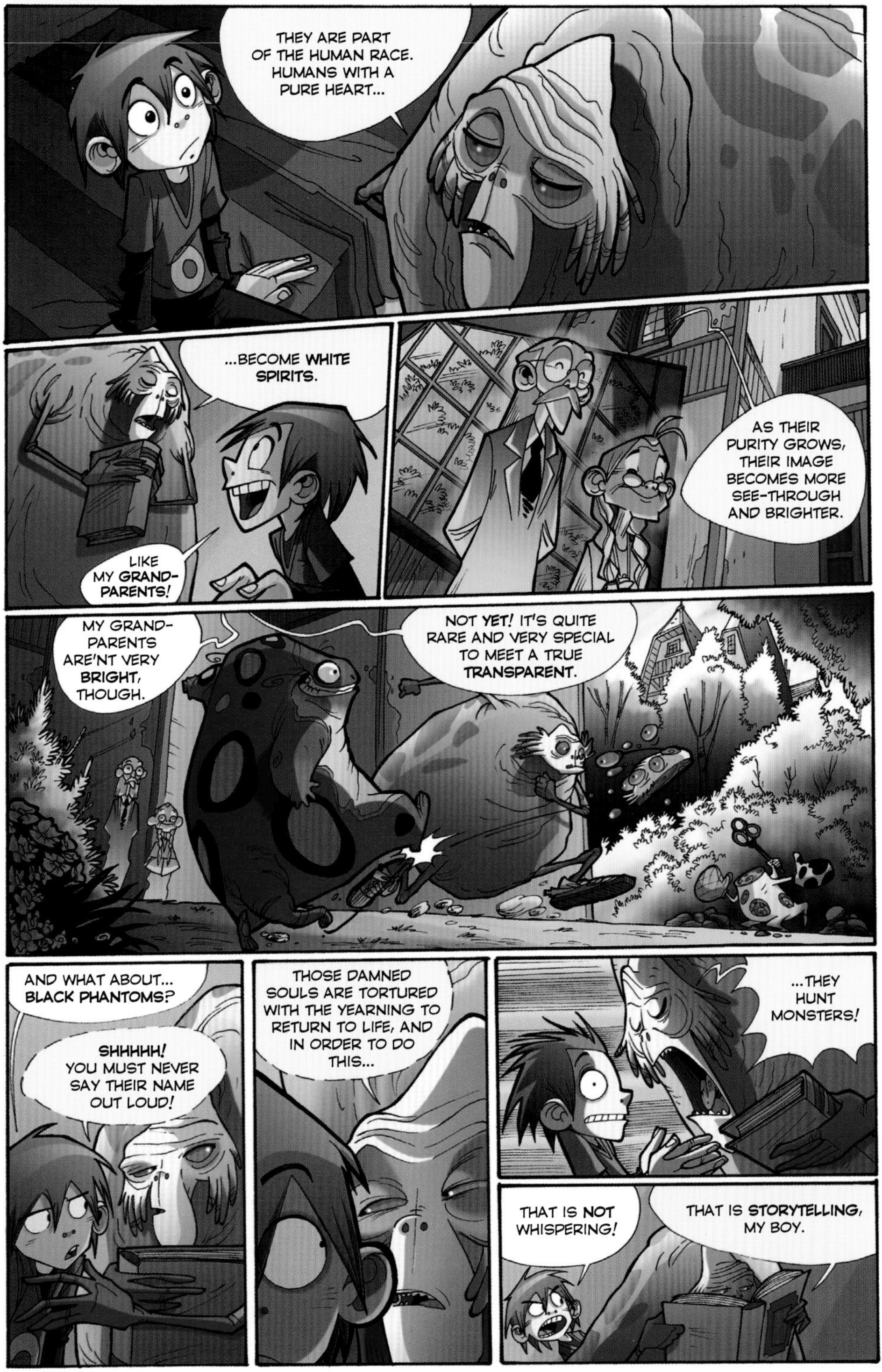
THEY ARE PART OF THE HUMAN RACE. HUMANS WITH A PURE HEART...
...BECOME WHITE SPIRITS.
LIKE MY GRAND-PARENTS!
AS THEIR PURITY GROWS, THEIR IMAGE BECOMES MORE SEE-THROUGH AND BRIGHTER.
MY GRAND-PARENTS ARE'NT VERY BRIGHT, THOUGH.
NOT YET! IT'S QUITE RARE AND VERY SPECIAL TO MEET A TRUE TRANSPARENT.
AND WHAT ABOUT... BLACK PHANTOMS?
SHHHHH! YOU MUST NEVER SAY THEIR NAME OUT LOUD!
THOSE DAMNED SOULS ARE TORTURED WITH THE YEARNING TO RETURN TO LIFE, AND IN ORDER TO DO THIS...
...THEY HUNT MONSTERS!
THAT IS NOT WHISPERING!
THAT IS STORYTELLING, MY BOY.

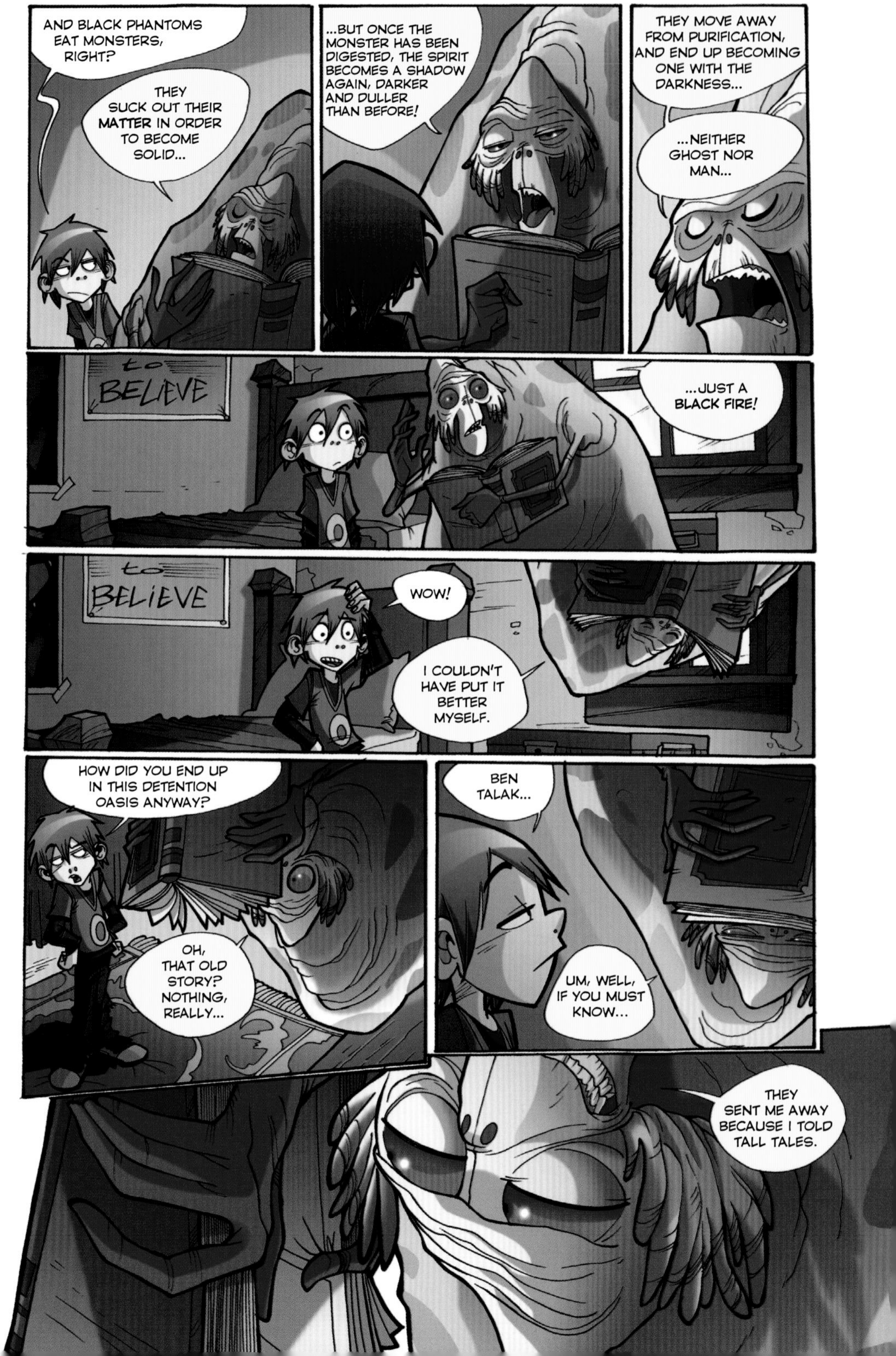
AND BLACK PHANTOMS EAT MONSTERS, RIGHT?
THEY SUCK OUT THEIR MATTER IN ORDER TO BECOME SOLID...
...BUT ONCE THE MONSTER HAS BEEN DIGESTED, THE SPIRIT BECOMES A SHADOW AGAIN, DARKER AND DULLER THAN BEFORE!
THEY MOVE AWAY FROM PURIFICATION, AND END UP BECOMING ONE WITH THE DARKNESS...
...NEITHER GHOST NOR MAN...
to BELIEVE
...JUST A BLACK FIRE!
to BELIEVE
WOW!
I COULDN'T HAVE PUT IT BETTER MYSELF.
HOW DID YOU END UP IN THIS DETENTION OASIS ANYWAY?
OH, THAT OLD STORY? NOTHING, REALLY...
BEN TALAK...
UM, WELL, IF YOU MUST KNOW...
THEY SENT ME AWAY BECAUSE I TOLD TALL TALES.

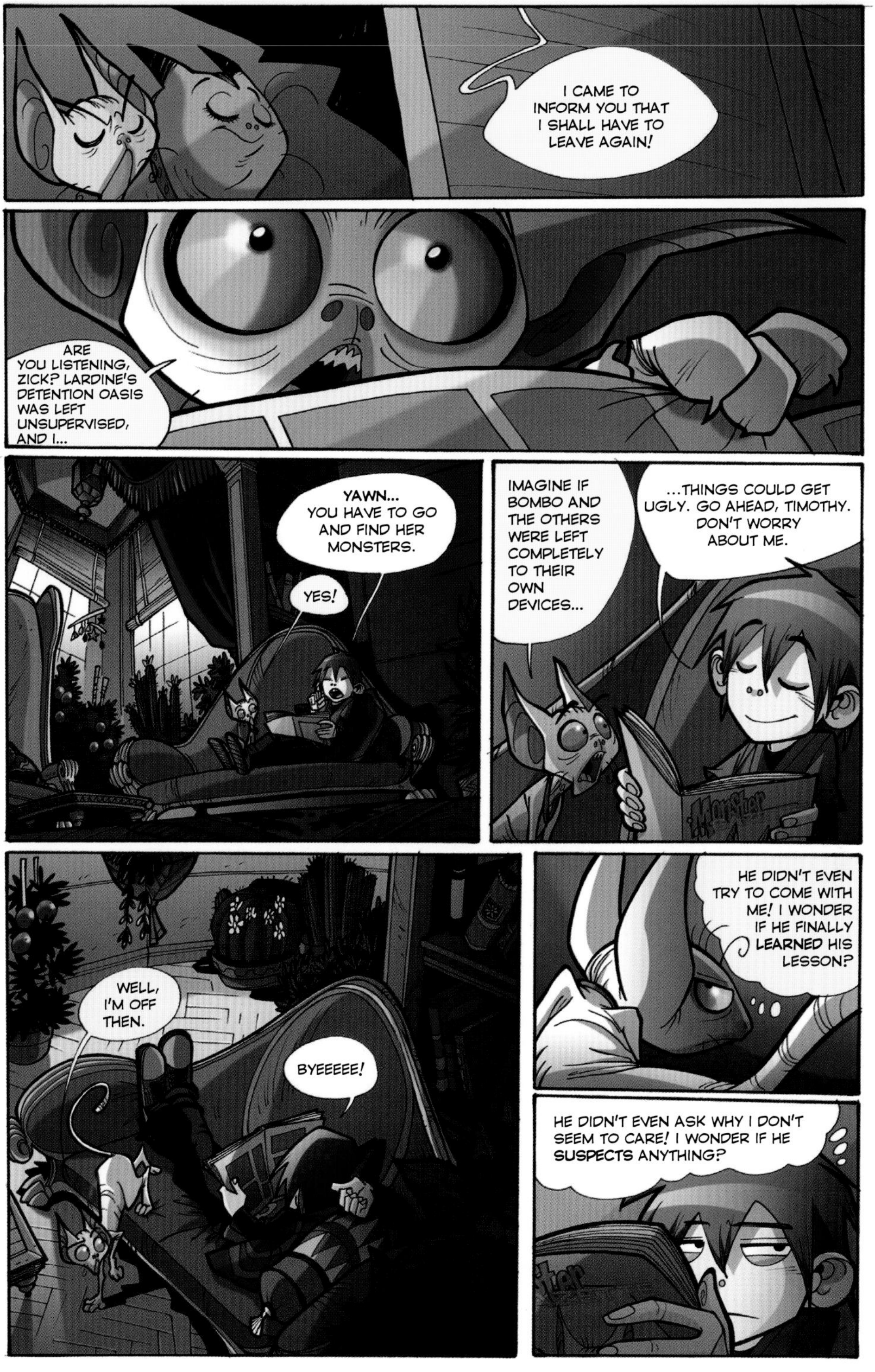
I CAME TO INFORM YOU THAT I SHALL HAVE TO LEAVE AGAIN!
ARE YOU LISTENING, ZICK? LARDINE'S DETENTION OASIS WAS LEFT UNSUPERVISED, AND I...
YAWN... YOU HAVE TO GO AND FIND HER MONSTERS.
YES!
IMAGINE IF BOMBO AND THE OTHERS WERE LEFT COMPLETELY TO THEIR OWN DEVICES...
...THINGS COULD GET UGLY. GO AHEAD, TIMOTHY. DON'T WORRY ABOUT ME.
WELL, I'M OFF THEN.
BYEEEEE!
HE DIDN'T EVEN TRY TO COME WITH ME! I WONDER IF HE FINALLY LEARNED HIS LESSON?
HE DIDN'T EVEN ASK WHY I DON'T SEEM TO CARE! I WONDER IF HE SUSPECTS ANYTHING?

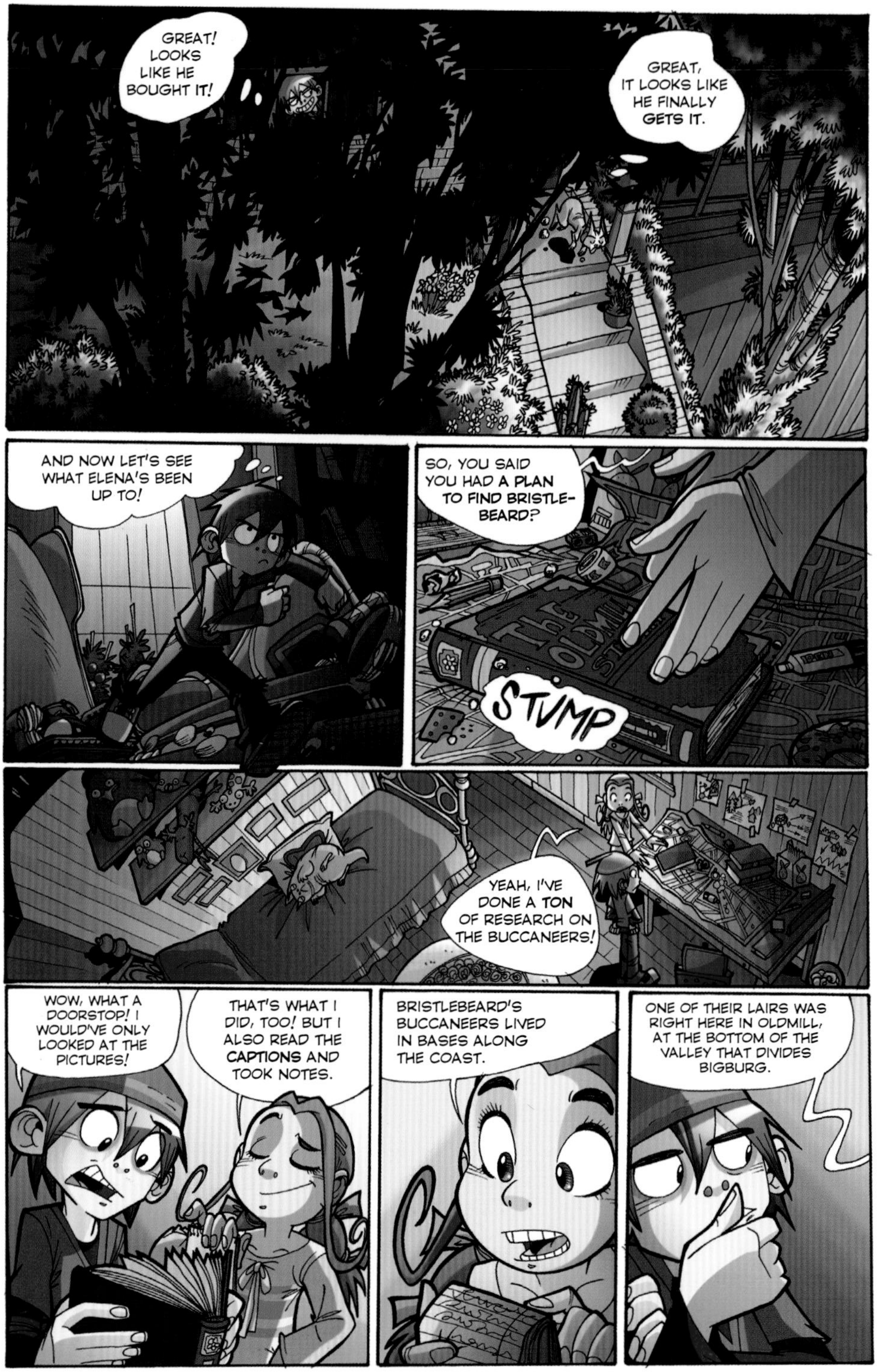
GREAT! LOOKS LIKE HE BOUGHT IT!
GREAT, IT LOOKS LIKE HE FINALLY GETS IT.
AND NOW LET'S SEE WHAT ELENA'S BEEN UP TO!
SO, YOU SAID YOU HAD A PLAN TO FIND BRISTLE-BEARD?
STUMP
YEAH, I'VE DONE A TON OF RESEARCH ON THE BUCCANEERS!
WOW, WHAT A DOORSTOP! I WOULD'VE ONLY LOOKED AT THE PICTURES!
THAT'S WHAT I DID, TOO! BUT I ALSO READ THE CAPTIONS AND TOOK NOTES.
BRISTLEBEARD'S BUCCANEERS LIVED IN BASES ALONG THE COAST.
ONE OF THEIR LAIRS WAS RIGHT HERE IN OLDMILL, AT THE BOTTOM OF THE VALLEY THAT DIVIDES BIGBURG.

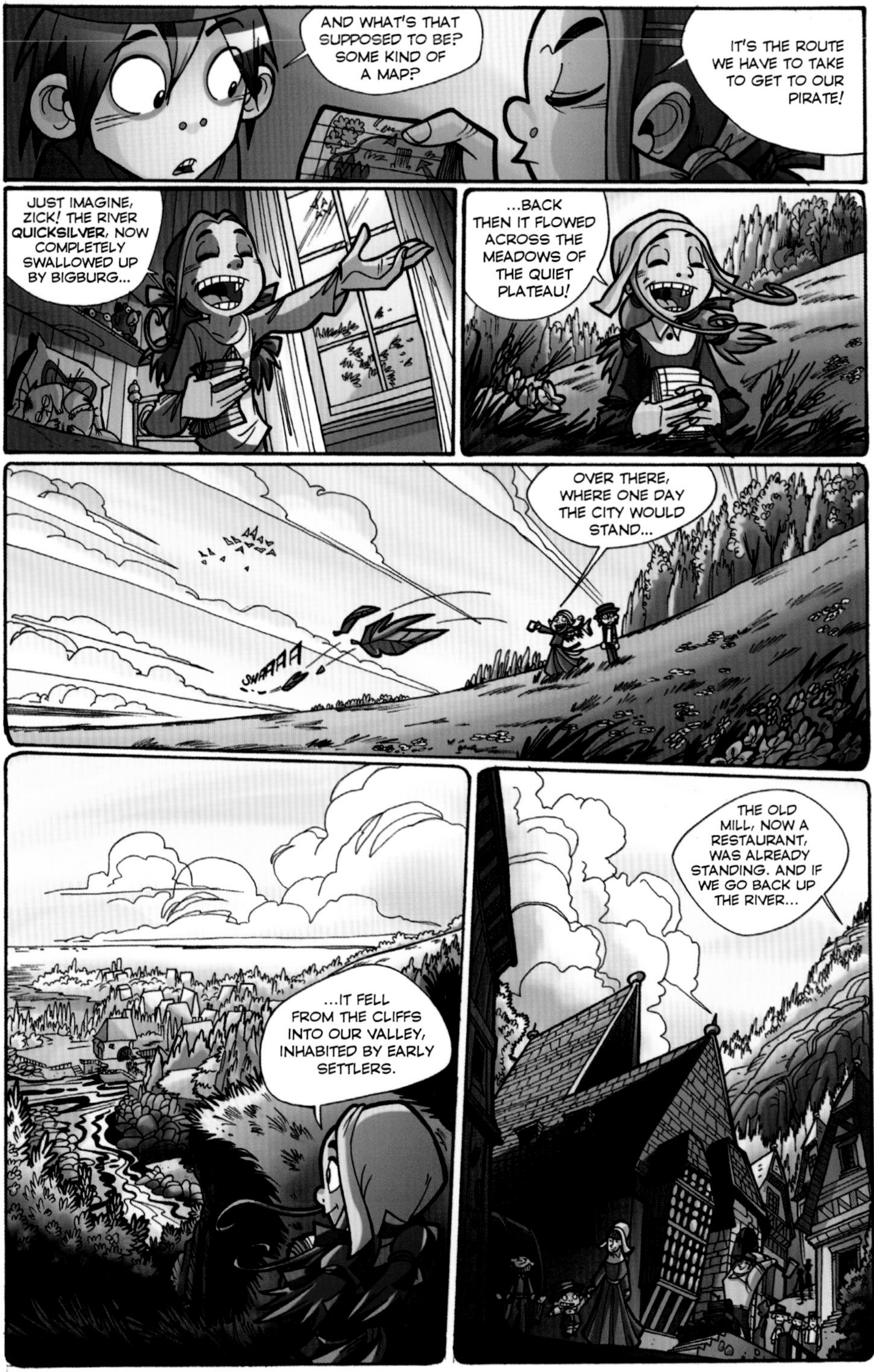
AND WHAT'S THAT SUPPOSED TO BE? SOME KIND OF A MAP?
IT'S THE ROUTE WE HAVE TO TAKE TO GET TO OUR PIRATE!
JUST IMAGINE, ZICK! THE RIVER QUICKSILVER, NOW COMPLETELY SWALLOWED UP BY BIGBURG...
...BACK THEN IT FLOWED ACROSS THE MEADOWS OF THE QUIET PLATEAU!
OVER THERE, WHERE ONE DAY THE CITY WOULD STAND...
SWFFFF
...IT FELL FROM THE CLIFFS INTO OUR VALLEY, INHABITED BY EARLY SETTLERS.
THE OLD MILL, NOW A RESTAURANT, WAS ALREADY STANDING. AND IF WE GO BACK UP THE RIVER...

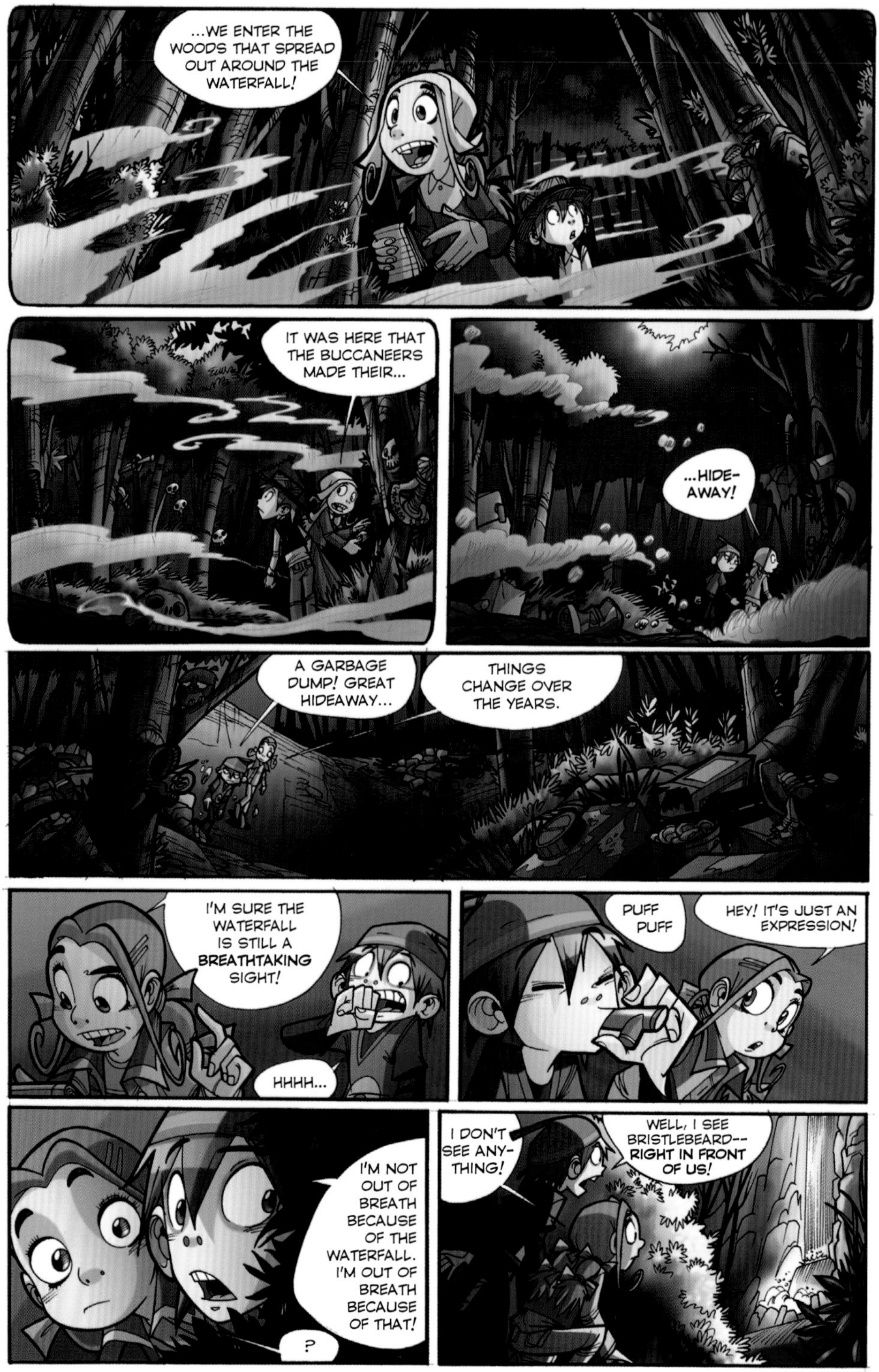
...WE ENTER THE WOODS THAT SPREAD OUT AROUND THE WATERFALL!
IT WAS HERE THAT THE BUCCANEERS MADE THEIR...
...HIDE-AWAY!
A GARBAGE DUMP! GREAT HIDEAWAY...
THINGS CHANGE OVER THE YEARS.
I'M SURE THE WATERFALL IS STILL A **BREATHTAKING** SIGHT!
HHHH...
PUFF PUFF
HEY! IT'S JUST AN EXPRESSION!
I'M NOT OUT OF BREATH BECAUSE OF THE WATERFALL. I'M OUT OF BREATH BECAUSE OF THAT!
?
I DON'T SEE ANY-THING!
WELL, I SEE BRISTLEBEARD-- **RIGHT IN FRONT OF US!**

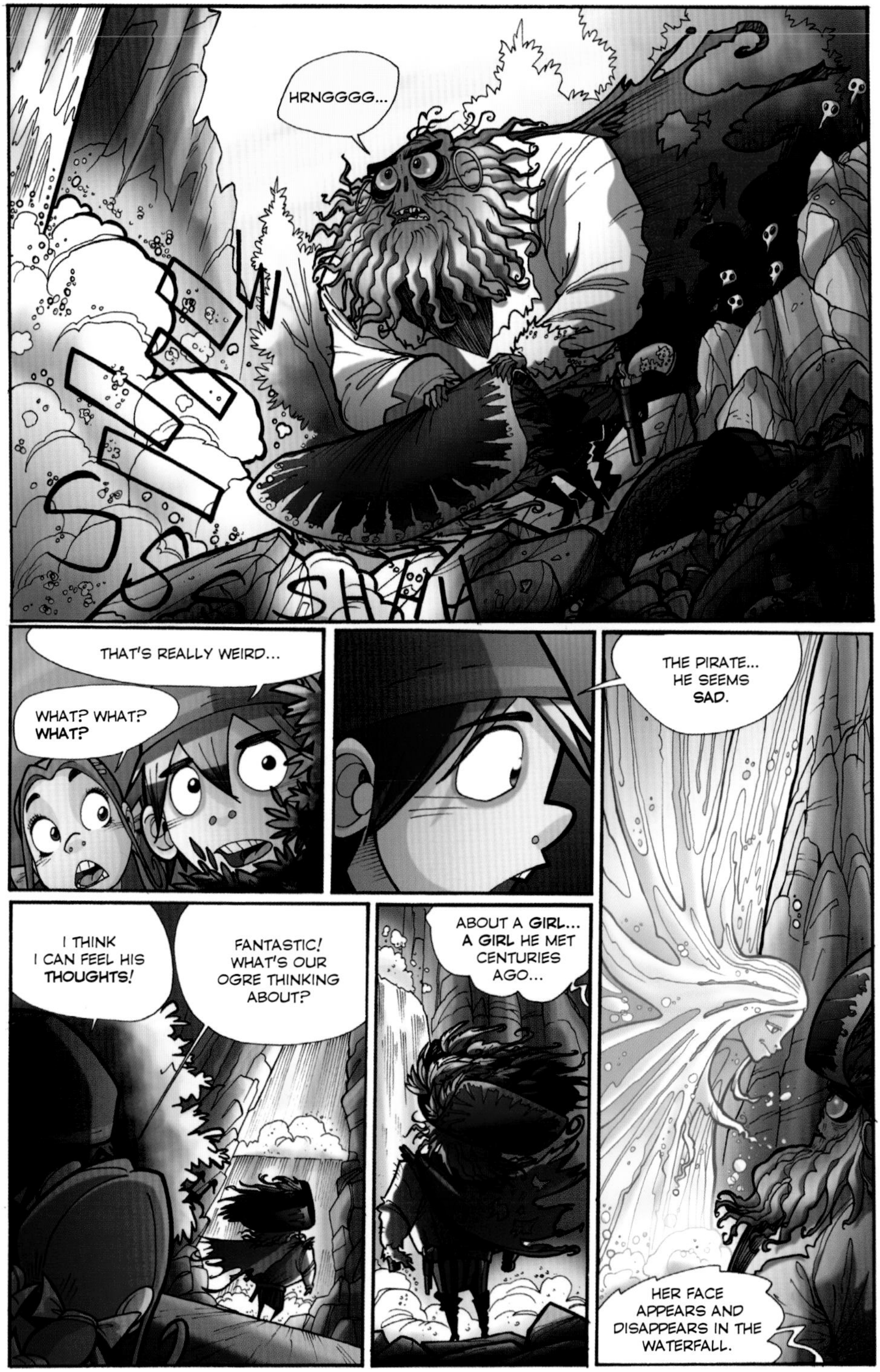
HRNGGGG...
THAT'S REALLY WEIRD...
WHAT? WHAT? WHAT?
THE PIRATE... HE SEEMS SAD.
I THINK I CAN FEEL HIS THOUGHTS!
FANTASTIC! WHAT'S OUR OGRE THINKING ABOUT?
ABOUT A GIRL... A GIRL HE MET CENTURIES AGO...
HER FACE APPEARS AND DISAPPEARS IN THE WATERFALL.

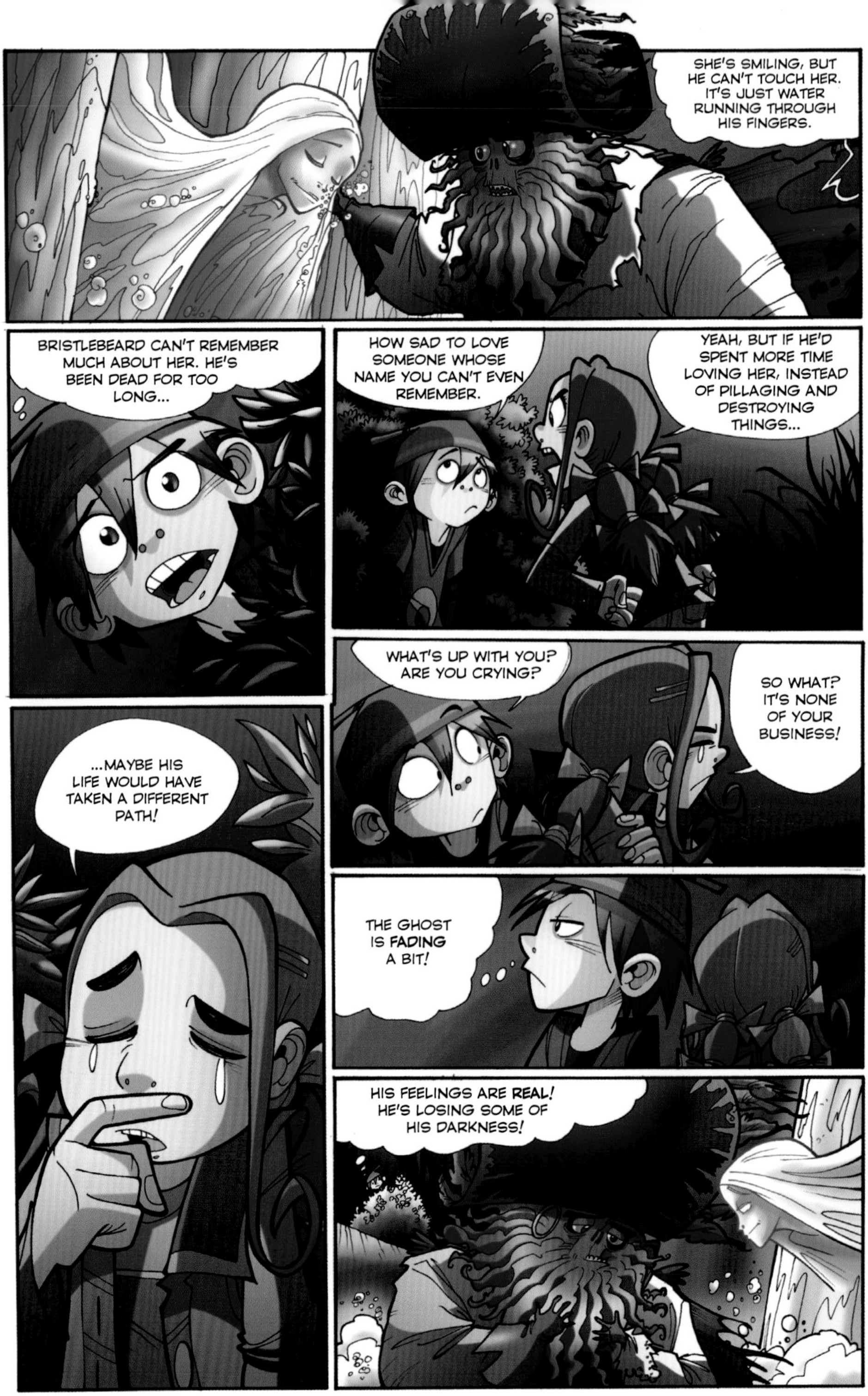

SHE'S SMILING, BUT HE CAN'T TOUCH HER. IT'S JUST WATER RUNNING THROUGH HIS FINGERS.
BRISTLEBEARD CAN'T REMEMBER MUCH ABOUT HER. HE'S BEEN DEAD FOR TOO LONG...
HOW SAD TO LOVE SOMEONE WHOSE NAME YOU CAN'T EVEN REMEMBER.
YEAH, BUT IF HE'D SPENT MORE TIME LOVING HER, INSTEAD OF PILLAGING AND DESTROYING THINGS...
...MAYBE HIS LIFE WOULD HAVE TAKEN A DIFFERENT PATH!
WHAT'S UP WITH YOU? ARE YOU CRYING?
SO WHAT? IT'S NONE OF YOUR BUSINESS!
THE GHOST IS FADING A BIT!
HIS FEELINGS ARE REAL! HE'S LOSING SOME OF HIS DARKNESS!

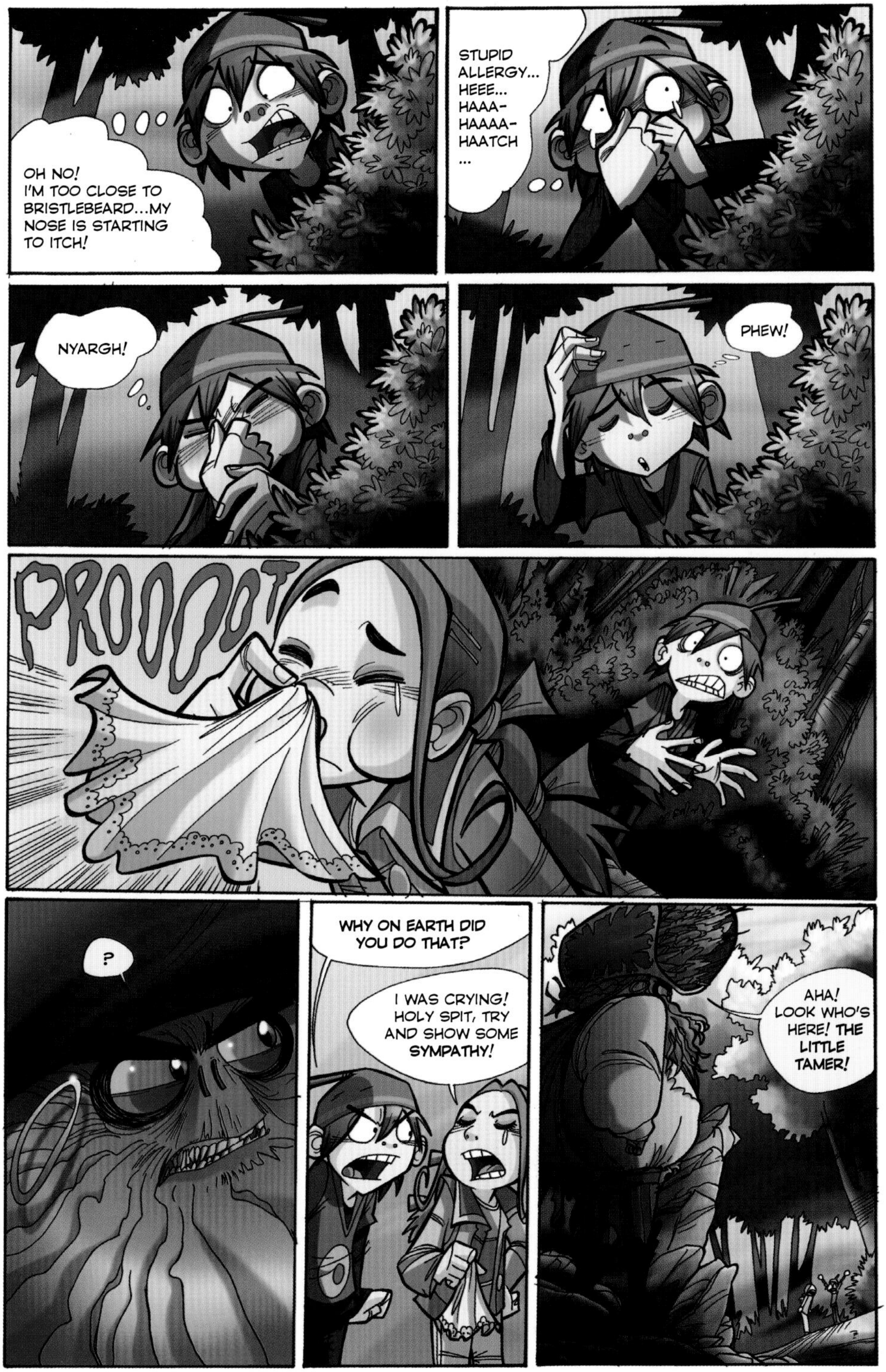
OH NO! I'M TOO CLOSE TO BRISTLEBEARD...MY NOSE IS STARTING TO ITCH!
STUPID ALLERGY... HEEE... HAAA-HAAAA-HAATCH ...
NYARGH!
PHEW!
PROOOOT
?
WHY ON EARTH DID YOU DO THAT?
I WAS CRYING! HOLY SPIT, TRY AND SHOW SOME SYMPATHY!
AHA! LOOK WHO'S HERE! THE LITTLE TAMER!

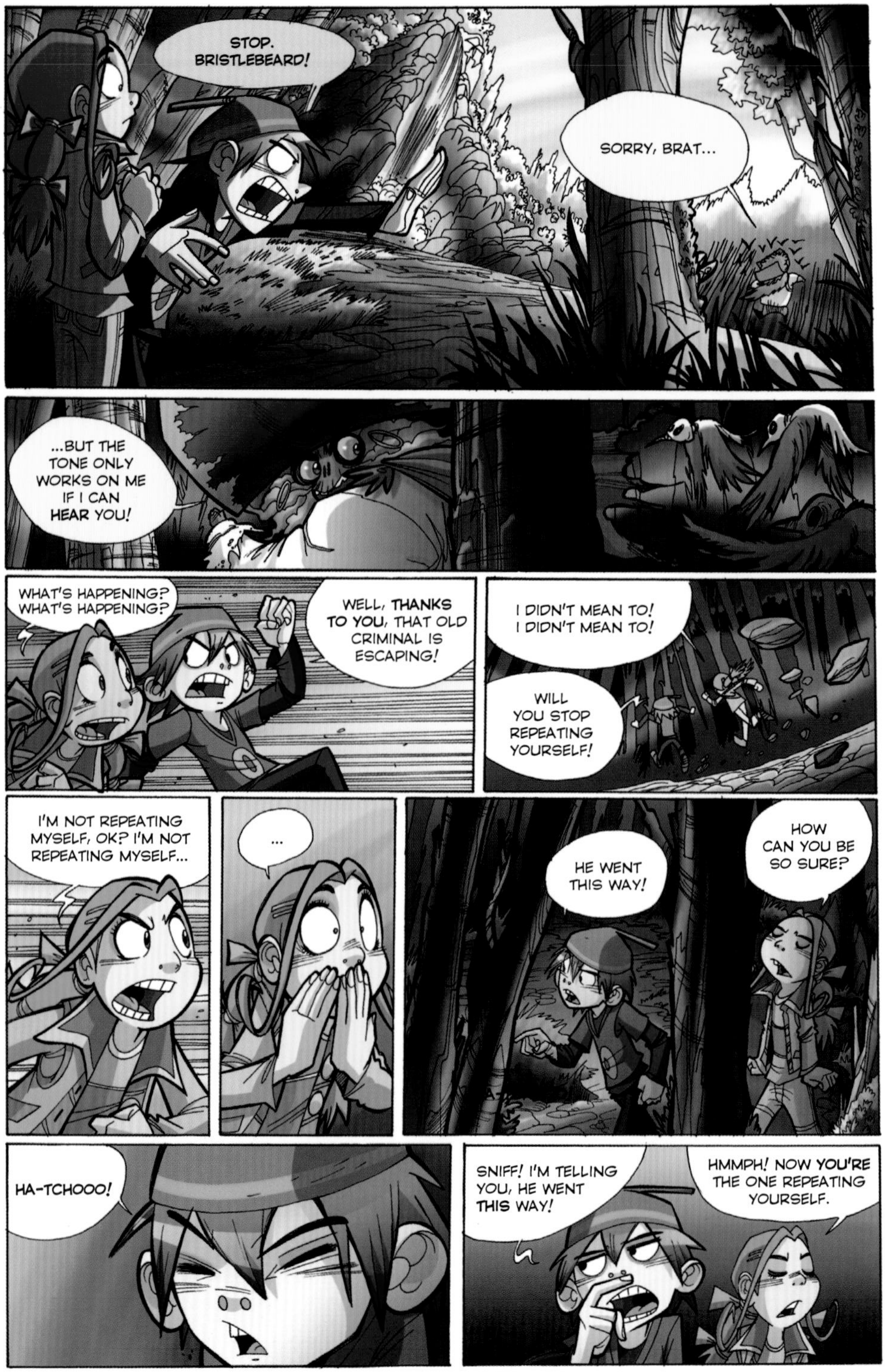
STOP. BRISTLEBEARD!
SORRY, BRAT...
...BUT THE TONE ONLY WORKS ON ME IF I CAN HEAR YOU!
WHAT'S HAPPENING? WHAT'S HAPPENING?
WELL, THANKS TO YOU, THAT OLD CRIMINAL IS ESCAPING!
I DIDN'T MEAN TO! I DIDN'T MEAN TO!
WILL YOU STOP REPEATING YOURSELF!
I'M NOT REPEATING MYSELF, OK? I'M NOT REPEATING MYSELF...
...
HE WENT THIS WAY!
HOW CAN YOU BE SO SURE?
HA-TCHOOO!
SNIFF! I'M TELLING YOU, HE WENT THIS WAY!
HMMPH! NOW YOU'RE THE ONE REPEATING YOURSELF.

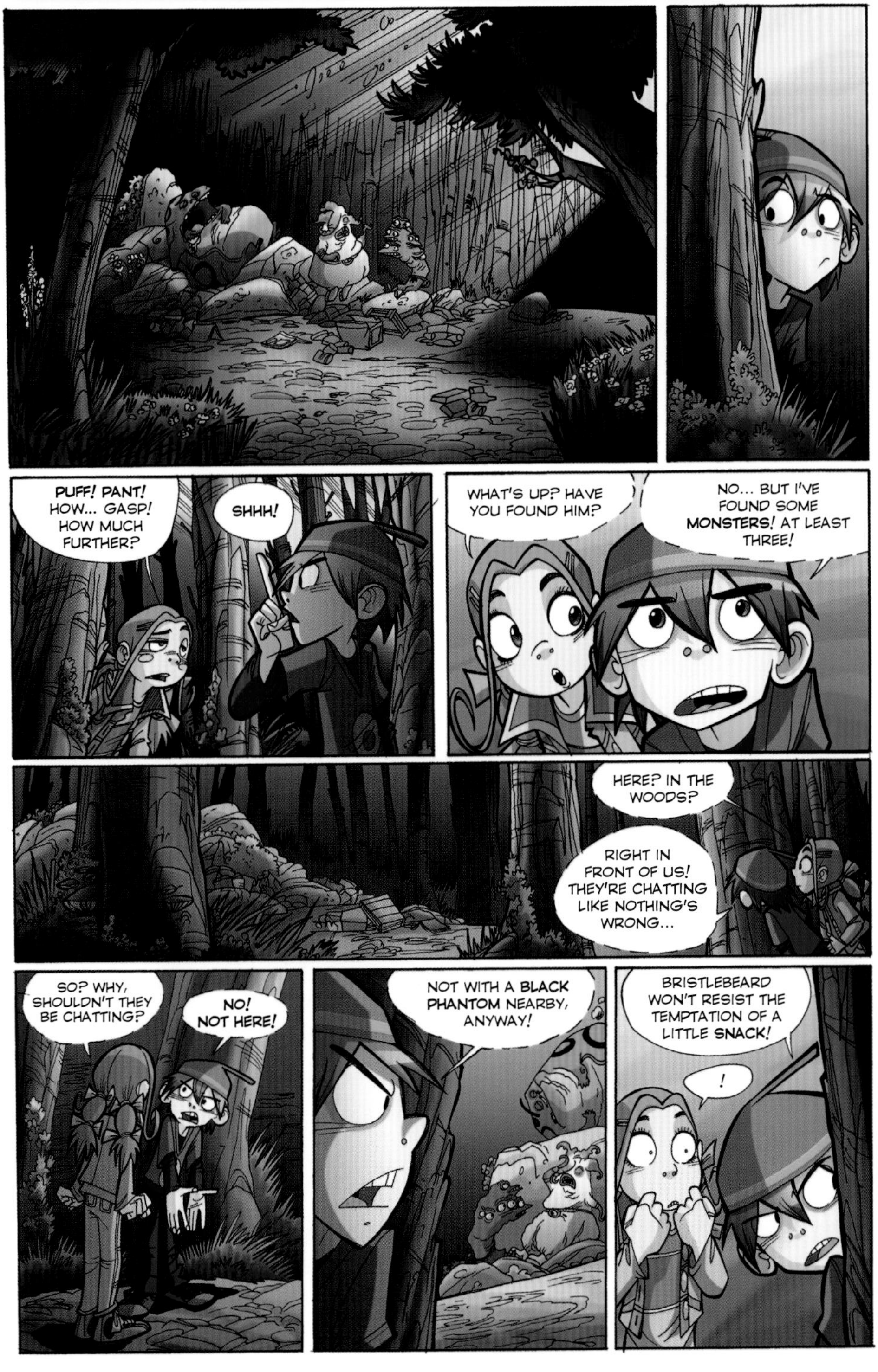
PUFF! PANT! HOW... GASP! HOW MUCH FURTHER?
SHHH!
WHAT'S UP? HAVE YOU FOUND HIM?
NO... BUT I'VE FOUND SOME MONSTERS! AT LEAST THREE!
HERE? IN THE WOODS?
RIGHT IN FRONT OF US! THEY'RE CHATTING LIKE NOTHING'S WRONG...
SO? WHY, SHOULDN'T THEY BE CHATTING?
NO! NOT HERE!
NOT WITH A BLACK PHANTOM NEARBY, ANYWAY!
BRISTLEBEARD WON'T RESIST THE TEMPTATION OF A LITTLE SNACK!
!

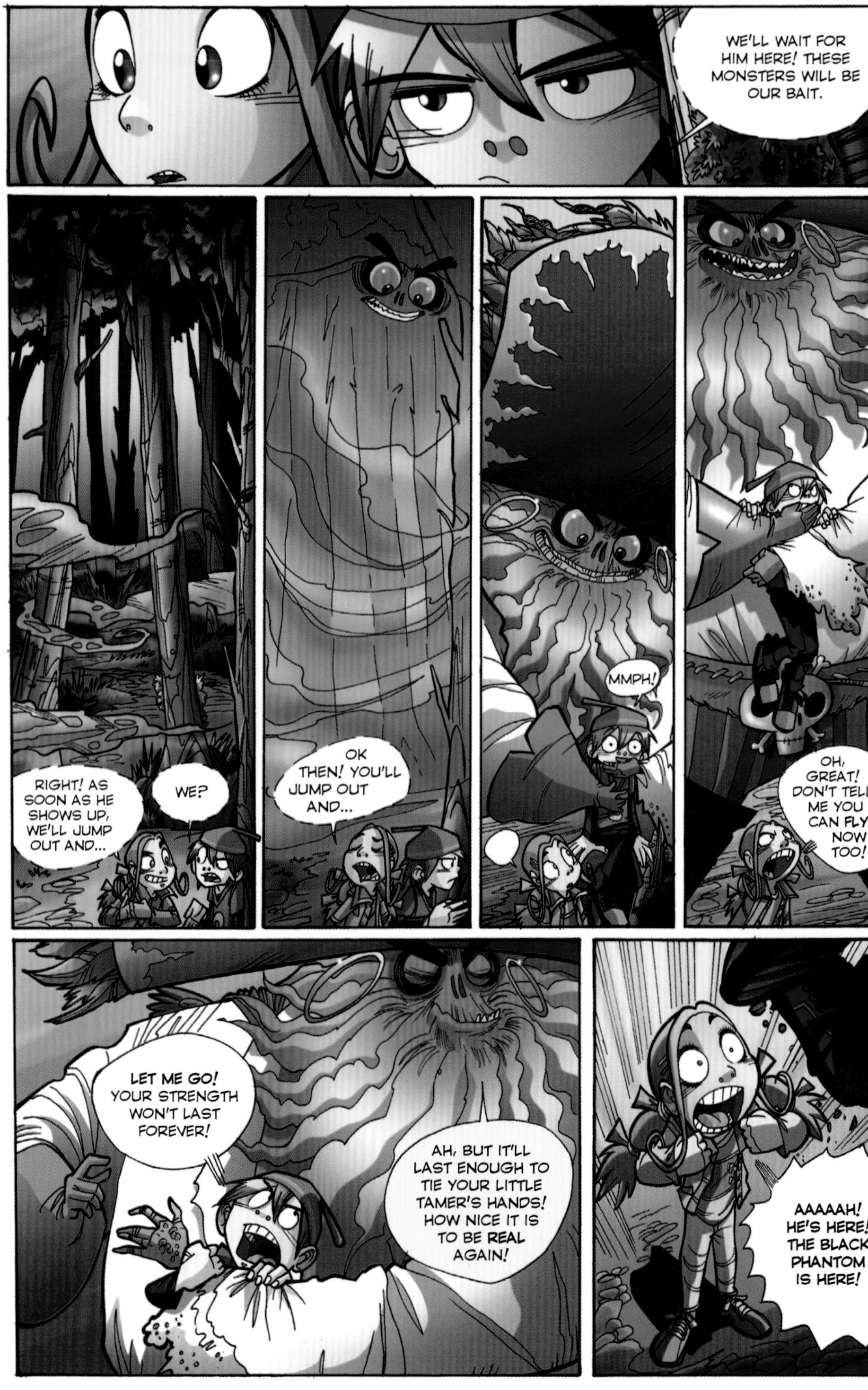
WE'LL WAIT FOR HIM HERE! THESE MONSTERS WILL BE OUR BAIT.
RIGHT! AS SOON AS HE SHOWS UP, WE'LL JUMP OUT AND...
WE?
OK THEN! YOU'LL JUMP OUT AND...
MMPH!
OH, GREAT! DON'T TELL ME YOU CAN FLY NOW TOO!
LET ME GO! YOUR STRENGTH WON'T LAST FOREVER!
AH, BUT IT'LL LAST ENOUGH TO TIE YOUR LITTLE TAMER'S HANDS! HOW NICE IT IS TO BE REAL AGAIN!
AAAAAH! HE'S HERE! THE BLACK PHANTOM IS HERE!

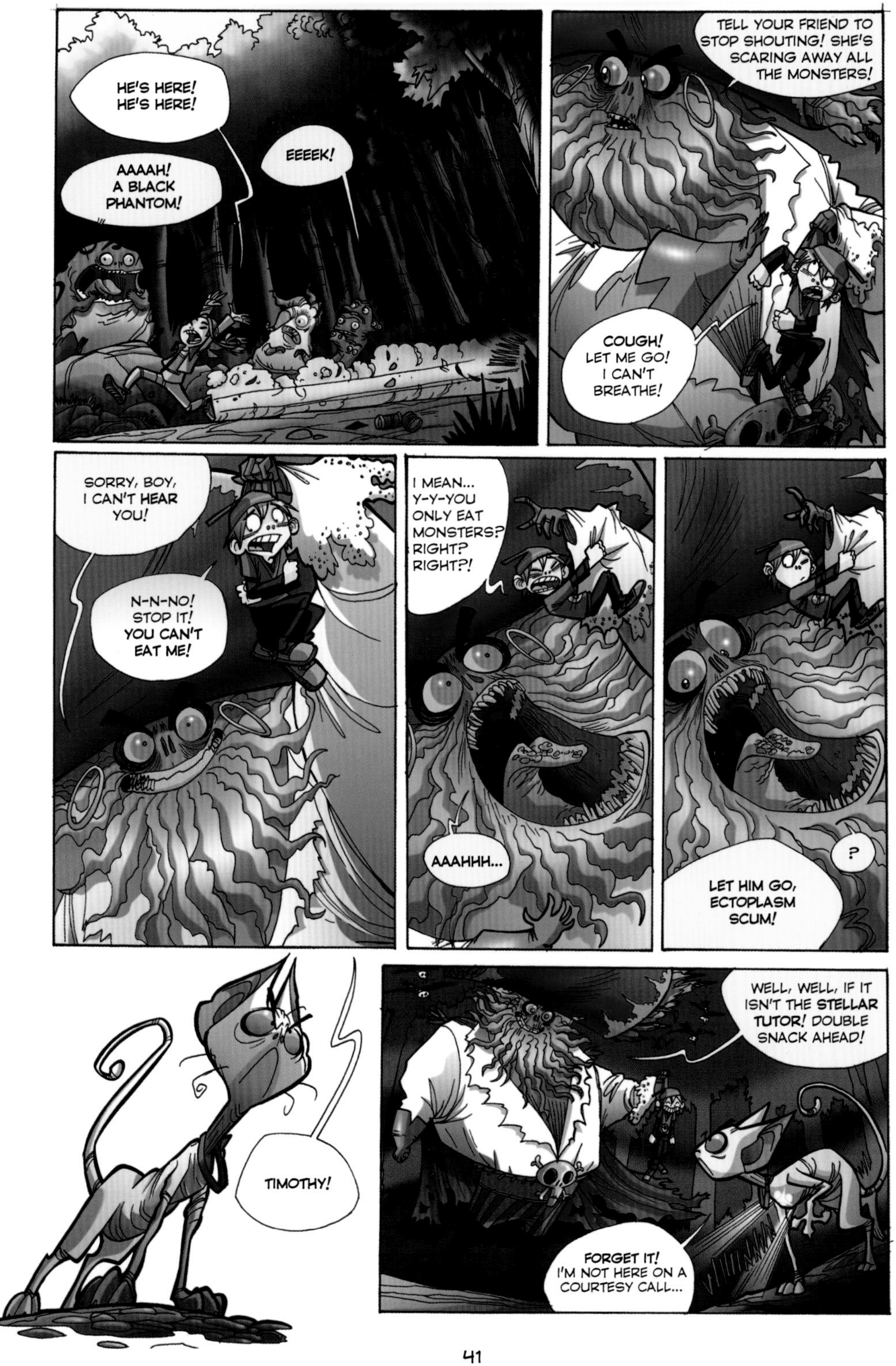
HE'S HERE! HE'S HERE!
AAAAH! A BLACK PHANTOM!
EEEEK!
TELL YOUR FRIEND TO STOP SHOUTING! SHE'S SCARING AWAY ALL THE MONSTERS!
COUGH! LET ME GO! I CAN'T BREATHE!
SORRY, BOY, I CAN'T HEAR YOU!
N-N-NO! STOP IT! YOU CAN'T EAT ME!
I MEAN... Y-Y-YOU ONLY EAT MONSTERS? RIGHT? RIGHT?!
AAAHHH...
?
LET HIM GO, ECTOPLASM SCUM!
TIMOTHY!
WELL, WELL, IF IT ISN'T THE STELLAR TUTOR! DOUBLE SNACK AHEAD!
FORGET IT! I'M NOT HERE ON A COURTESY CALL...

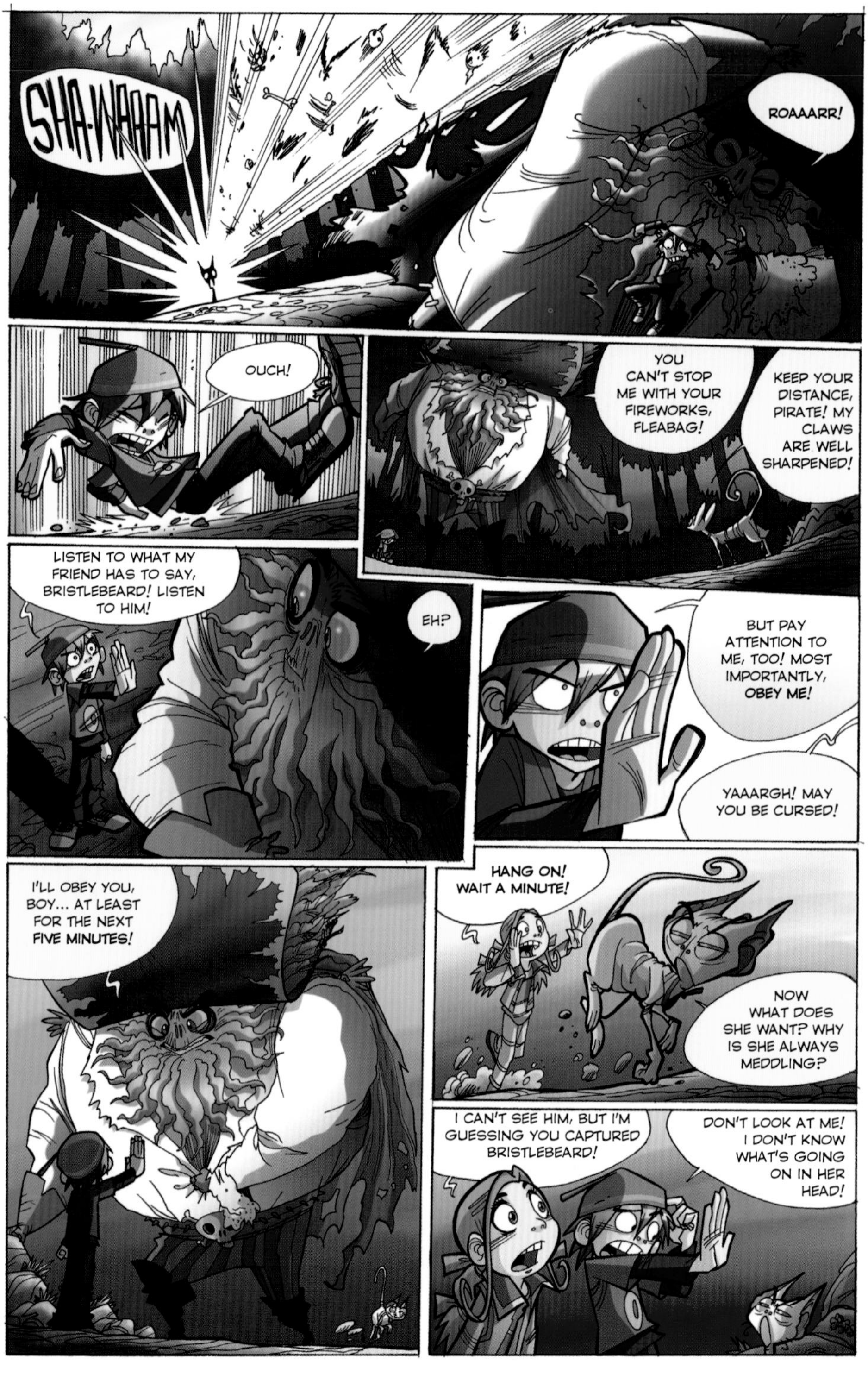
SHA-WAAAM
ROAAARR!
OUCH!
YOU CAN'T STOP ME WITH YOUR FIREWORKS, FLEABAG!
KEEP YOUR DISTANCE, PIRATE! MY CLAWS ARE WELL SHARPENED!
LISTEN TO WHAT MY FRIEND HAS TO SAY, BRISTLEBEARD! LISTEN TO HIM!
EH?
BUT PAY ATTENTION TO ME, TOO! MOST IMPORTANTLY, OBEY ME!
YAAARGH! MAY YOU BE CURSED!
I'LL OBEY YOU, BOY... AT LEAST FOR THE NEXT FIVE MINUTES!
HANG ON! WAIT A MINUTE!
NOW WHAT DOES SHE WANT? WHY IS SHE ALWAYS MEDDLING?
I CAN'T SEE HIM, BUT I'M GUESSING YOU CAPTURED BRISTLEBEARD!
DON'T LOOK AT ME! I DON'T KNOW WHAT'S GOING ON IN HER HEAD!

I JUST WANT TO SAY THAT THIS SPIRIT CAN'T BE ALL BAD!

DID YOU HEAR THE LITTLE LADY? I'M JUST A BIT PECKISH, THAT'S ALL!

I MEAN... THIS GUY ACTUALLY CRIED WHEN HE SAW THE FACE OF THE GIRL HE LOVED!

HEY, HOW THE DEVIL DOES SHE KNOW THAT I...

BRISTLEBEARD HAS KNOWN LOVE! A FEELING THAT GOES BEYOND LIFE AND DEATH!

AND WHAT DO YOU KNOW ABOUT THAT, GIRL?

HOLD STILL!

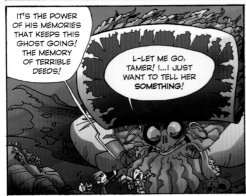

IT'S THE POWER OF HIS MEMORIES THAT KEEPS THIS GHOST GOING! THE MEMORY OF TERRIBLE DEEDS!

L-LET ME GO, TAMER! I...I JUST WANT TO TELL HER SOMETHING!

BUT THOSE MEMORIES ONLY FILL HIS STOMACH... NOT HIS CONSCIENCE!

HOW DARE SHE SPEAK LIKE THAT! I'LL TEAR HER TO PIECES! I SWEAR...

AT LEAST NOT AS MUCH AS THE MEMORY OF A LOST LOVE!

I... I... ...

IF HE'D MADE DIFFERENT CHOICES WHEN HE WAS ALIVE, THEN MAYBE SHE...

I...

...THEN MAYBE SHE WOULD BE HERE WITH HIM TODAY!

...

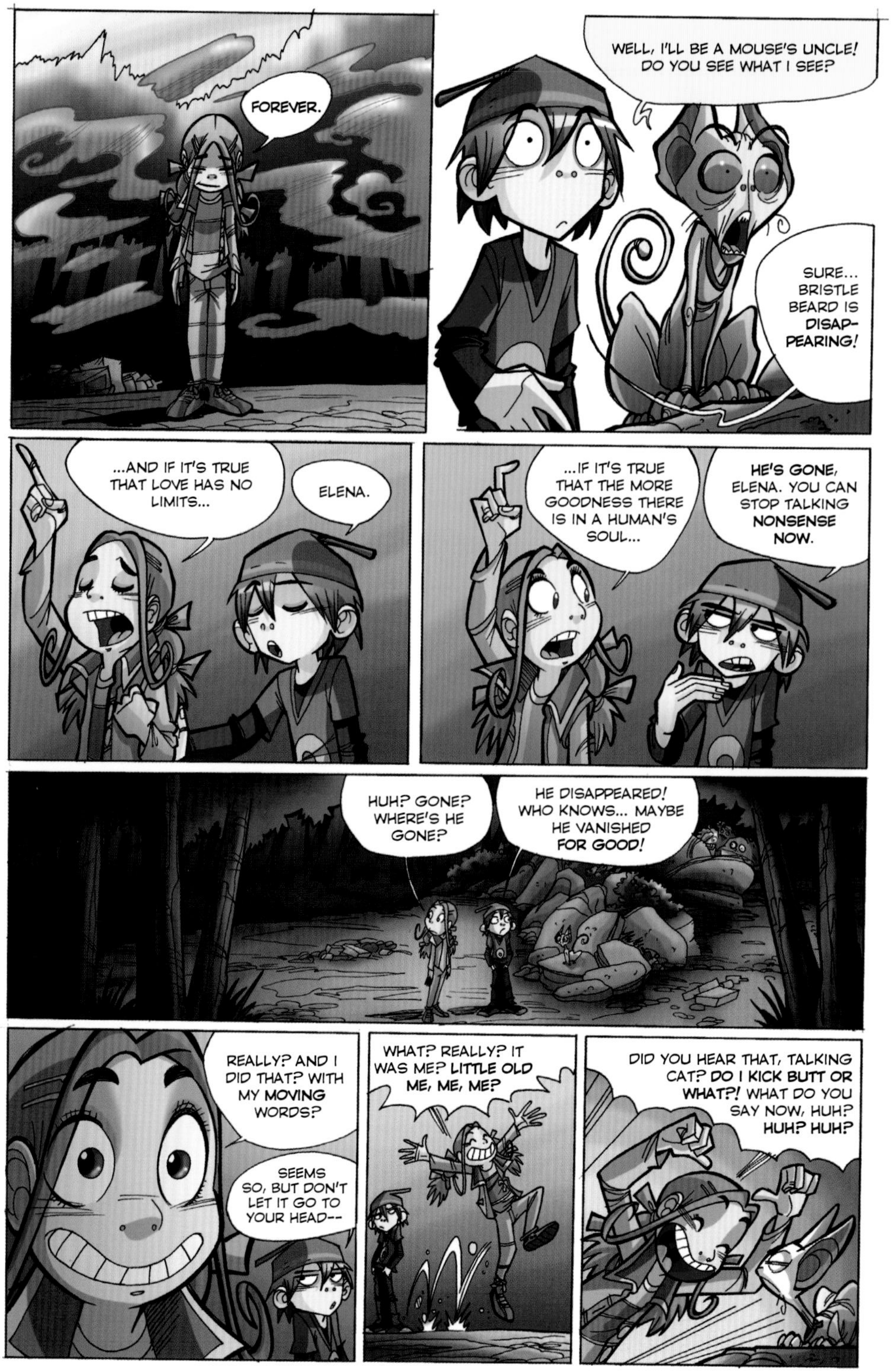
FOREVER.
WELL, I'LL BE A MOUSE'S UNCLE! DO YOU SEE WHAT I SEE?
SURE... BRISTLE BEARD IS DISAP-PEARING!
...AND IF IT'S TRUE THAT LOVE HAS NO LIMITS...
ELENA.
...IF IT'S TRUE THAT THE MORE GOODNESS THERE IS IN A HUMAN'S SOUL...
HE'S GONE, ELENA. YOU CAN STOP TALKING NONSENSE NOW.
HUH? GONE? WHERE'S HE GONE?
HE DISAPPEARED! WHO KNOWS... MAYBE HE VANISHED FOR GOOD!
REALLY? AND I DID THAT? WITH MY MOVING WORDS?
SEEMS SO, BUT DON'T LET IT GO TO YOUR HEAD--
WHAT? REALLY? IT WAS ME? LITTLE OLD ME, ME, ME?
DID YOU HEAR THAT, TALKING CAT? DO I KICK BUTT OR WHAT?! WHAT DO YOU SAY NOW, HUH? HUH? HUH?

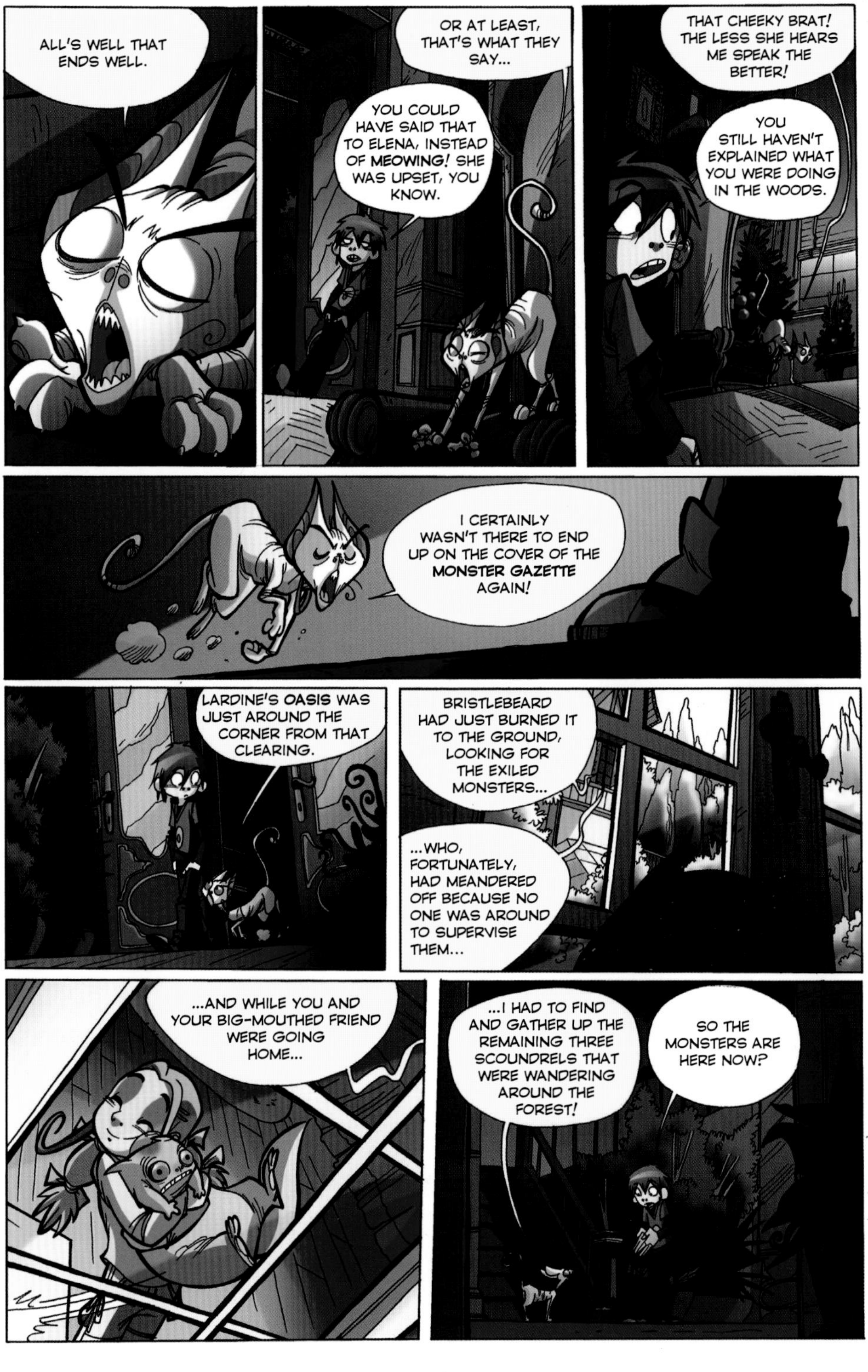
ALL'S WELL THAT ENDS WELL.
OR AT LEAST, THAT'S WHAT THEY SAY...
YOU COULD HAVE SAID THAT TO ELENA, INSTEAD OF MEOWING! SHE WAS UPSET, YOU KNOW.
THAT CHEEKY BRAT! THE LESS SHE HEARS ME SPEAK THE BETTER!
YOU STILL HAVEN'T EXPLAINED WHAT YOU WERE DOING IN THE WOODS.
I CERTAINLY WASN'T THERE TO END UP ON THE COVER OF THE MONSTER GAZETTE AGAIN!
LARDINE'S OASIS WAS JUST AROUND THE CORNER FROM THAT CLEARING.
BRISTLEBEARD HAD JUST BURNED IT TO THE GROUND, LOOKING FOR THE EXILED MONSTERS...
...WHO, FORTUNATELY, HAD MEANDERED OFF BECAUSE NO ONE WAS AROUND TO SUPERVISE THEM...
...AND WHILE YOU AND YOUR BIG-MOUTHED FRIEND WERE GOING HOME...
...I HAD TO FIND AND GATHER UP THE REMAINING THREE SCOUNDRELS THAT WERE WANDERING AROUND THE FOREST!
SO THE MONSTERS ARE HERE NOW?

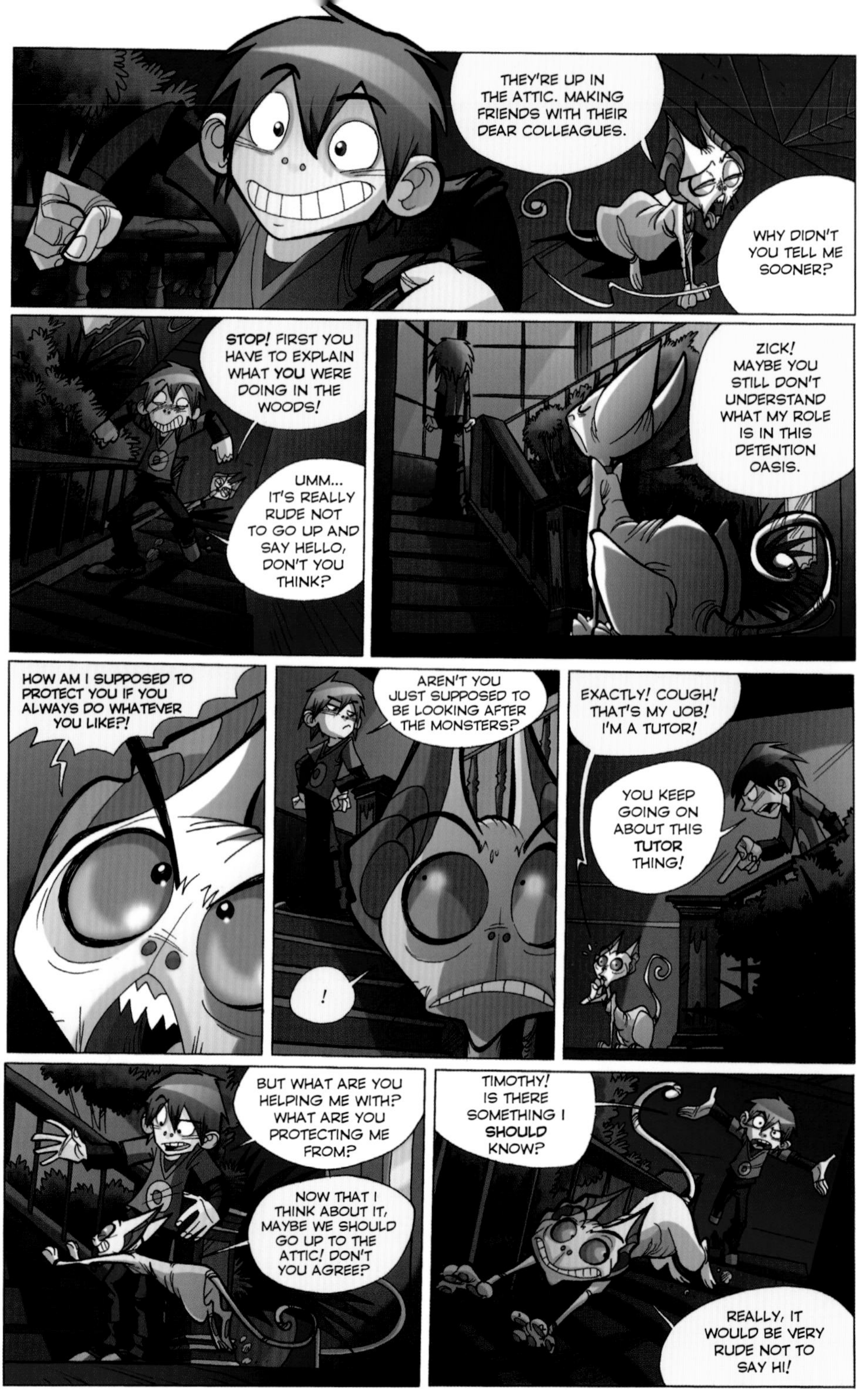
THEY'RE UP IN THE ATTIC. MAKING FRIENDS WITH THEIR DEAR COLLEAGUES.
WHY DIDN'T YOU TELL ME SOONER?
STOP! FIRST YOU HAVE TO EXPLAIN WHAT YOU WERE DOING IN THE WOODS!
UMM... IT'S REALLY RUDE NOT TO GO UP AND SAY HELLO, DON'T YOU THINK?
ZICK! MAYBE YOU STILL DON'T UNDERSTAND WHAT MY ROLE IS IN THIS DETENTION OASIS.
HOW AM I SUPPOSED TO PROTECT YOU IF YOU ALWAYS DO WHATEVER YOU LIKE?!
AREN'T YOU JUST SUPPOSED TO BE LOOKING AFTER THE MONSTERS?
!
EXACTLY! COUGH! THAT'S MY JOB! I'M A TUTOR!
YOU KEEP GOING ON ABOUT THIS TUTOR THING!
BUT WHAT ARE YOU HELPING ME WITH? WHAT ARE YOU PROTECTING ME FROM?
NOW THAT I THINK ABOUT IT, MAYBE WE SHOULD GO UP TO THE ATTIC! DON'T YOU AGREE?
TIMOTHY! IS THERE SOMETHING I SHOULD KNOW?
REALLY, IT WOULD BE VERY RUDE NOT TO SAY HI!

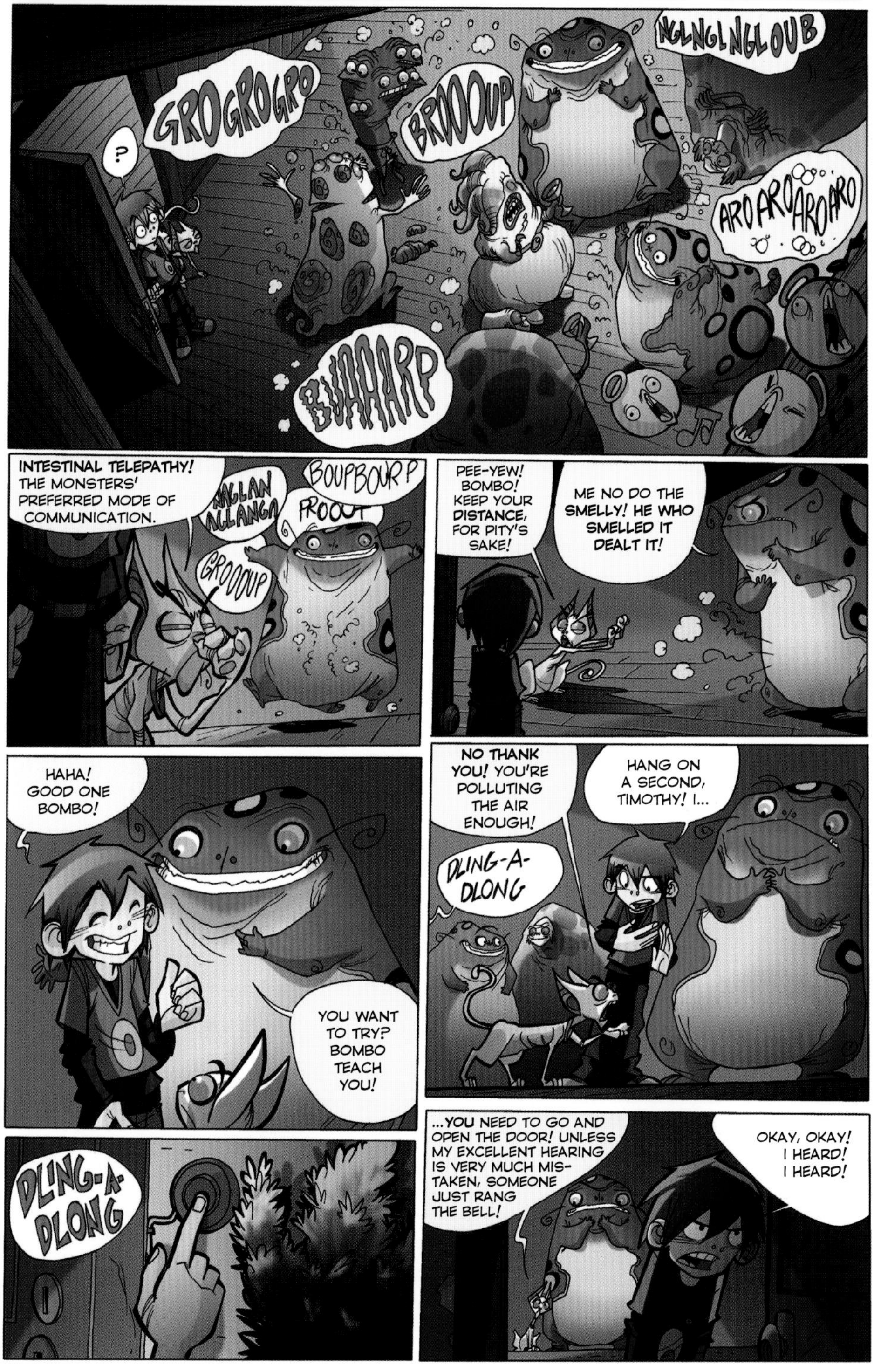
?
GROGROGRO
BROOOUP
NGLNGLNGLOUB
AROAROAROARO
BUAAARP
INTESTINAL TELEPATHY! THE MONSTERS' PREFERRED MODE OF COMMUNICATION.
NGLLAN NGLLANGA
BOUPBOURP
FROOOT
GROOOUP
PEE-YEW! BOMBO! KEEP YOUR DISTANCE, FOR PITY'S SAKE!
ME NO DO THE SMELLY! HE WHO SMELLED IT DEALT IT!
HAHA! GOOD ONE BOMBO!
YOU WANT TO TRY? BOMBO TEACH YOU!
NO THANK YOU! YOU'RE POLLUTING THE AIR ENOUGH!
HANG ON A SECOND, TIMOTHY! I...
DLING-A-DLONG
DLING-A-DLONG
...YOU NEED TO GO AND OPEN THE DOOR! UNLESS MY EXCELLENT HEARING IS VERY MUCH MIS-TAKEN, SOMEONE JUST RANG THE BELL!
OKAY, OKAY! I HEARD! I HEARD!

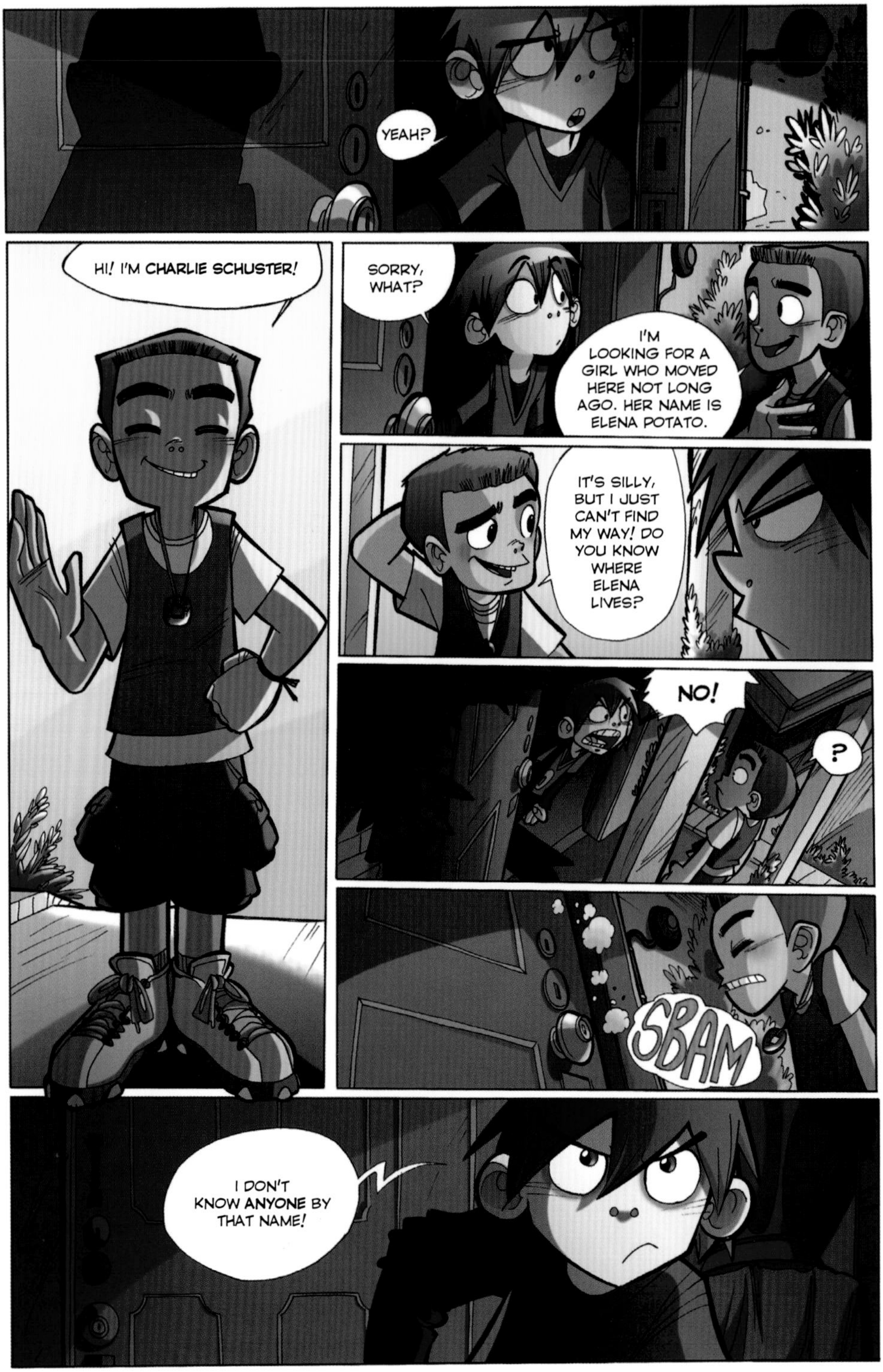
YEAH?
HI! I'M CHARLIE SCHUSTER!
SORRY, WHAT?
I'M LOOKING FOR A GIRL WHO MOVED HERE NOT LONG AGO. HER NAME IS ELENA POTATO.
IT'S SILLY, BUT I JUST CAN'T FIND MY WAY! DO YOU KNOW WHERE ELENA LIVES?
NO!
?
SBAM
I DON'T KNOW ANYONE BY THAT NAME!

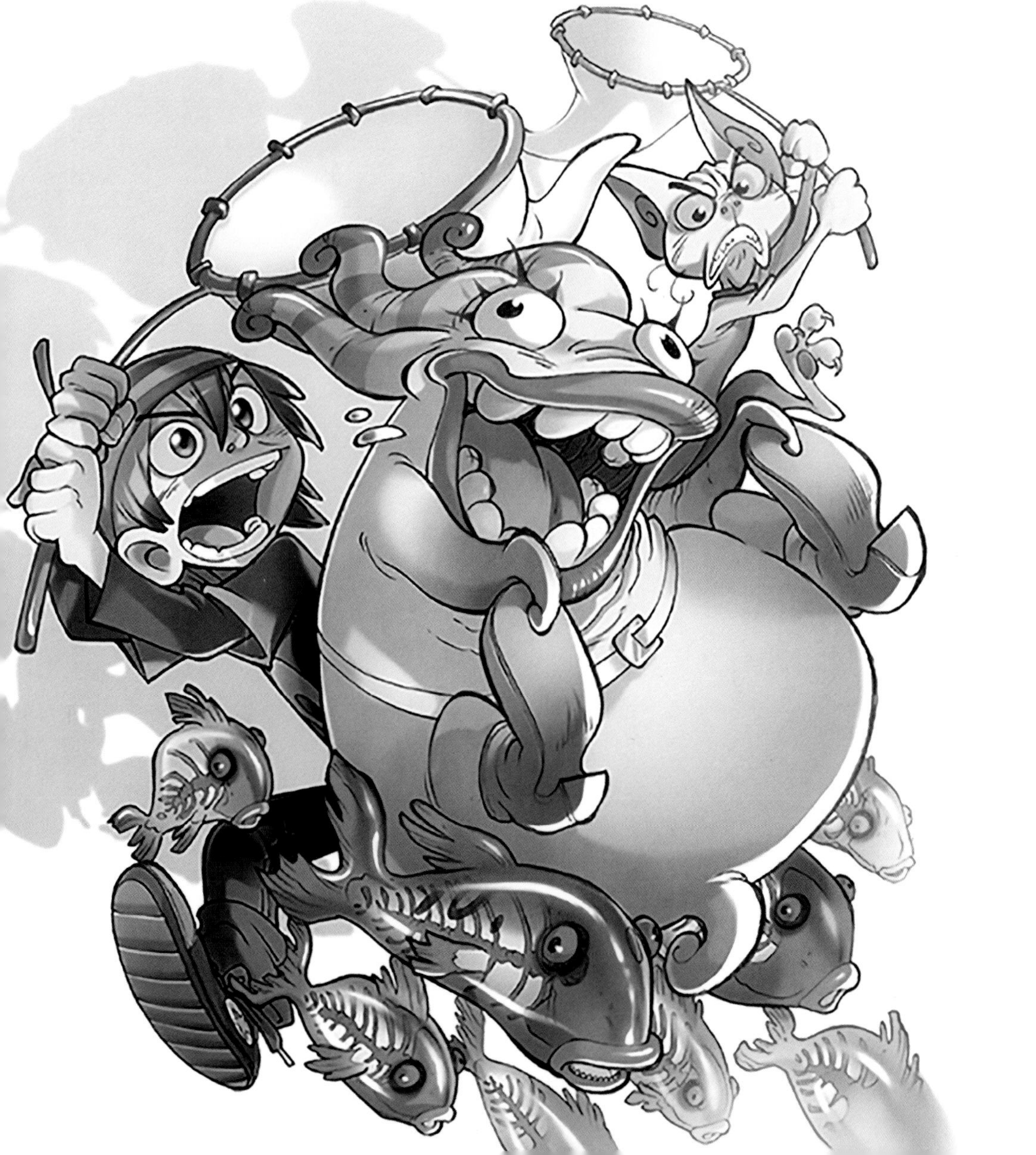

PART 2

HERE COMES CHARLIE SCHUSTER

Plot: Katja Centomo
Script: Francesco Artibani
Pencils and Inks: Alessio Coppola
Design Supervisor: Alessandro Barbucci
Colors: Sergio Algozzino, Barbara Bargiggia,
Pamela Brughera, Cecilia Giumento,
and Paolo Maddaleni

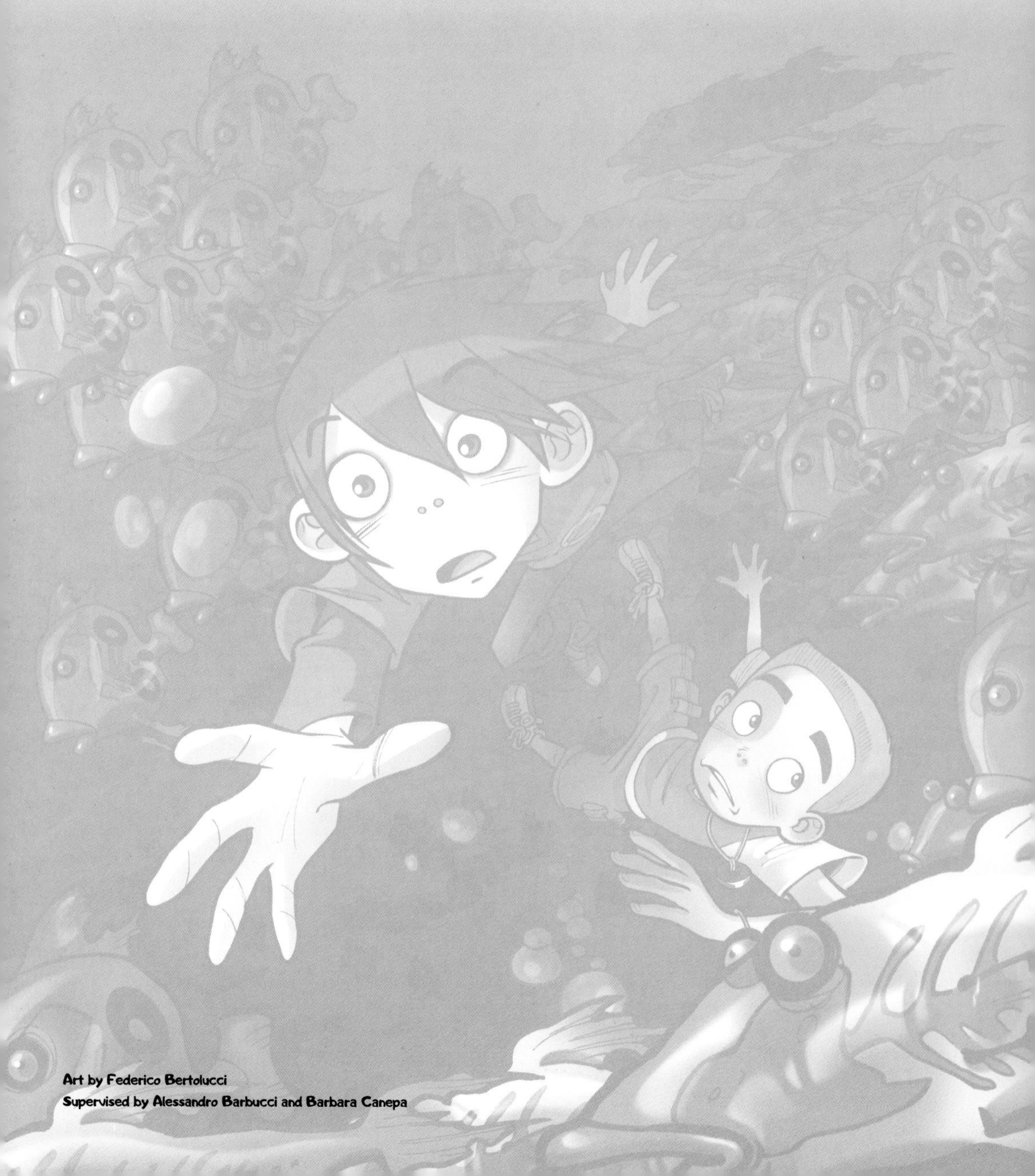

Art by Federico Bertolucci
Supervised by Alessandro Barbucci and Barbara Canepa

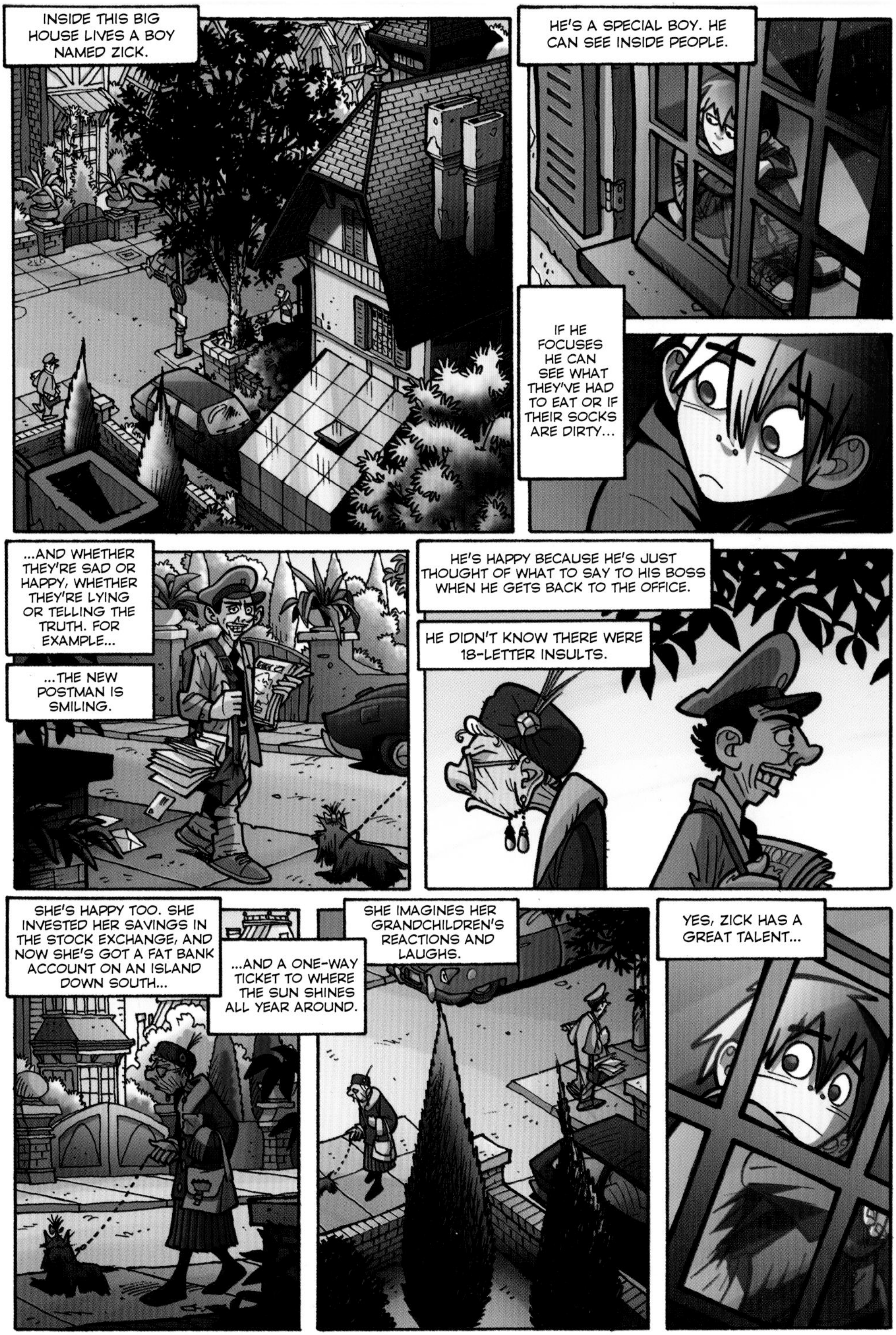
INSIDE THIS BIG HOUSE LIVES A BOY NAMED ZICK.
HE'S A SPECIAL BOY. HE CAN SEE INSIDE PEOPLE.
IF HE FOCUSES HE CAN SEE WHAT THEY'VE HAD TO EAT OR IF THEIR SOCKS ARE DIRTY...
...AND WHETHER THEY'RE SAD OR HAPPY, WHETHER THEY'RE LYING OR TELLING THE TRUTH. FOR EXAMPLE...
...THE NEW POSTMAN IS SMILING.
HE'S HAPPY BECAUSE HE'S JUST THOUGHT OF WHAT TO SAY TO HIS BOSS WHEN HE GETS BACK TO THE OFFICE.
HE DIDN'T KNOW THERE WERE 18-LETTER INSULTS.
SHE'S HAPPY TOO. SHE INVESTED HER SAVINGS IN THE STOCK EXCHANGE, AND NOW SHE'S GOT A FAT BANK ACCOUNT ON AN ISLAND DOWN SOUTH...
...AND A ONE-WAY TICKET TO WHERE THE SUN SHINES ALL YEAR AROUND.
SHE IMAGINES HER GRANDCHILDREN'S REACTIONS AND LAUGHS.
YES, ZICK HAS A GREAT TALENT...

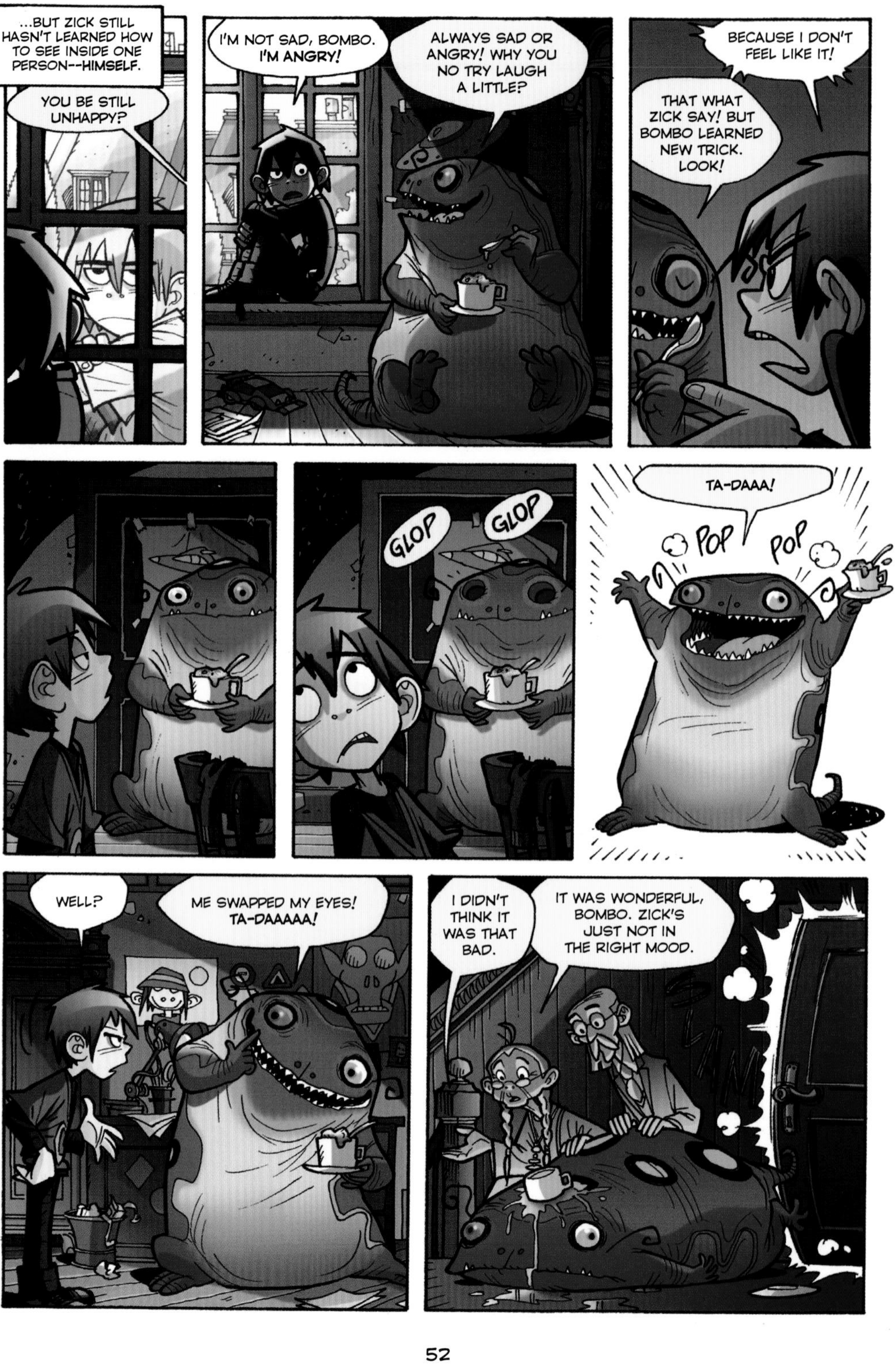

...BUT ZICK STILL HASN'T LEARNED HOW TO SEE INSIDE ONE PERSON--**HIMSELF**.
YOU BE STILL UNHAPPY?
I'M NOT SAD, BOMBO. **I'M ANGRY!**
ALWAYS SAD OR ANGRY! WHY YOU NO TRY LAUGH A LITTLE?
BECAUSE I DON'T FEEL LIKE IT!
THAT WHAT ZICK SAY! BUT BOMBO LEARNED NEW TRICK. LOOK!
GLOP
GLOP
TA-DAAA!
POP
POP
WELL?
ME SWAPPED MY EYES! **TA-DAAAAA!**
I DIDN'T THINK IT WAS THAT BAD.
IT WAS WONDERFUL, BOMBO. ZICK'S JUST NOT IN THE RIGHT MOOD.

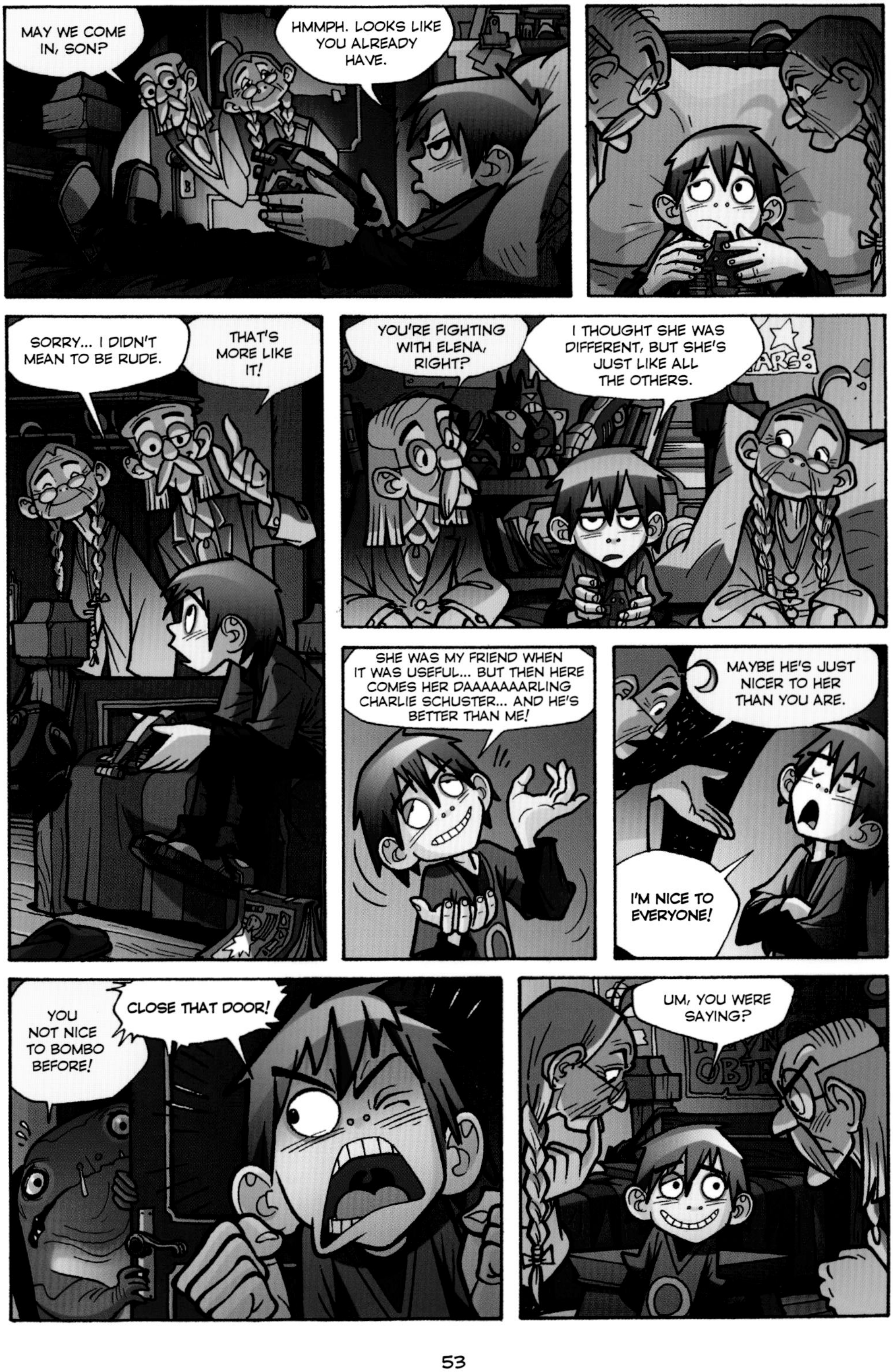
MAY WE COME IN, SON?
HMMPH. LOOKS LIKE YOU ALREADY HAVE.
SORRY... I DIDN'T MEAN TO BE RUDE.
THAT'S MORE LIKE IT!
YOU'RE FIGHTING WITH ELENA, RIGHT?
I THOUGHT SHE WAS DIFFERENT, BUT SHE'S JUST LIKE ALL THE OTHERS.
SHE WAS MY FRIEND WHEN IT WAS USEFUL... BUT THEN HERE COMES HER DAAAAAAARLING CHARLIE SCHUSTER... AND HE'S BETTER THAN ME!
MAYBE HE'S JUST NICER TO HER THAN YOU ARE.
I'M NICE TO EVERYONE!
YOU NOT NICE TO BOMBO BEFORE!
CLOSE THAT DOOR!
UM, YOU WERE SAYING?

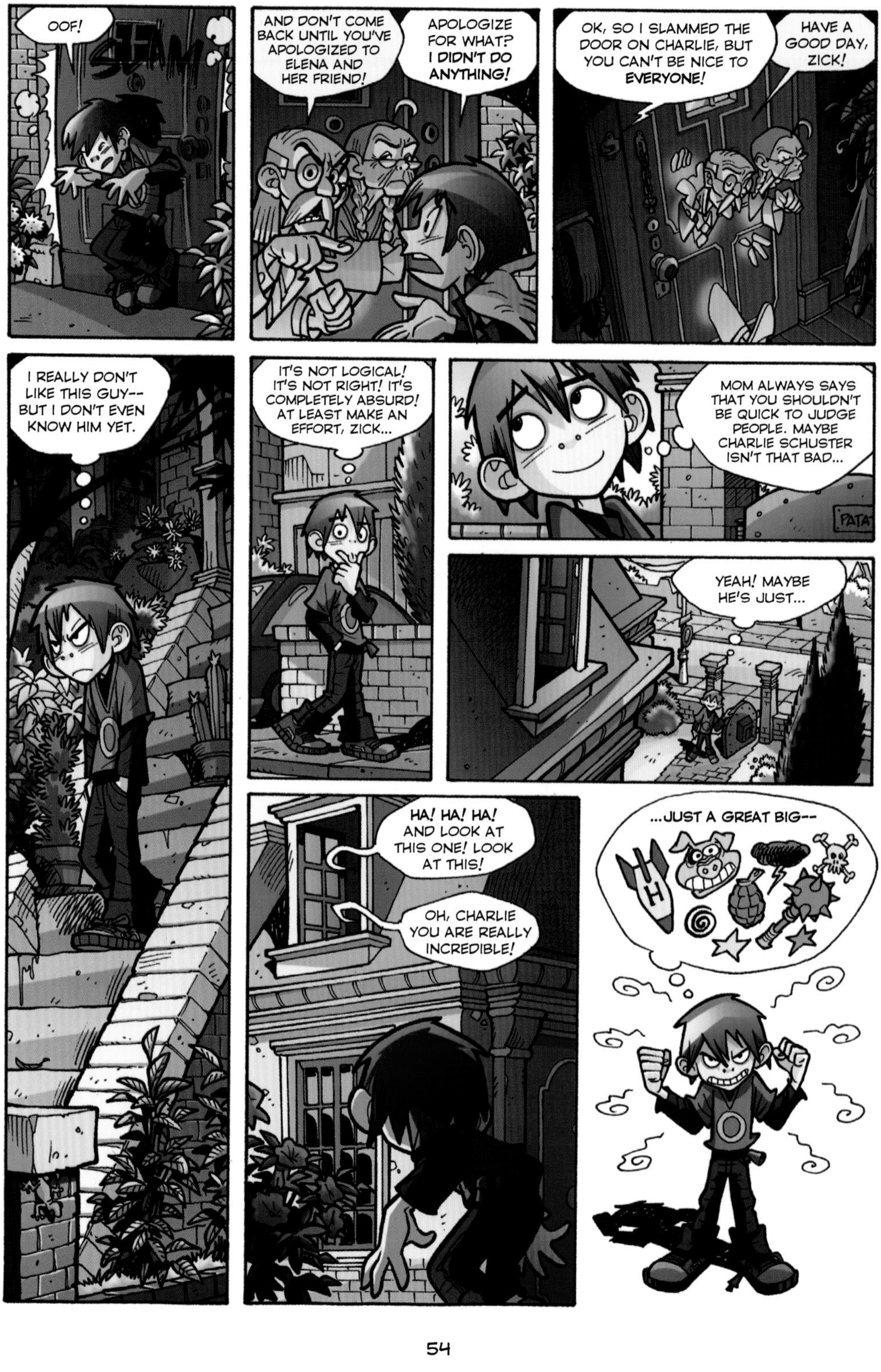
OOF!
SLAM
AND DON'T COME BACK UNTIL YOU'VE APOLOGIZED TO ELENA AND HER FRIEND!
APOLOGIZE FOR WHAT? I DIDN'T DO ANYTHING!
OK, SO I SLAMMED THE DOOR ON CHARLIE, BUT YOU CAN'T BE NICE TO EVERYONE!
HAVE A GOOD DAY, ZICK!
I REALLY DON'T LIKE THIS GUY-- BUT I DON'T EVEN KNOW HIM YET.
IT'S NOT LOGICAL! IT'S NOT RIGHT! IT'S COMPLETELY ABSURD! AT LEAST MAKE AN EFFORT, ZICK...
MOM ALWAYS SAYS THAT YOU SHOULDN'T BE QUICK TO JUDGE PEOPLE. MAYBE CHARLIE SCHUSTER ISN'T THAT BAD...
YEAH! MAYBE HE'S JUST...
HA! HA! HA! AND LOOK AT THIS ONE! LOOK AT THIS!
OH, CHARLIE YOU ARE REALLY INCREDIBLE!
...JUST A GREAT BIG--

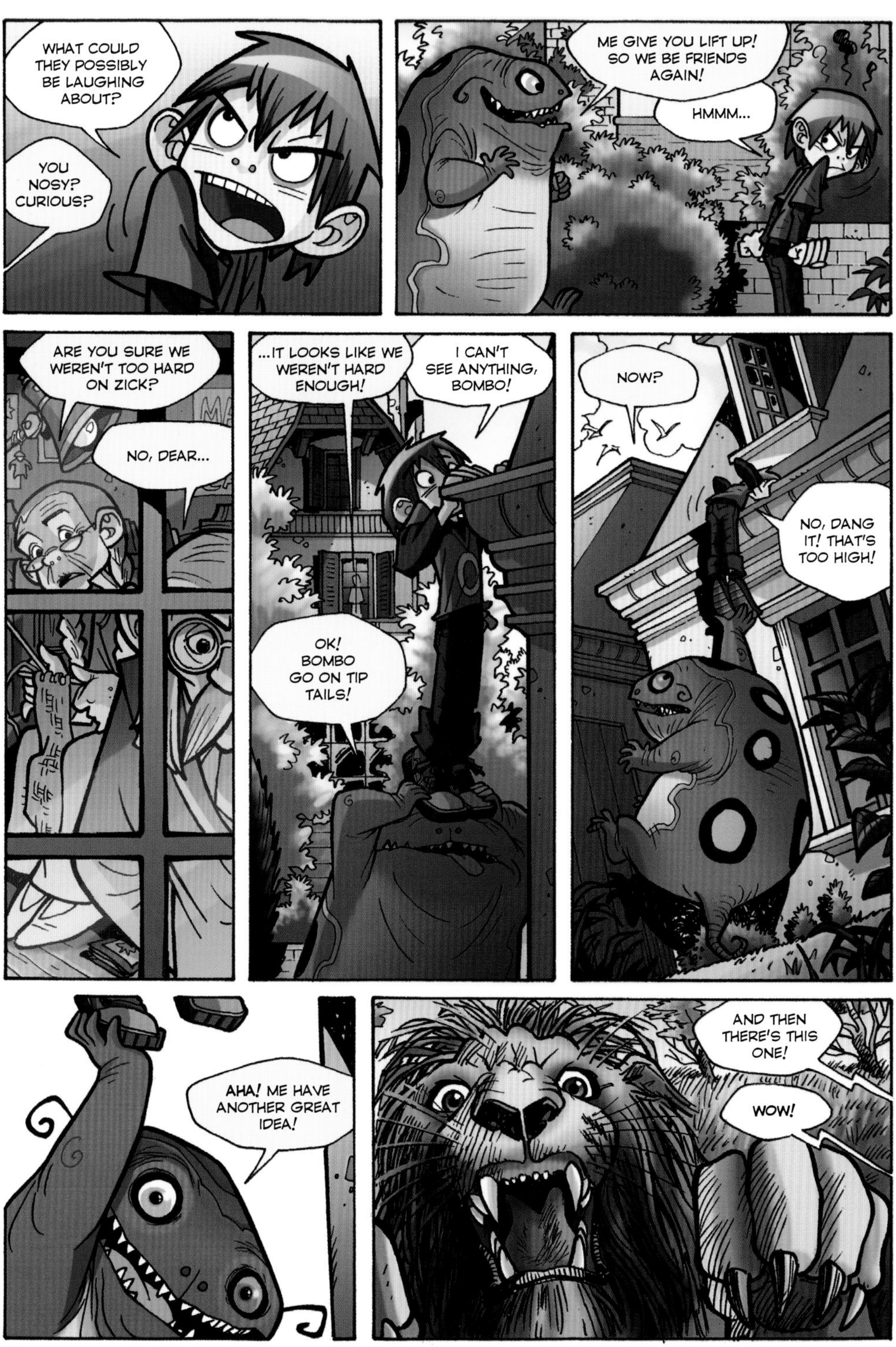
WHAT COULD THEY POSSIBLY BE LAUGHING ABOUT?
YOU NOSY? CURIOUS?
ME GIVE YOU LIFT UP! SO WE BE FRIENDS AGAIN!
HMMM...
ARE YOU SURE WE WEREN'T TOO HARD ON ZICK?
NO, DEAR...
...IT LOOKS LIKE WE WEREN'T HARD ENOUGH!
I CAN'T SEE ANYTHING, BOMBO!
OK! BOMBO GO ON TIP TAILS!
NOW?
NO, DANG IT! THAT'S TOO HIGH!
AHA! ME HAVE ANOTHER GREAT IDEA!
AND THEN THERE'S THIS ONE!
WOW!

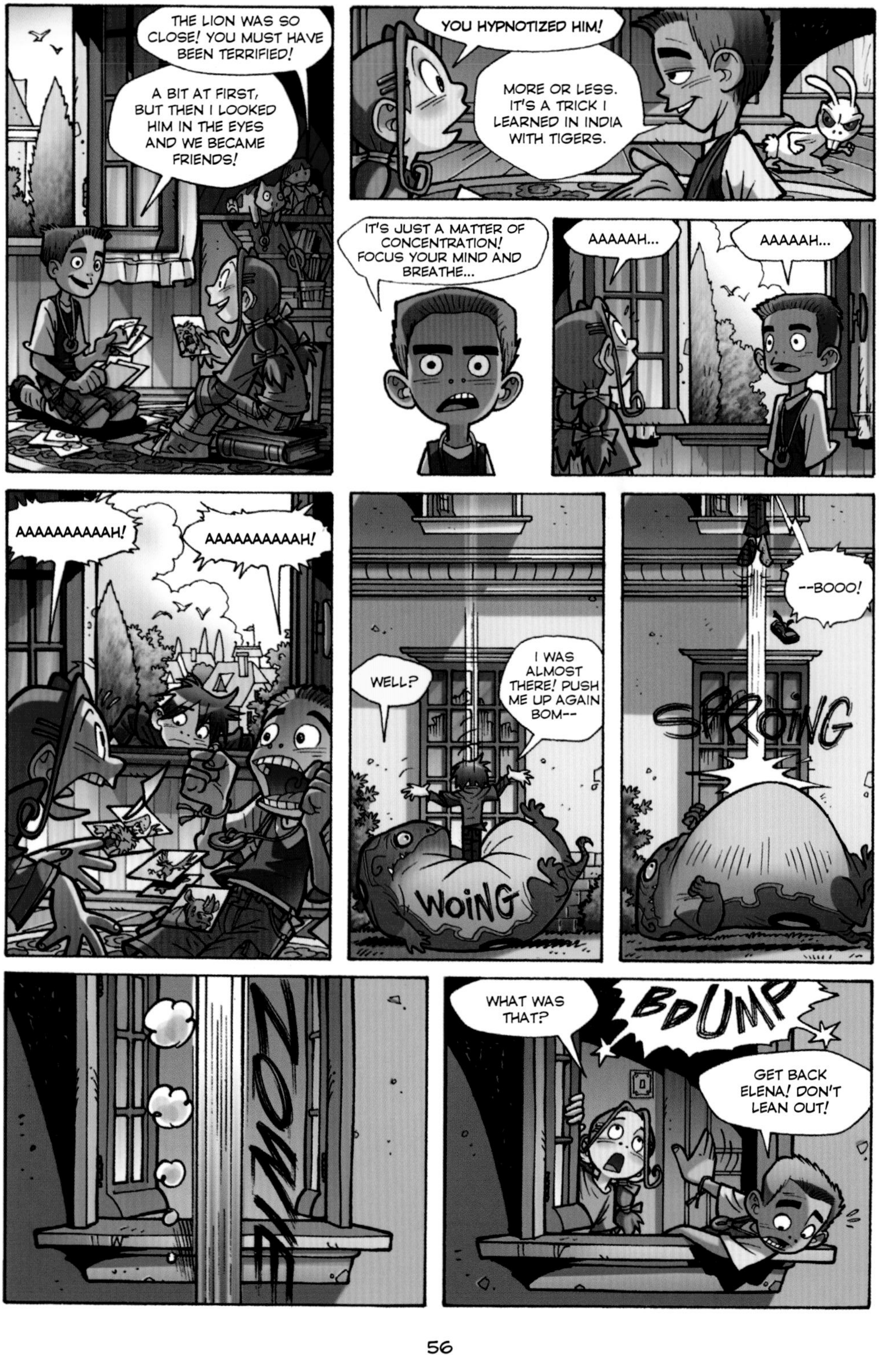
THE LION WAS SO CLOSE! YOU MUST HAVE BEEN TERRIFIED!
A BIT AT FIRST, BUT THEN I LOOKED HIM IN THE EYES AND WE BECAME FRIENDS!
YOU HYPNOTIZED HIM!
MORE OR LESS. IT'S A TRICK I LEARNED IN INDIA WITH TIGERS.
IT'S JUST A MATTER OF CONCENTRATION! FOCUS YOUR MIND AND BREATHE...
AAAAAH...
AAAAAH...
AAAAAAAAAAH!
AAAAAAAAAAH!
WELL?
I WAS ALMOST THERE! PUSH ME UP AGAIN BOM--
WOING
--BOOO!
SPROING
ZOOM
WHAT WAS THAT?
BDUMP
GET BACK ELENA! DON'T LEAN OUT!

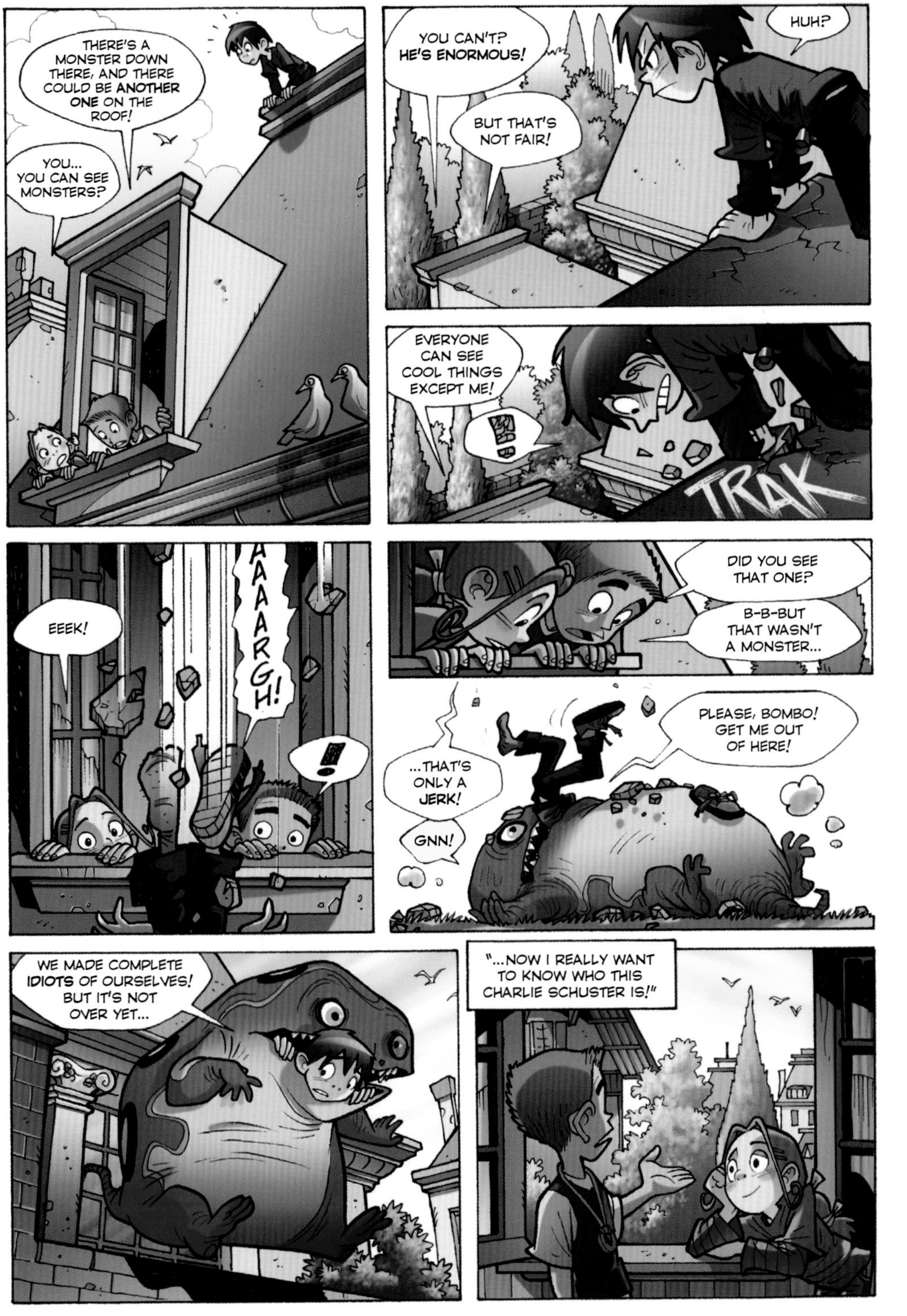
THERE'S A MONSTER DOWN THERE, AND THERE COULD BE ANOTHER ONE ON THE ROOF!
YOU... YOU CAN SEE MONSTERS?
YOU CAN'T? HE'S ENORMOUS!
HUH?
BUT THAT'S NOT FAIR!
EVERYONE CAN SEE COOL THINGS EXCEPT ME!
!
TRAK
EEEK!
AAAAARGH!
!
DID YOU SEE THAT ONE?
B-B-BUT THAT WASN'T A MONSTER...
...THAT'S ONLY A JERK!
PLEASE, BOMBO! GET ME OUT OF HERE!
GNN!
WE MADE COMPLETE IDIOTS OF OURSELVES! BUT IT'S NOT OVER YET...
"...NOW I REALLY WANT TO KNOW WHO THIS CHARLIE SCHUSTER IS!"

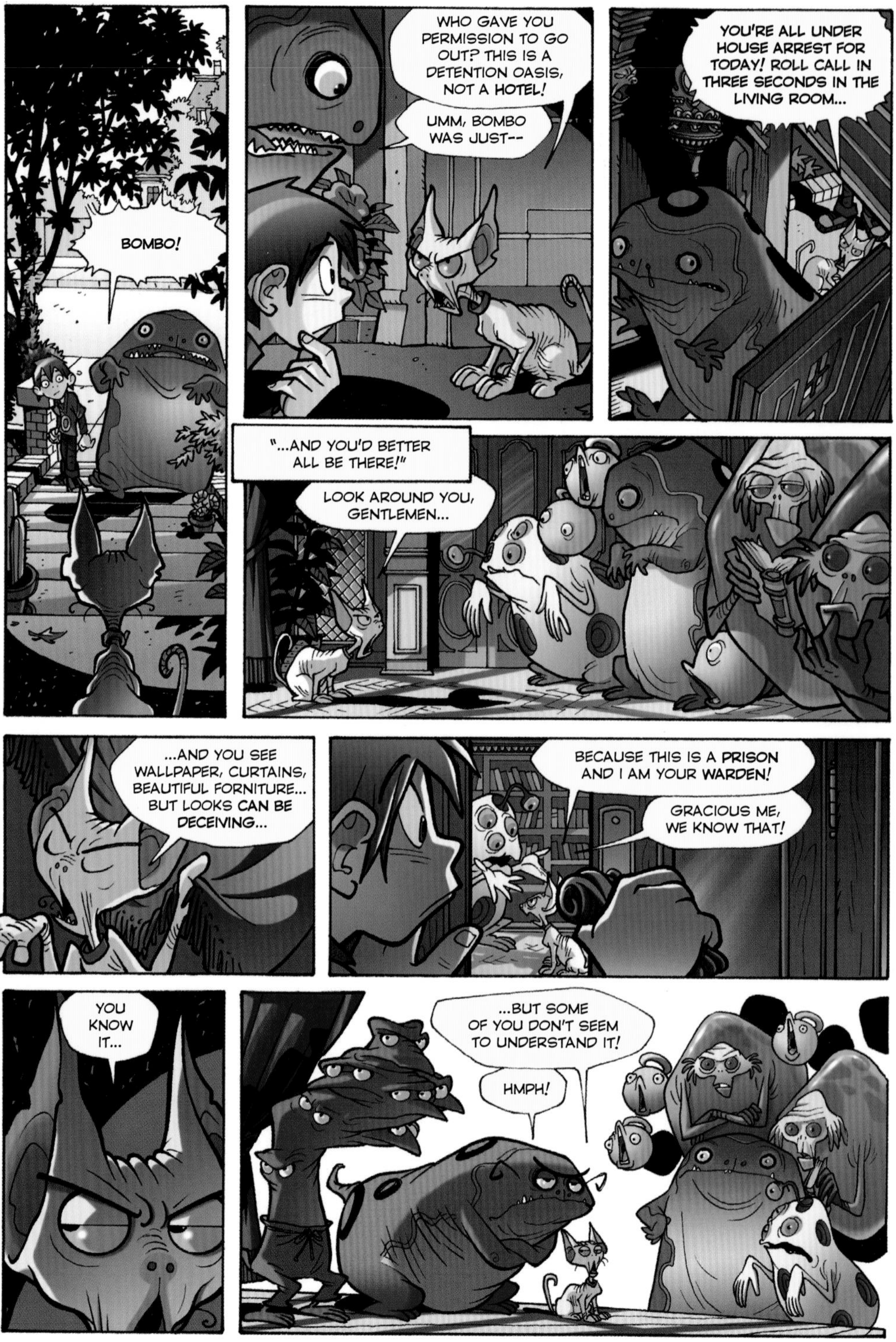
BOMBO!
WHO GAVE YOU PERMISSION TO GO OUT? THIS IS A DETENTION OASIS, NOT A HOTEL!
UMM, BOMBO WAS JUST--
YOU'RE ALL UNDER HOUSE ARREST FOR TODAY! ROLL CALL IN THREE SECONDS IN THE LIVING ROOM...
"...AND YOU'D BETTER ALL BE THERE!"
LOOK AROUND YOU, GENTLEMEN...
...AND YOU SEE WALLPAPER, CURTAINS, BEAUTIFUL FORNITURE... BUT LOOKS CAN BE DECEIVING...
BECAUSE THIS IS A PRISON AND I AM YOUR WARDEN!
GRACIOUS ME, WE KNOW THAT!
YOU KNOW IT...
...BUT SOME OF YOU DON'T SEEM TO UNDERSTAND IT!
HMPH!

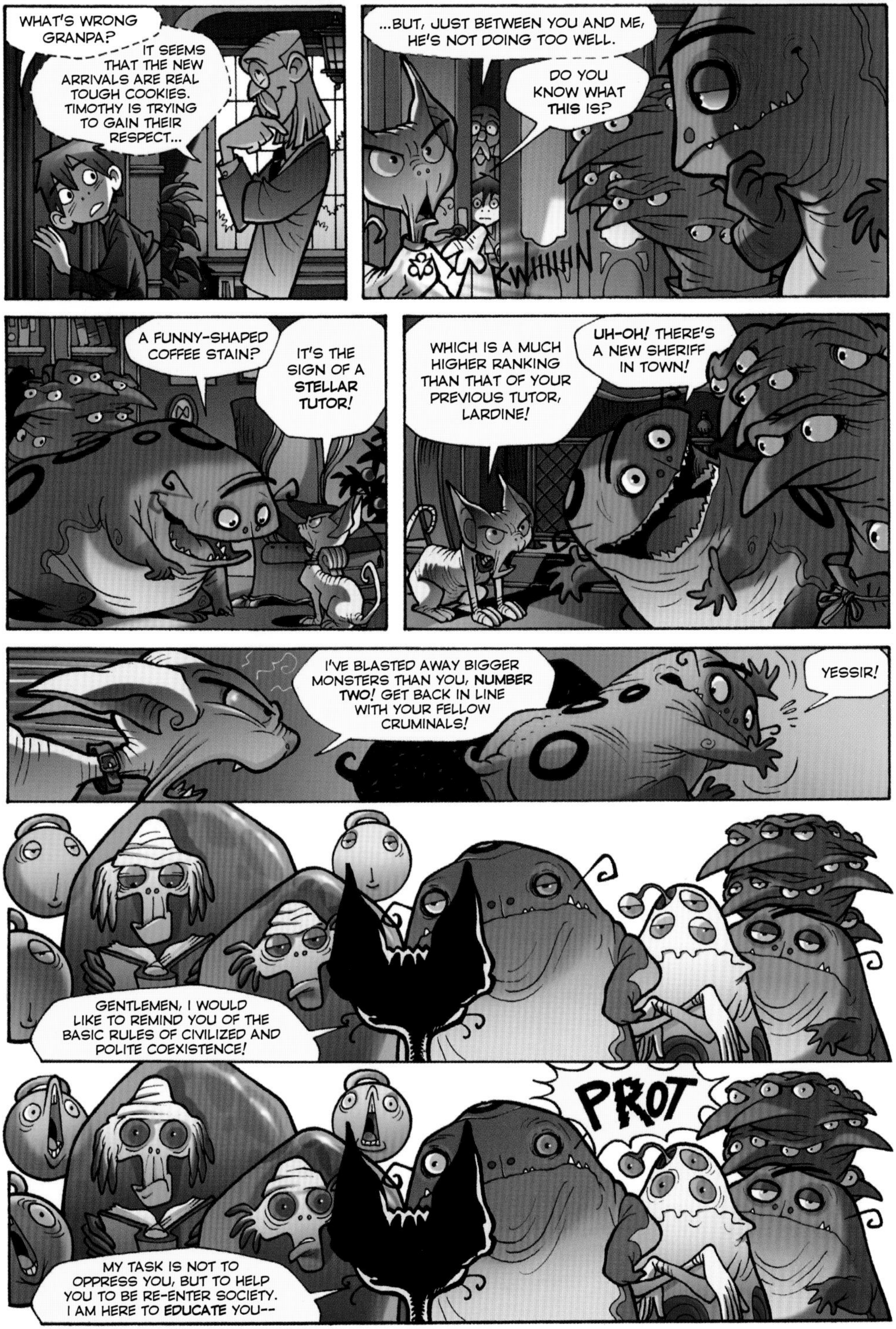
WHAT'S WRONG GRANPA?
IT SEEMS THAT THE NEW ARRIVALS ARE REAL TOUGH COOKIES. TIMOTHY IS TRYING TO GAIN THEIR RESPECT...
...BUT, JUST BETWEEN YOU AND ME, HE'S NOT DOING TOO WELL.
DO YOU KNOW WHAT **THIS** IS?
KWIIIIIN
A FUNNY-SHAPED COFFEE STAIN?
IT'S THE SIGN OF A **STELLAR TUTOR**!
WHICH IS A MUCH HIGHER RANKING THAN THAT OF YOUR PREVIOUS TUTOR, LARDINE!
UH-OH! THERE'S A NEW SHERIFF IN TOWN!
I'VE BLASTED AWAY BIGGER MONSTERS THAN YOU, **NUMBER TWO**! GET BACK IN LINE WITH YOUR FELLOW CRUMINALS!
YESSIR!
GENTLEMEN, I WOULD LIKE TO REMIND YOU OF THE BASIC RULES OF CIVILIZED AND POLITE COEXISTENCE!
PROT
MY TASK IS NOT TO OPPRESS YOU, BUT TO HELP YOU TO BE RE-ENTER SOCIETY. I AM HERE TO **EDUCATE** YOU--

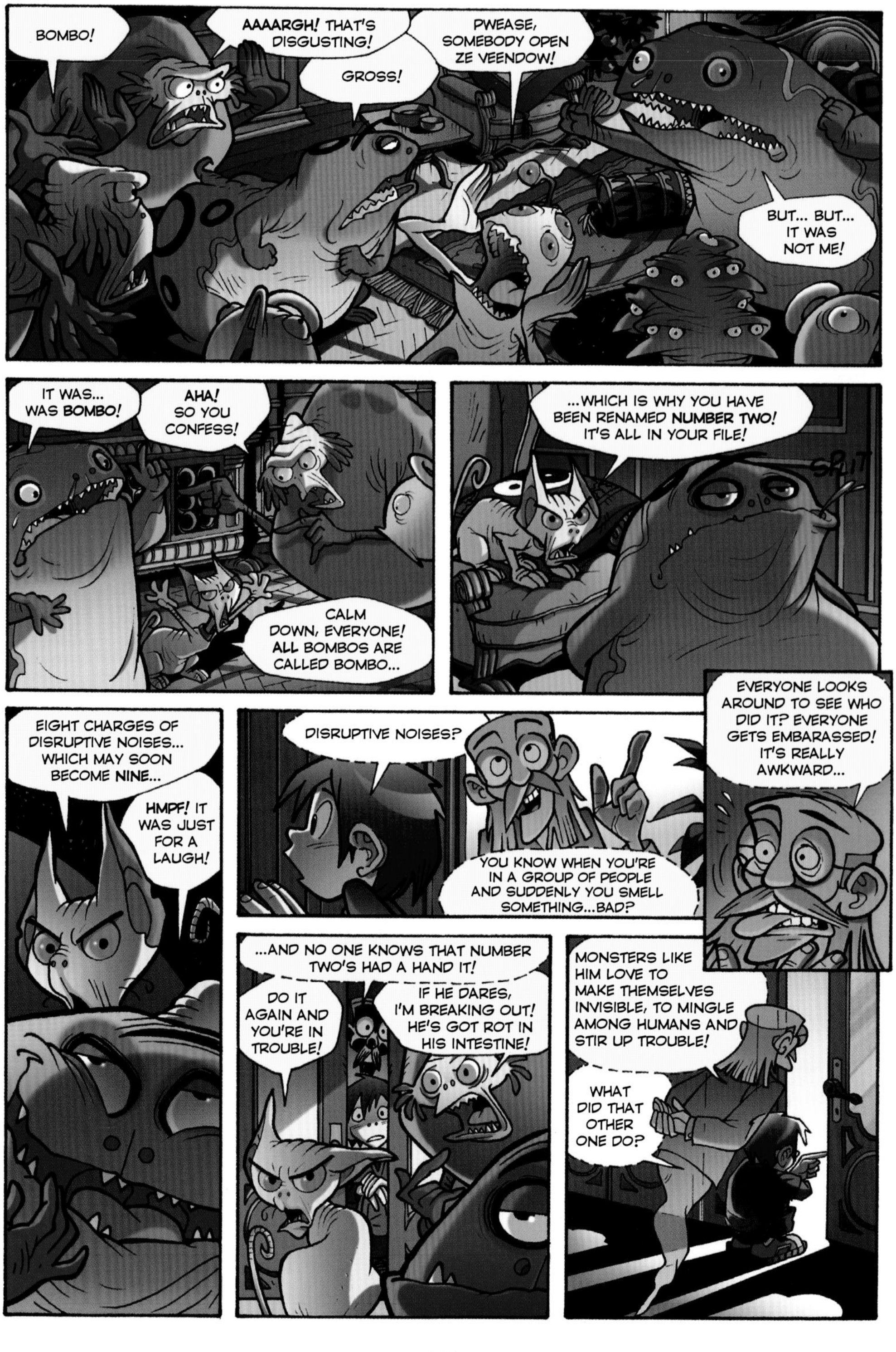
BOMBO!
AAAARGH! THAT'S DISGUSTING!
GROSS!
PWEASE, SOMEBODY OPEN ZE VEENDOW!
BUT... BUT... IT WAS NOT ME!
IT WAS... WAS BOMBO!
AHA! SO YOU CONFESS!
CALM DOWN, EVERYONE! ALL BOMBOS ARE CALLED BOMBO...
...WHICH IS WHY YOU HAVE BEEN RENAMED NUMBER TWO! IT'S ALL IN YOUR FILE!
SPLIT
EIGHT CHARGES OF DISRUPTIVE NOISES... WHICH MAY SOON BECOME NINE...
HMPF! IT WAS JUST FOR A LAUGH!
DISRUPTIVE NOISES?
YOU KNOW WHEN YOU'RE IN A GROUP OF PEOPLE AND SUDDENLY YOU SMELL SOMETHING...BAD?
EVERYONE LOOKS AROUND TO SEE WHO DID IT? EVERYONE GETS EMBARASSED! IT'S REALLY AWKWARD...
...AND NO ONE KNOWS THAT NUMBER TWO'S HAD A HAND IT!
DO IT AGAIN AND YOU'RE IN TROUBLE!
IF HE DARES, I'M BREAKING OUT! HE'S GOT ROT IN HIS INTESTINE!
MONSTERS LIKE HIM LOVE TO MAKE THEMSELVES INVISIBLE, TO MINGLE AMONG HUMANS AND STIR UP TROUBLE!
WHAT DID THAT OTHER ONE DO?

GET BACK TO YOUR PLACES! IMMEDIATELY!

ABSOLUTELY NOT!

SEE? THEY'RE THE ONES WHO DON'T WANT ME!

WHAT ARE YOU WAITING FOR, MR. KORRIKARRO?

I'M GOING! I'M GOING!

NO, HOLD UP! WHY SHOULD I ALWAYS HAVE TO TAKE ORDERS?

FOR HEAVEN'S SAKE... ANOTHER ONE OF HIS CRISES!

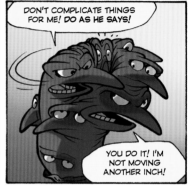

DON'T COMPLICATE THINGS FOR ME! DO AS HE SAYS!

YOU DO IT! I'M NOT MOVING ANOTHER INCH!

YOU AREN'T IN CHARGE HERE! TAKE THAT!

YOU WANT A FIGHT? YOU DON'T KNOW WHO YOU'RE DEALING WITH!

CLAK!

YOU SEE, ZICK... ZAMURROS ARE COLLECTIVE MONSTERS...

HEY! WHY DON'T YOU PICK ON SOMEONE YOUR OWN SIZE!

AND WHY DON'T YOU MIND YOUR OWN BUSINESS?

...HAPPY, SOCIABLE, AND WELL-BALANCED CREATURES...

STUNF

URGH!

...EXCEPT FOR HIM, OBVIOUSLY!

EEEEK! AAAAH!

BON BON

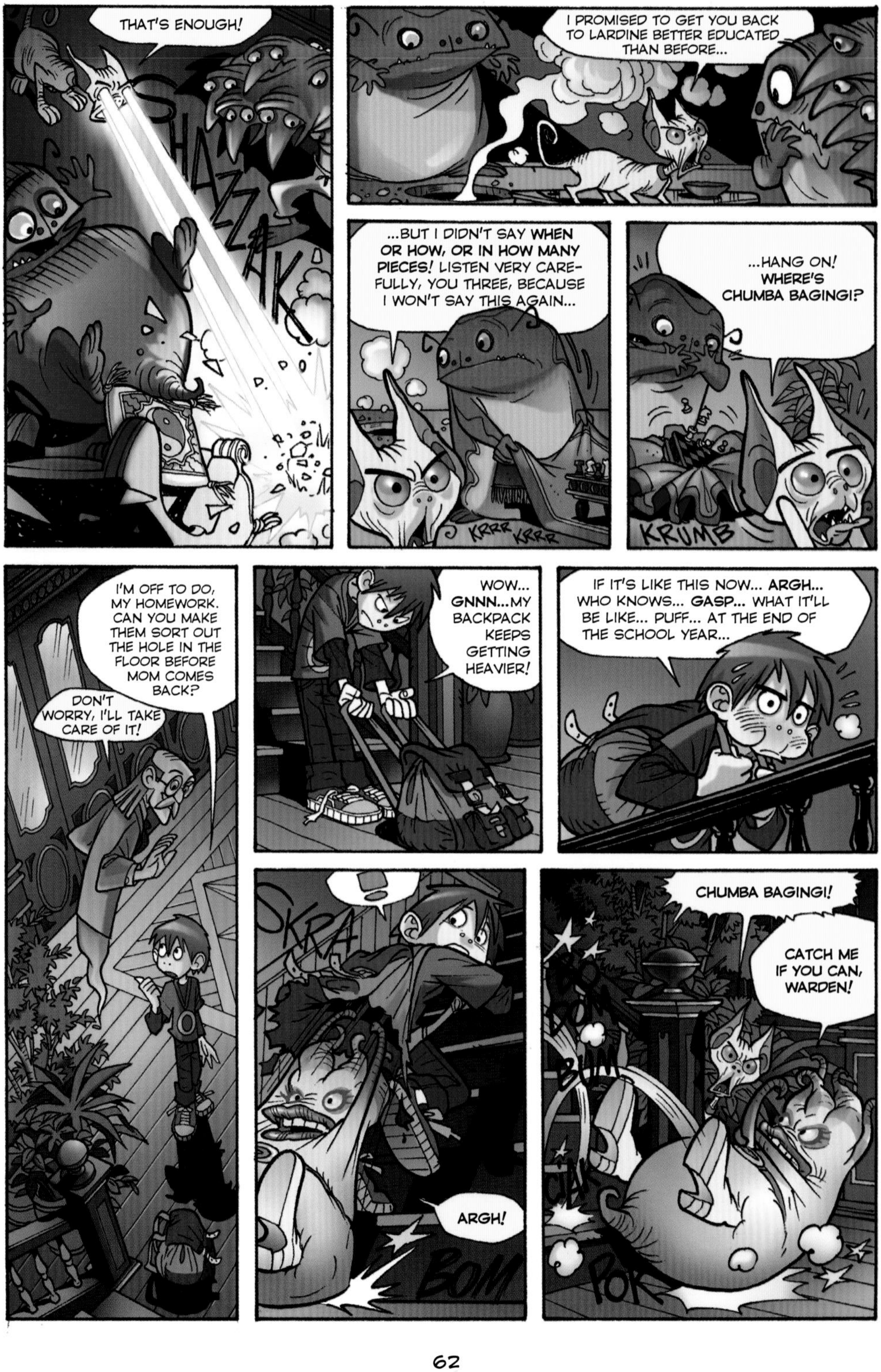
THAT'S ENOUGH!
SHAZZZAK
I PROMISED TO GET YOU BACK TO LARDINE BETTER EDUCATED THAN BEFORE...
...BUT I DIDN'T SAY WHEN OR HOW, OR IN HOW MANY PIECES! LISTEN VERY CAREFULLY, YOU THREE, BECAUSE I WON'T SAY THIS AGAIN...
KRRR KRRR
...HANG ON! WHERE'S CHUMBA BAGINGI?
KRUMB
I'M OFF TO DO, MY HOMEWORK. CAN YOU MAKE THEM SORT OUT THE HOLE IN THE FLOOR BEFORE MOM COMES BACK?
DON'T WORRY, I'LL TAKE CARE OF IT!
WOW... GNNN...MY BACKPACK KEEPS GETTING HEAVIER!
IF IT'S LIKE THIS NOW... ARGH... WHO KNOWS... GASP... WHAT IT'LL BE LIKE... PUFF... AT THE END OF THE SCHOOL YEAR...
SKRA
ARGH!
BOM
CHUMBA BAGINGI!
CATCH ME IF YOU CAN, WARDEN!
BOM
POK

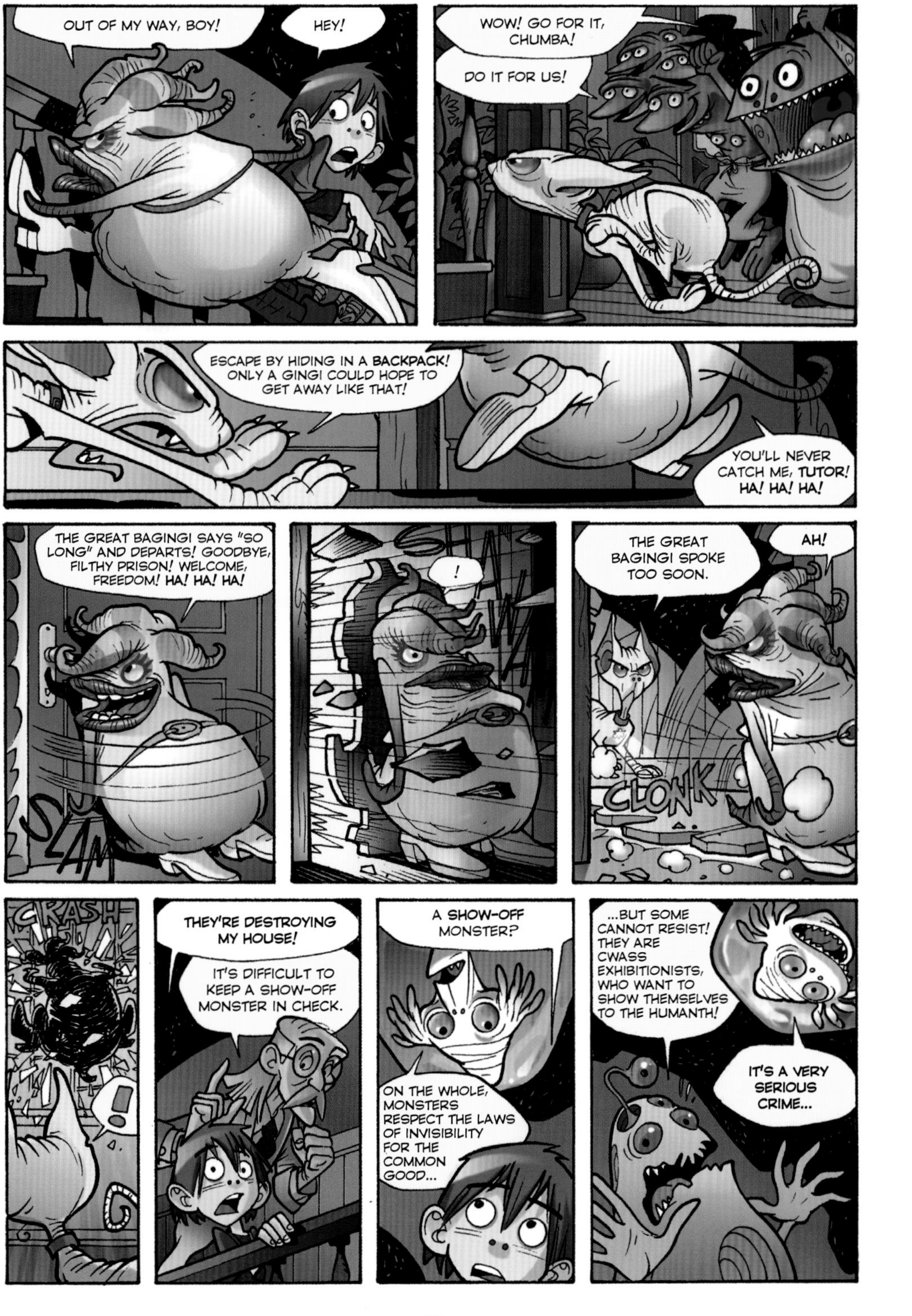

OUT OF MY WAY, BOY!
HEY!
WOW! GO FOR IT, CHUMBA!
DO IT FOR US!
ESCAPE BY HIDING IN A BACKPACK! ONLY A GINGI COULD HOPE TO GET AWAY LIKE THAT!
YOU'LL NEVER CATCH ME, TUTOR! HA! HA! HA!
THE GREAT BAGINGI SAYS "SO LONG" AND DEPARTS! GOODBYE, FILTHY PRISON! WELCOME, FREEDOM! HA! HA! HA!
SLAM
!
THE GREAT BAGINGI SPOKE TOO SOON.
AH!
CLONK
CRASH
!
THEY'RE DESTROYING MY HOUSE!
IT'S DIFFICULT TO KEEP A SHOW-OFF MONSTER IN CHECK.
A SHOW-OFF MONSTER?
ON THE WHOLE, MONSTERS RESPECT THE LAWS OF INVISIBILITY FOR THE COMMON GOOD...
...BUT SOME CANNOT RESIST! THEY ARE CWASS EXHIBITIONISTS, WHO WANT TO SHOW THEMSELVES TO THE HUMANTH!
IT'S A VERY SERIOUS CRIME...

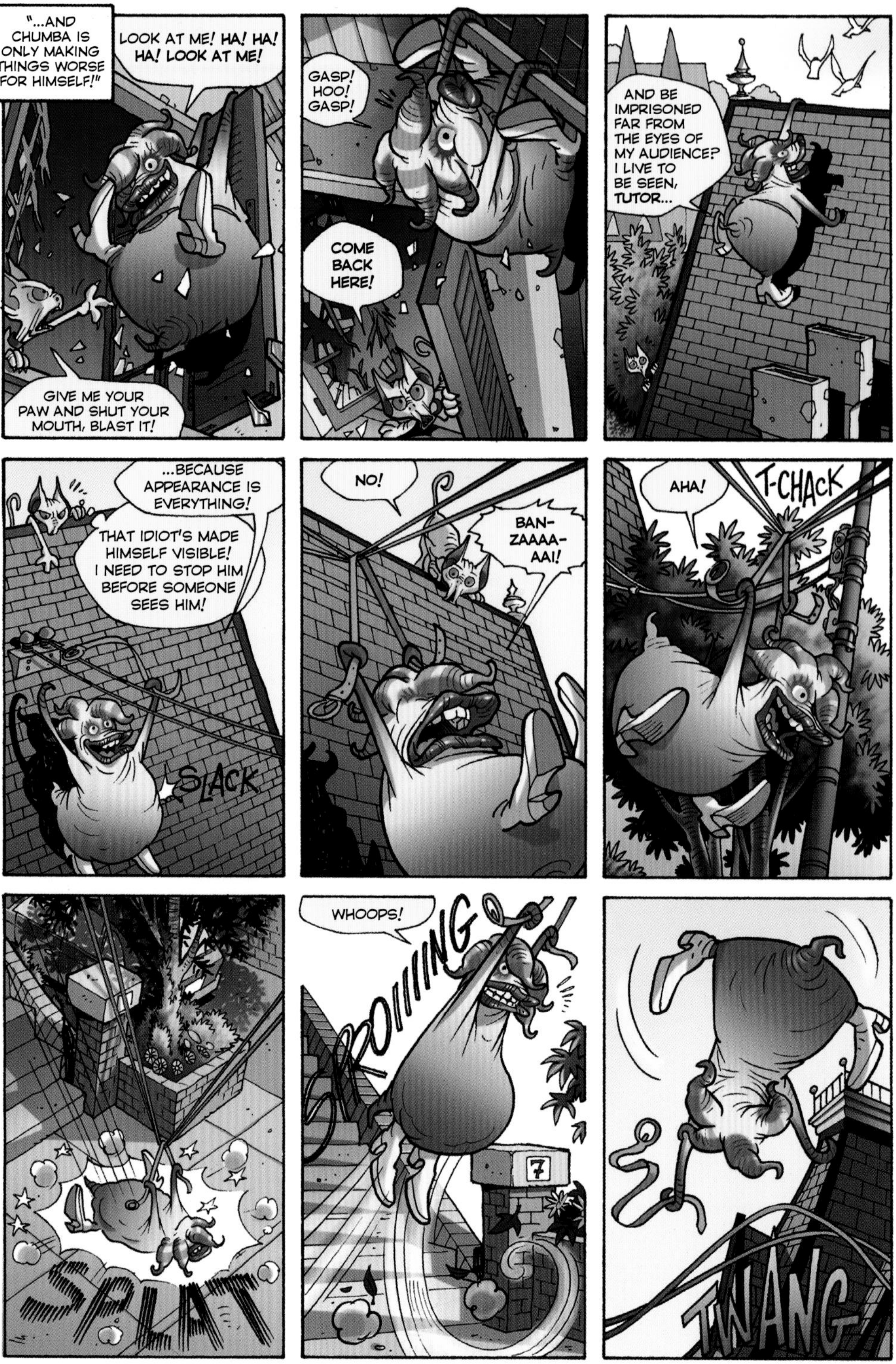
"...AND CHUMBA IS ONLY MAKING THINGS WORSE FOR HIMSELF!"
LOOK AT ME! HA! HA! HA! LOOK AT ME!
GIVE ME YOUR PAW AND SHUT YOUR MOUTH, BLAST IT!
GASP! HOO! GASP!
COME BACK HERE!
AND BE IMPRISONED FAR FROM THE EYES OF MY AUDIENCE? I LIVE TO BE SEEN, TUTOR...
...BECAUSE APPEARANCE IS EVERYTHING!
THAT IDIOT'S MADE HIMSELF VISIBLE! I NEED TO STOP HIM BEFORE SOMEONE SEES HIM!
SLACK
NO!
BAN-ZAAAAA-AAI!
AHA!
T-CHACK
SPLAT
WHOOPS!
SPROIIIING
7
TWANG

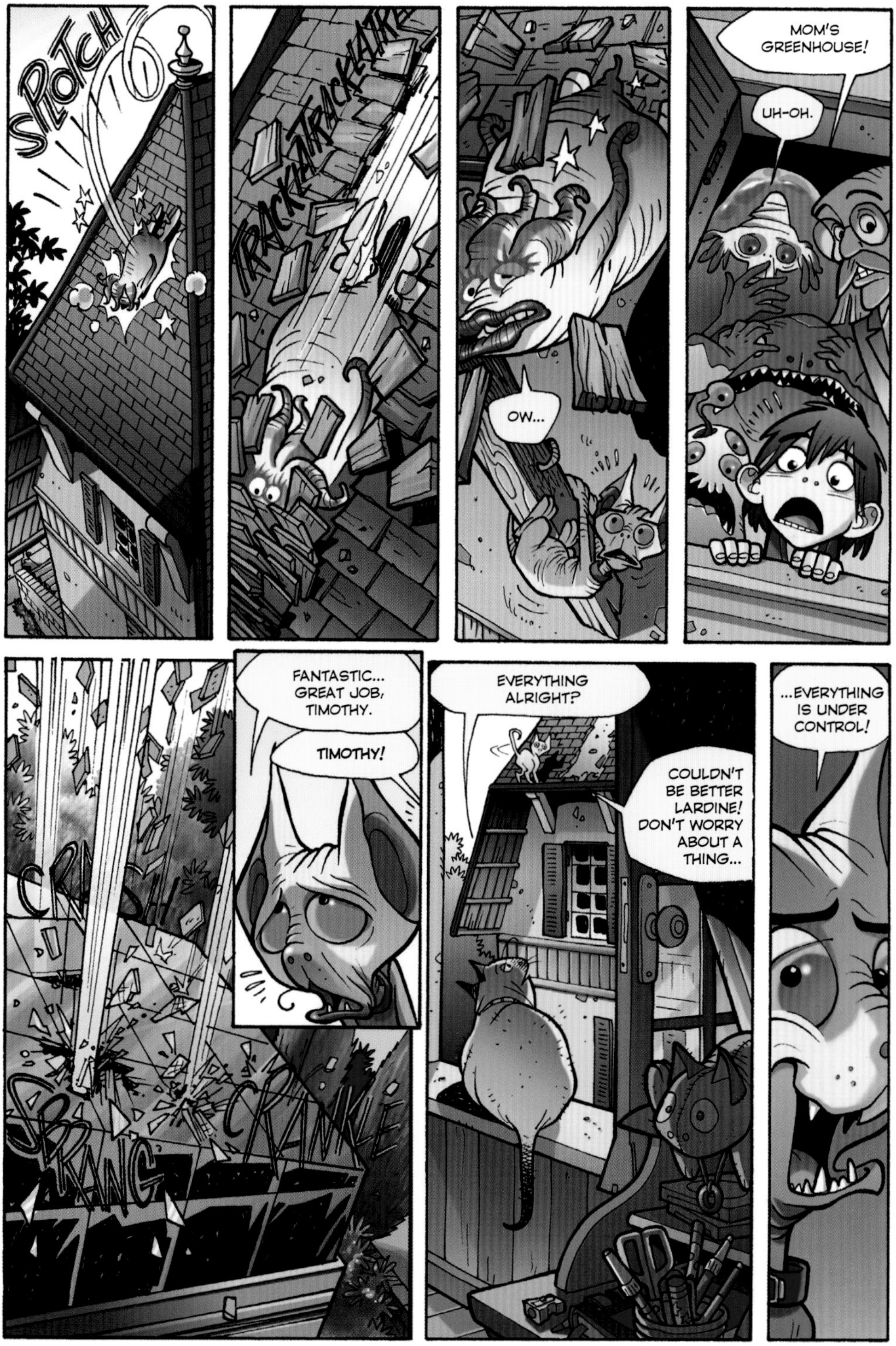
SPLOTCH
OW...
MOM'S GREENHOUSE!
UH-OH.
SPRANG
CRANKLE
FANTASTIC... GREAT JOB, TIMOTHY.
TIMOTHY!
EVERYTHING ALRIGHT?
COULDN'T BE BETTER LARDINE! DON'T WORRY ABOUT A THING...
...EVERYTHING IS UNDER CONTROL!

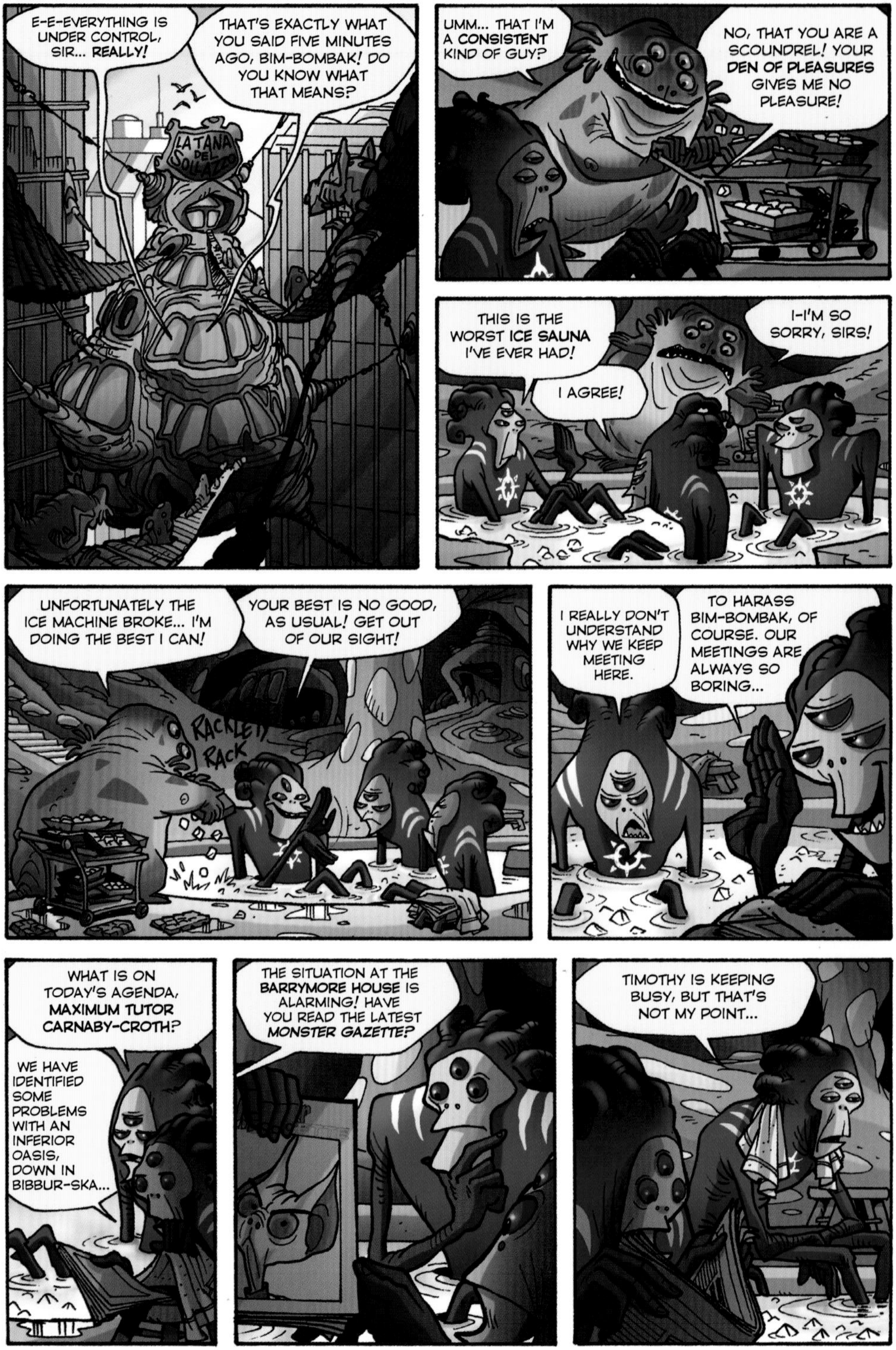
E-E-EVERYTHING IS UNDER CONTROL, SIR... REALLY!
THAT'S EXACTLY WHAT YOU SAID FIVE MINUTES AGO, BIM-BOMBAK! DO YOU KNOW WHAT THAT MEANS?
LA TANA DEL SOLLAZZO
UMM... THAT I'M A CONSISTENT KIND OF GUY?
NO, THAT YOU ARE A SCOUNDREL! YOUR DEN OF PLEASURES GIVES ME NO PLEASURE!
THIS IS THE WORST ICE SAUNA I'VE EVER HAD!
I AGREE!
I-I'M SO SORRY, SIRS!
UNFORTUNATELY THE ICE MACHINE BROKE... I'M DOING THE BEST I CAN!
YOUR BEST IS NO GOOD, AS USUAL! GET OUT OF OUR SIGHT!
RACKLETY RACK
I REALLY DON'T UNDERSTAND WHY WE KEEP MEETING HERE.
TO HARASS BIM-BOMBAK, OF COURSE. OUR MEETINGS ARE ALWAYS SO BORING...
WHAT IS ON TODAY'S AGENDA, MAXIMUM TUTOR CARNABY-CROTH?
WE HAVE IDENTIFIED SOME PROBLEMS WITH AN INFERIOR OASIS, DOWN IN BIBBUR-SKA...
THE SITUATION AT THE BARRYMORE HOUSE IS ALARMING! HAVE YOU READ THE LATEST MONSTER GAZETTE?
TIMOTHY IS KEEPING BUSY, BUT THAT'S NOT MY POINT...

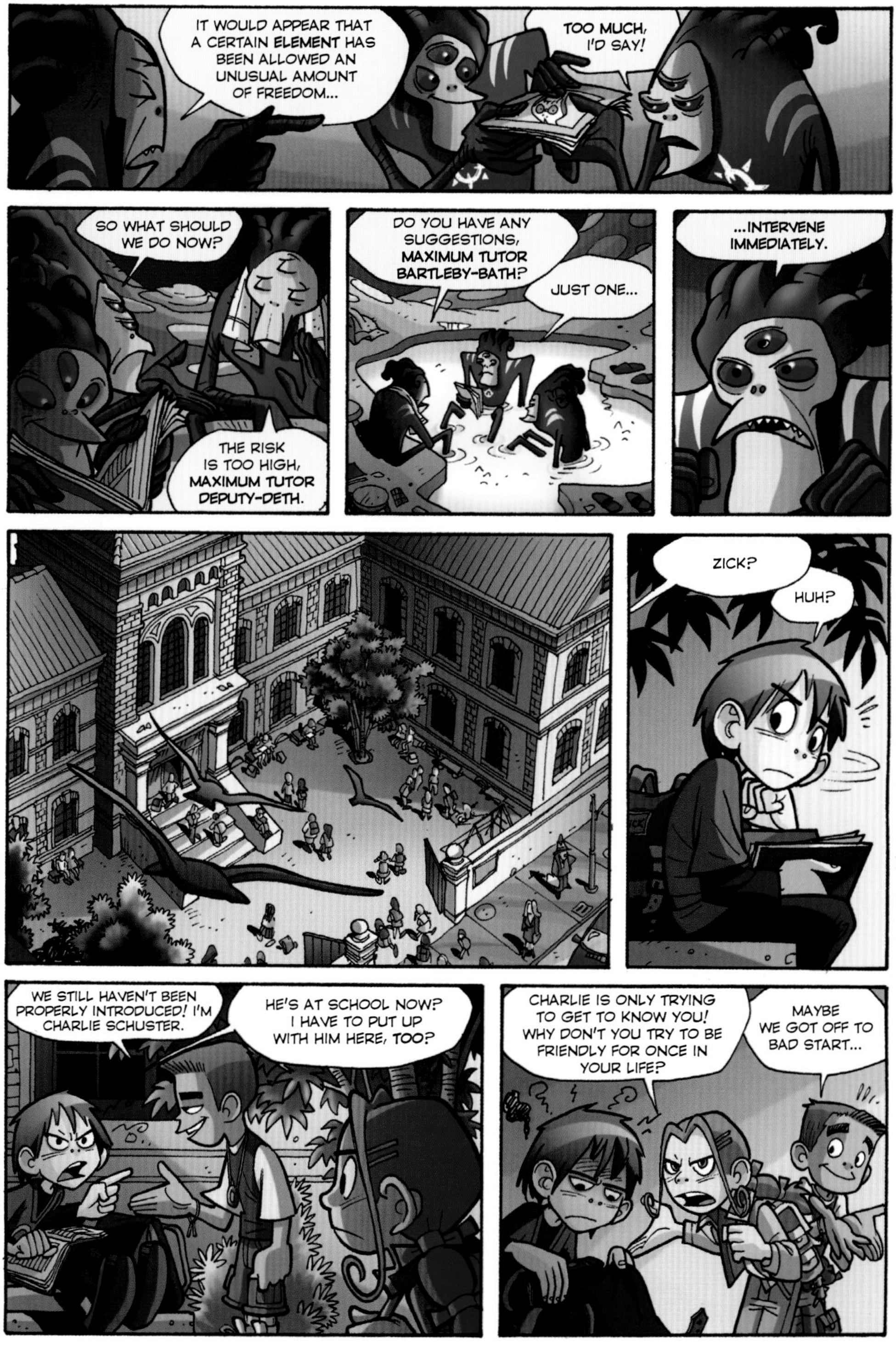

IT WOULD APPEAR THAT A CERTAIN ELEMENT HAS BEEN ALLOWED AN UNUSUAL AMOUNT OF FREEDOM...
TOO MUCH, I'D SAY!
SO WHAT SHOULD WE DO NOW?
THE RISK IS TOO HIGH, MAXIMUM TUTOR DEPUTY-DETH.
DO YOU HAVE ANY SUGGESTIONS, MAXIMUM TUTOR BARTLEBY-BATH?
JUST ONE...
...INTERVENE IMMEDIATELY.
ZICK?
HUH?
WE STILL HAVEN'T BEEN PROPERLY INTRODUCED! I'M CHARLIE SCHUSTER.
HE'S AT SCHOOL NOW? I HAVE TO PUT UP WITH HIM HERE, TOO?
CHARLIE IS ONLY TRYING TO GET TO KNOW YOU! WHY DON'T YOU TRY TO BE FRIENDLY FOR ONCE IN YOUR LIFE?
MAYBE WE GOT OFF TO BAD START...

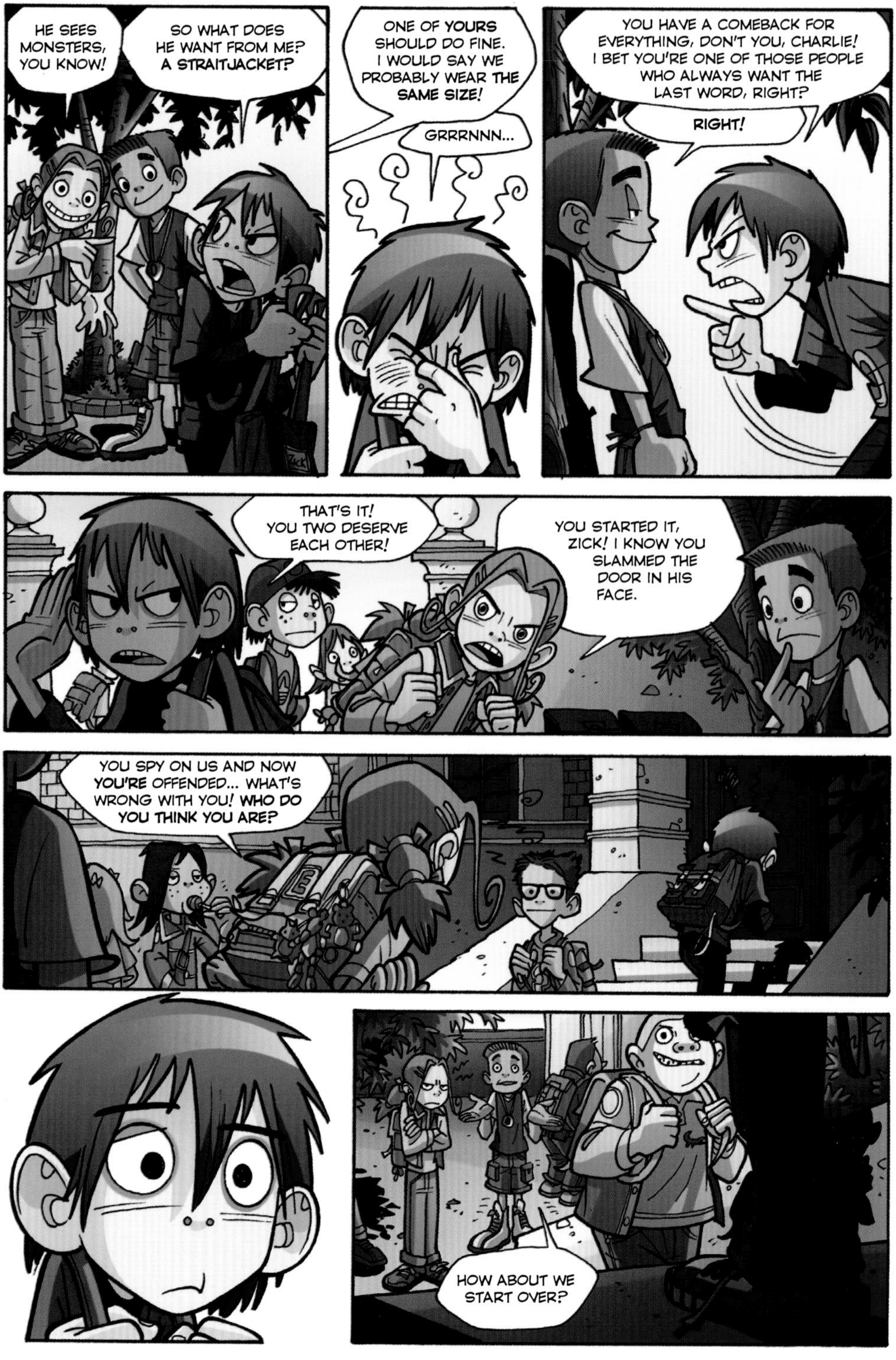

HE SEES MONSTERS, YOU KNOW!
SO WHAT DOES HE WANT FROM ME? A STRAITJACKET?
ONE OF YOURS SHOULD DO FINE. I WOULD SAY WE PROBABLY WEAR THE SAME SIZE!
GRRRNNN...
YOU HAVE A COMEBACK FOR EVERYTHING, DON'T YOU, CHARLIE! I BET YOU'RE ONE OF THOSE PEOPLE WHO ALWAYS WANT THE LAST WORD, RIGHT?
RIGHT!
THAT'S IT! YOU TWO DESERVE EACH OTHER!
YOU STARTED IT, ZICK! I KNOW YOU SLAMMED THE DOOR IN HIS FACE.
YOU SPY ON US AND NOW YOU'RE OFFENDED... WHAT'S WRONG WITH YOU! WHO DO YOU THINK YOU ARE?
HOW ABOUT WE START OVER?

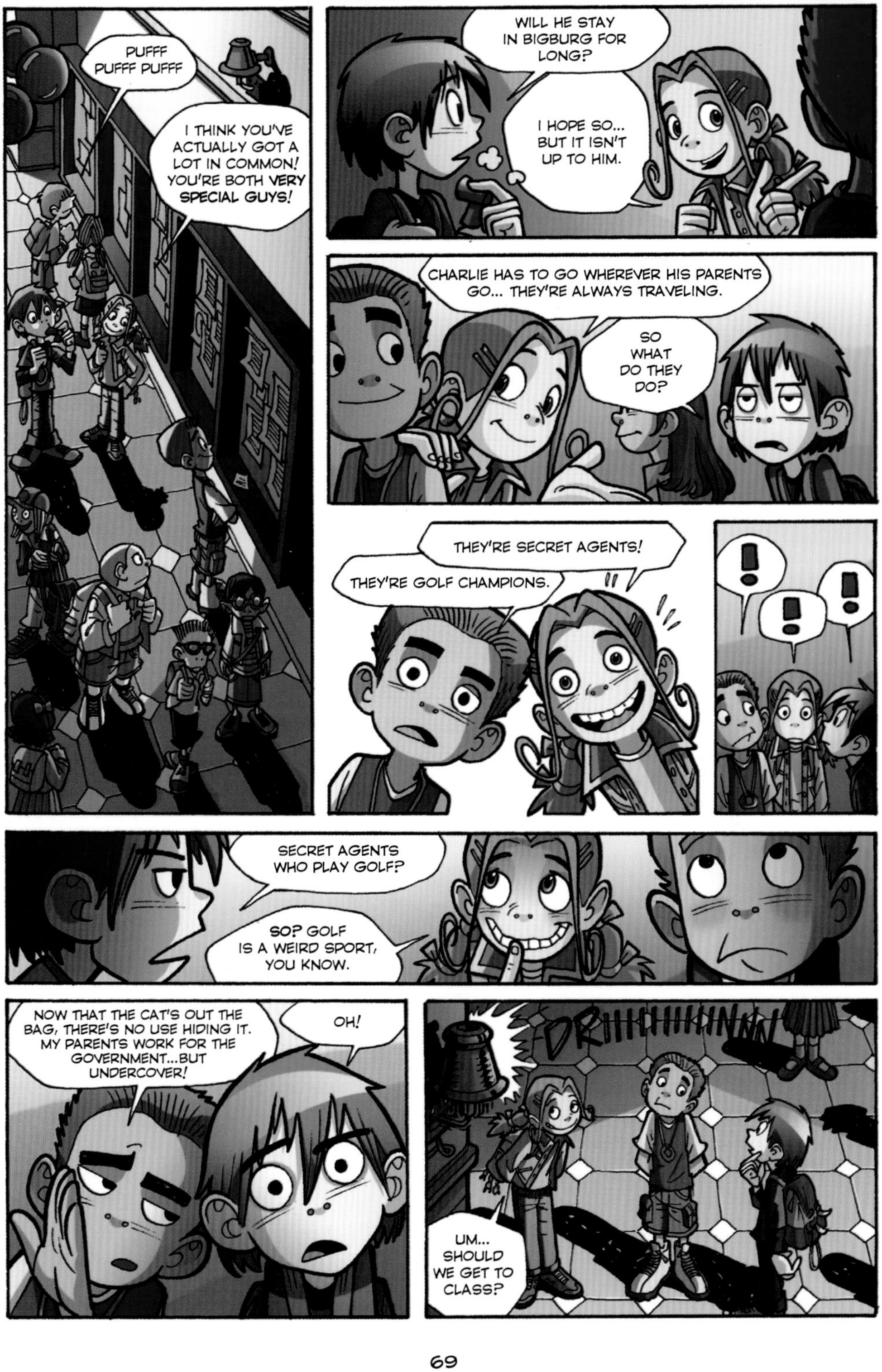
PUFFF
PUFFF PUFFF
I THINK YOU'VE ACTUALLY GOT A LOT IN COMMON! YOU'RE BOTH **VERY SPECIAL GUYS**!
WILL HE STAY IN BIGBURG FOR LONG?
I HOPE SO... BUT IT ISN'T UP TO HIM.
CHARLIE HAS TO GO WHEREVER HIS PARENTS GO... THEY'RE ALWAYS TRAVELING.
SO WHAT DO THEY DO?
THEY'RE SECRET AGENTS!
THEY'RE GOLF CHAMPIONS.
!
!
!
SECRET AGENTS WHO PLAY GOLF?
SO? GOLF IS A WEIRD SPORT, YOU KNOW.
NOW THAT THE CAT'S OUT THE BAG, THERE'S NO USE HIDING IT. MY PARENTS WORK FOR THE GOVERNMENT...BUT UNDERCOVER!
OH!
DRIIIIIIIIINNN
UM... SHOULD WE GET TO CLASS?

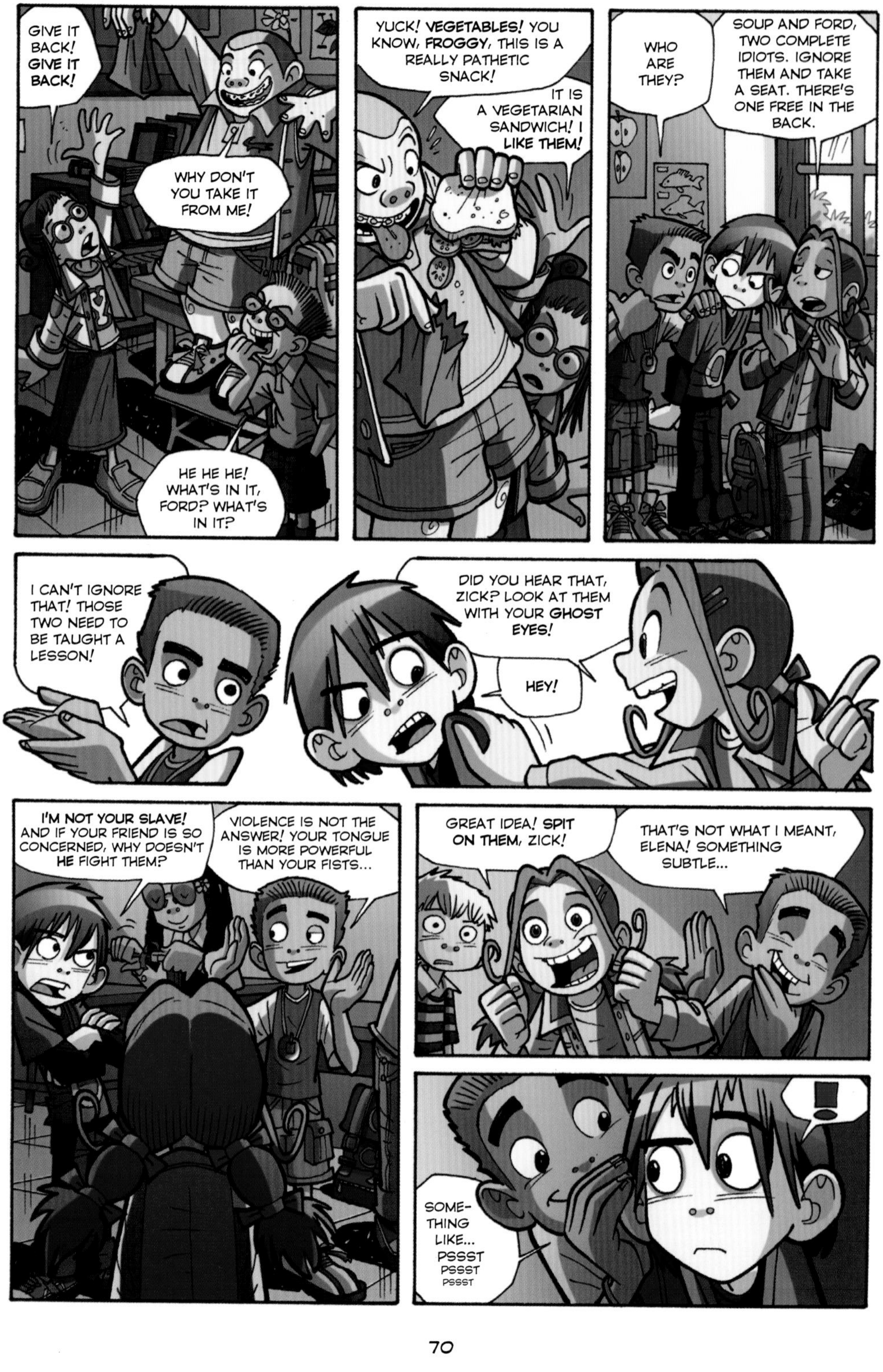
GIVE IT BACK! GIVE IT BACK!
WHY DON'T YOU TAKE IT FROM ME!
HE HE HE! WHAT'S IN IT, FORD? WHAT'S IN IT?
YUCK! VEGETABLES! YOU KNOW, FROGGY, THIS IS A REALLY PATHETIC SNACK!
IT IS A VEGETARIAN SANDWICH! I LIKE THEM!
WHO ARE THEY?
SOUP AND FORD, TWO COMPLETE IDIOTS. IGNORE THEM AND TAKE A SEAT. THERE'S ONE FREE IN THE BACK.
I CAN'T IGNORE THAT! THOSE TWO NEED TO BE TAUGHT A LESSON!
DID YOU HEAR THAT, ZICK? LOOK AT THEM WITH YOUR GHOST EYES!
HEY!
I'M NOT YOUR SLAVE! AND IF YOUR FRIEND IS SO CONCERNED, WHY DOESN'T HE FIGHT THEM?
VIOLENCE IS NOT THE ANSWER! YOUR TONGUE IS MORE POWERFUL THAN YOUR FISTS...
GREAT IDEA! SPIT ON THEM, ZICK!
THAT'S NOT WHAT I MEANT, ELENA! SOMETHING SUBTLE...
!
SOME-THING LIKE... PSSST PSSST PSSST

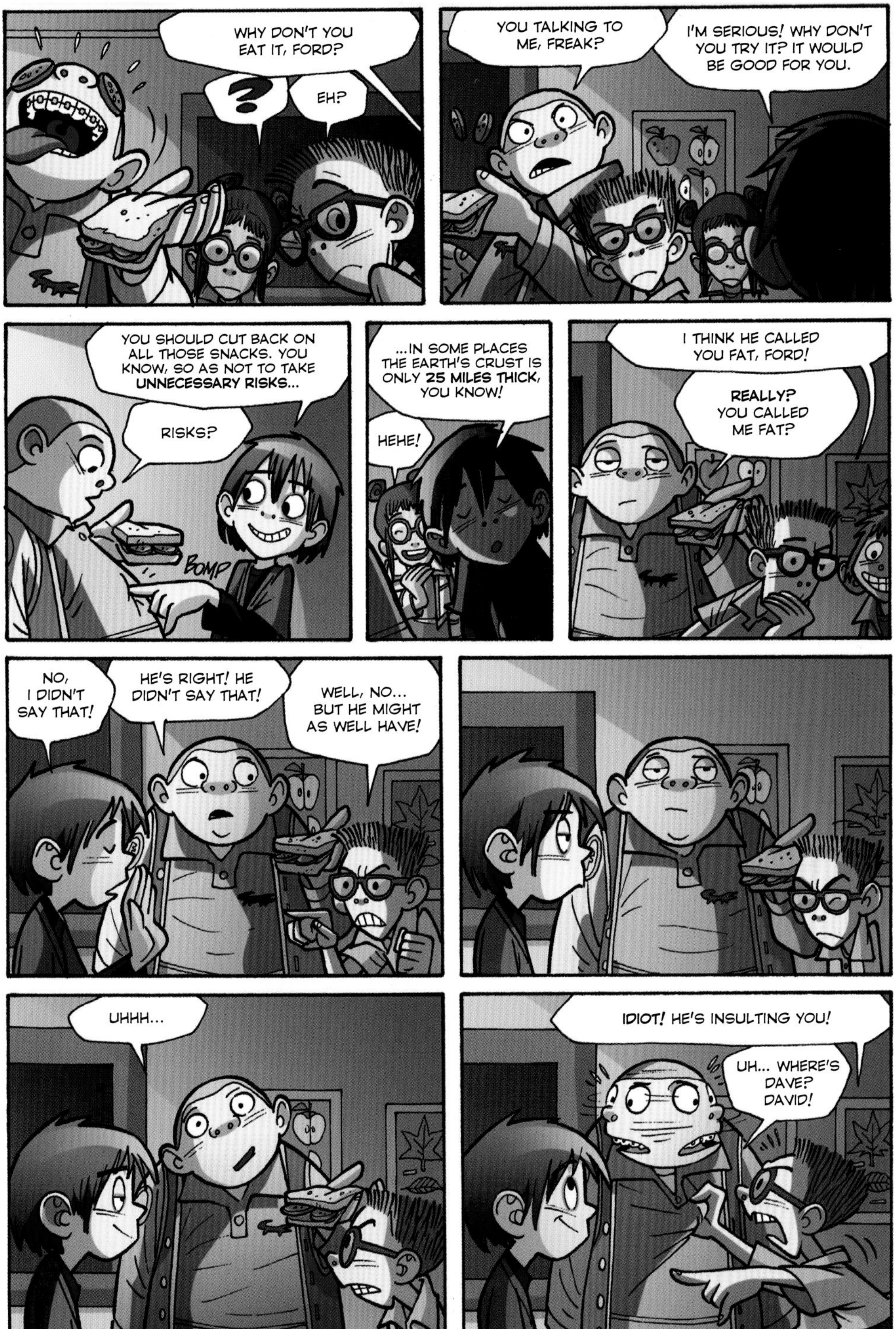
WHY DON'T YOU EAT IT, FORD?
?
EH?
YOU TALKING TO ME, FREAK?
I'M SERIOUS! WHY DON'T YOU TRY IT? IT WOULD BE GOOD FOR YOU.
YOU SHOULD CUT BACK ON ALL THOSE SNACKS. YOU KNOW, SO AS NOT TO TAKE UNNECESSARY RISKS...
RISKS?
BOMP
...IN SOME PLACES THE EARTH'S CRUST IS ONLY 25 MILES THICK, YOU KNOW!
HEHE!
I THINK HE CALLED YOU FAT, FORD!
REALLY? YOU CALLED ME FAT?
NO, I DIDN'T SAY THAT!
HE'S RIGHT! HE DIDN'T SAY THAT!
WELL, NO... BUT HE MIGHT AS WELL HAVE!
UHHH...
IDIOT! HE'S INSULTING YOU!
UH... WHERE'S DAVE? DAVID!

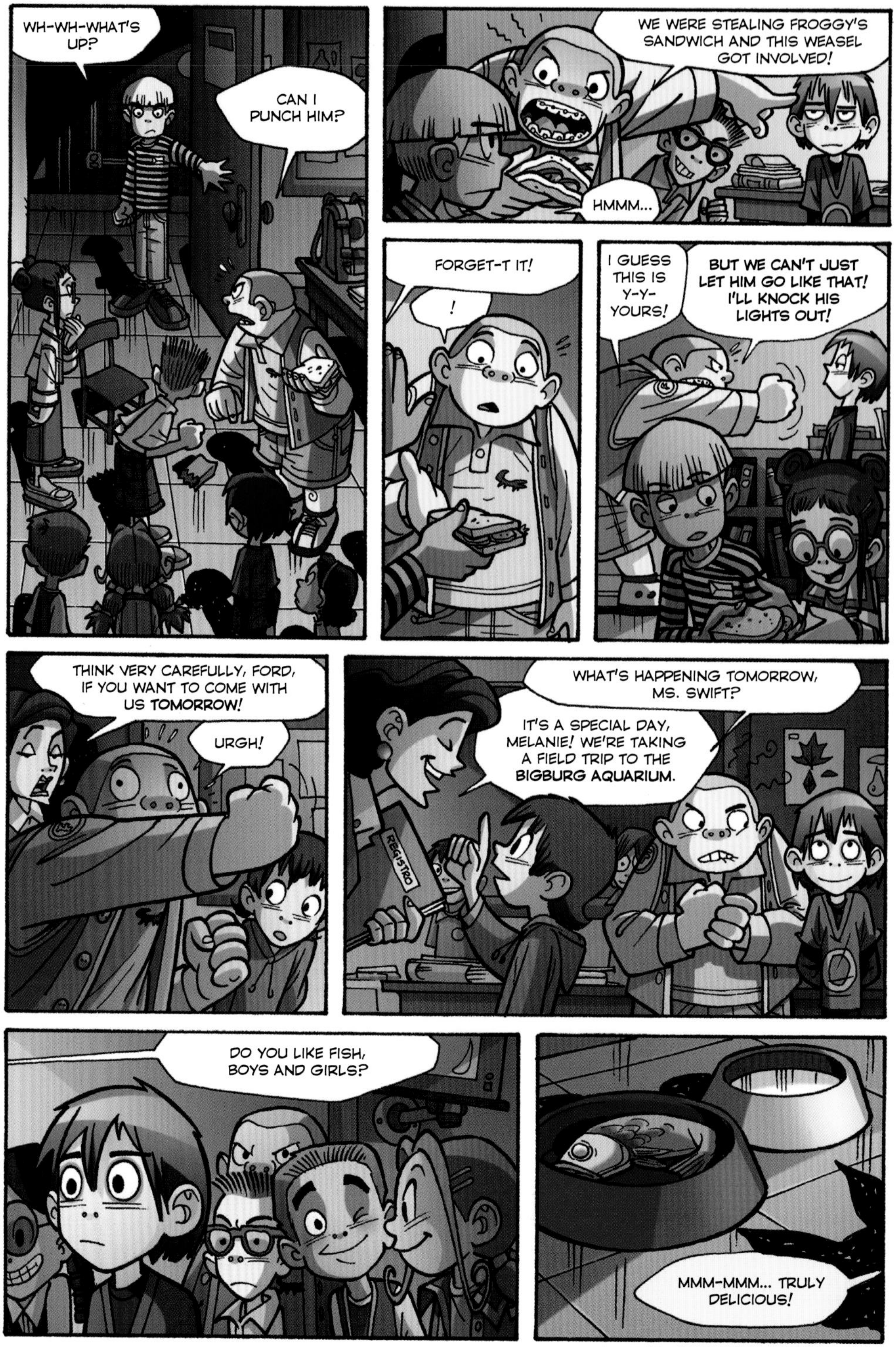
WH-WH-WHAT'S UP?
CAN I PUNCH HIM?
WE WERE STEALING FROGGY'S SANDWICH AND THIS WEASEL GOT INVOLVED!
HMMM...
FORGET-T IT!
!
I GUESS THIS IS Y-Y-YOURS!
BUT WE CAN'T JUST LET HIM GO LIKE THAT! I'LL KNOCK HIS LIGHTS OUT!
THINK VERY CAREFULLY, FORD, IF YOU WANT TO COME WITH US TOMORROW!
URGH!
WHAT'S HAPPENING TOMORROW, MS. SWIFT?
IT'S A SPECIAL DAY, MELANIE! WE'RE TAKING A FIELD TRIP TO THE BIGBURG AQUARIUM.
REGISTRO
DO YOU LIKE FISH, BOYS AND GIRLS?
MMM-MMM... TRULY DELICIOUS!

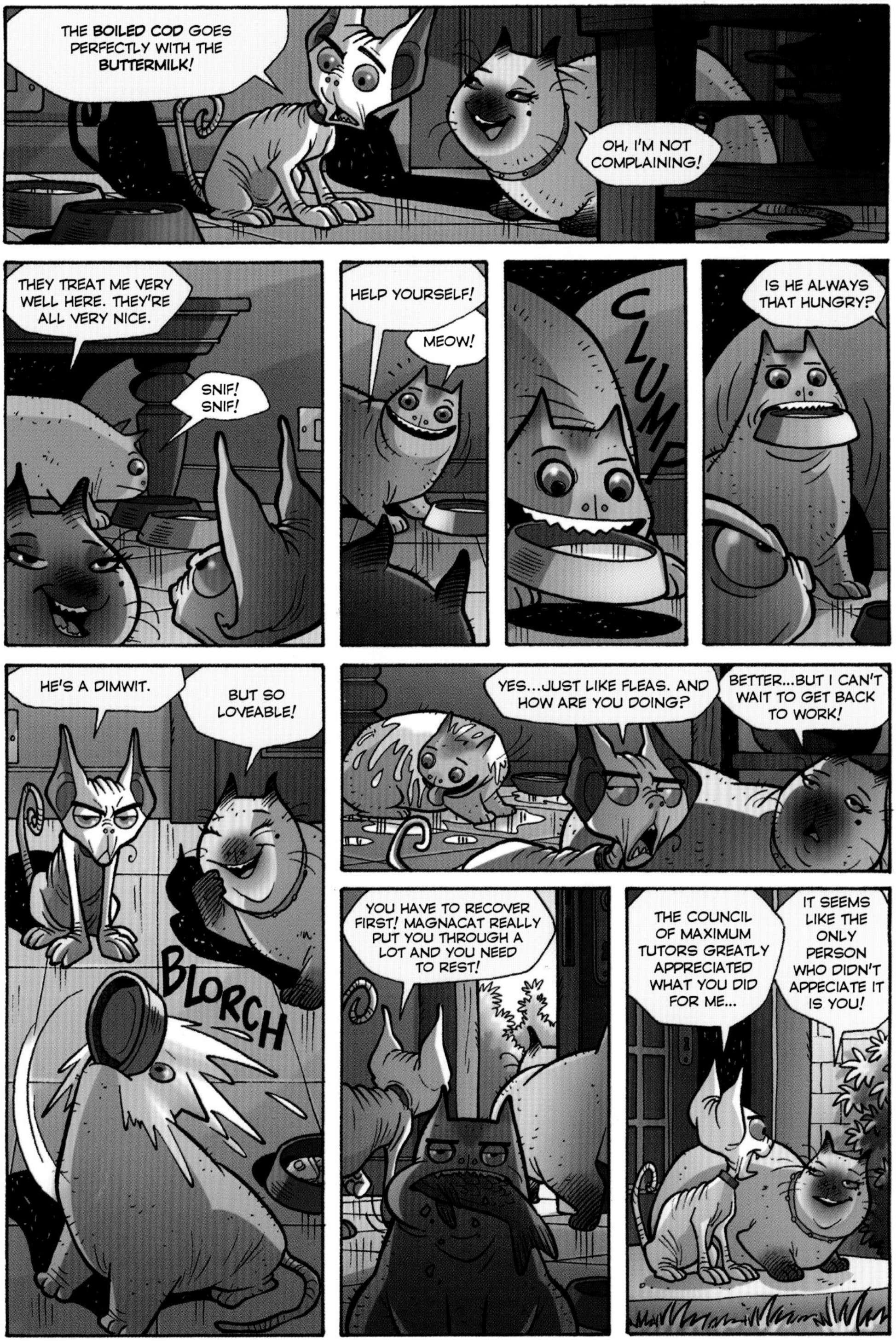
THE BOILED COD GOES PERFECTLY WITH THE BUTTERMILK!
OH, I'M NOT COMPLAINING!
THEY TREAT ME VERY WELL HERE. THEY'RE ALL VERY NICE.
SNIF! SNIF!
HELP YOURSELF!
MEOW!
CLUMP
IS HE ALWAYS THAT HUNGRY?
HE'S A DIMWIT.
BUT SO LOVEABLE!
BLORCH
YES...JUST LIKE FLEAS. AND HOW ARE YOU DOING?
BETTER...BUT I CAN'T WAIT TO GET BACK TO WORK!
YOU HAVE TO RECOVER FIRST! MAGNACAT REALLY PUT YOU THROUGH A LOT AND YOU NEED TO REST!
THE COUNCIL OF MAXIMUM TUTORS GREATLY APPRECIATED WHAT YOU DID FOR ME...
IT SEEMS LIKE THE ONLY PERSON WHO DIDN'T APPRECIATE IT IS YOU!

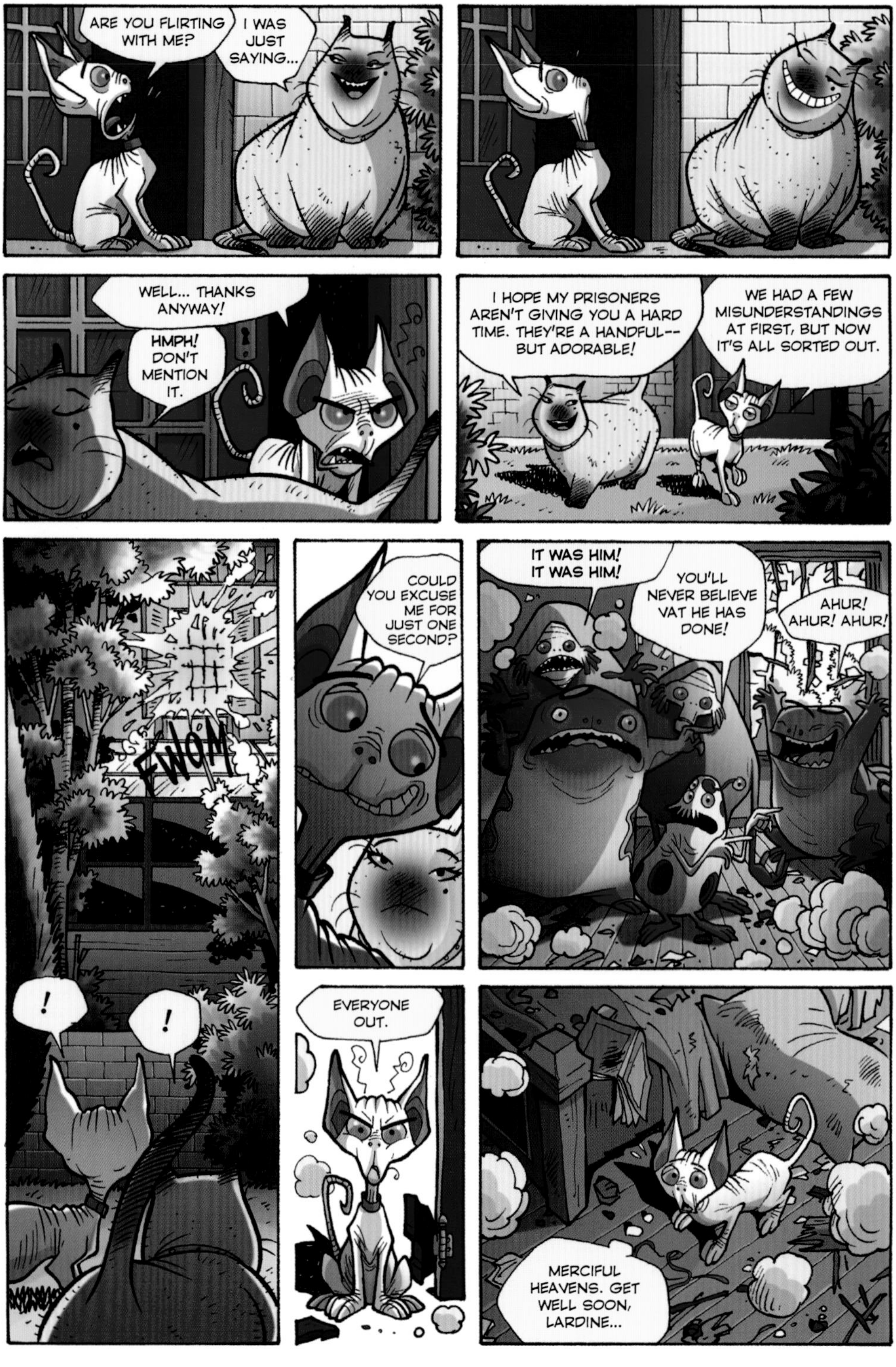
ARE YOU FLIRTING WITH ME?
I WAS JUST SAYING...
WELL... THANKS ANYWAY!
HMPH! DON'T MENTION IT.
I HOPE MY PRISONERS AREN'T GIVING YOU A HARD TIME. THEY'RE A HANDFUL-- BUT ADORABLE!
WE HAD A FEW MISUNDERSTANDINGS AT FIRST, BUT NOW IT'S ALL SORTED OUT.
FWOM
!
!
COULD YOU EXCUSE ME FOR JUST ONE SECOND?
IT WAS HIM! IT WAS HIM!
YOU'LL NEVER BELIEVE VAT HE HAS DONE!
AHUR! AHUR! AHUR!
EVERYONE OUT.
MERCIFUL HEAVENS. GET WELL SOON, LARDINE...

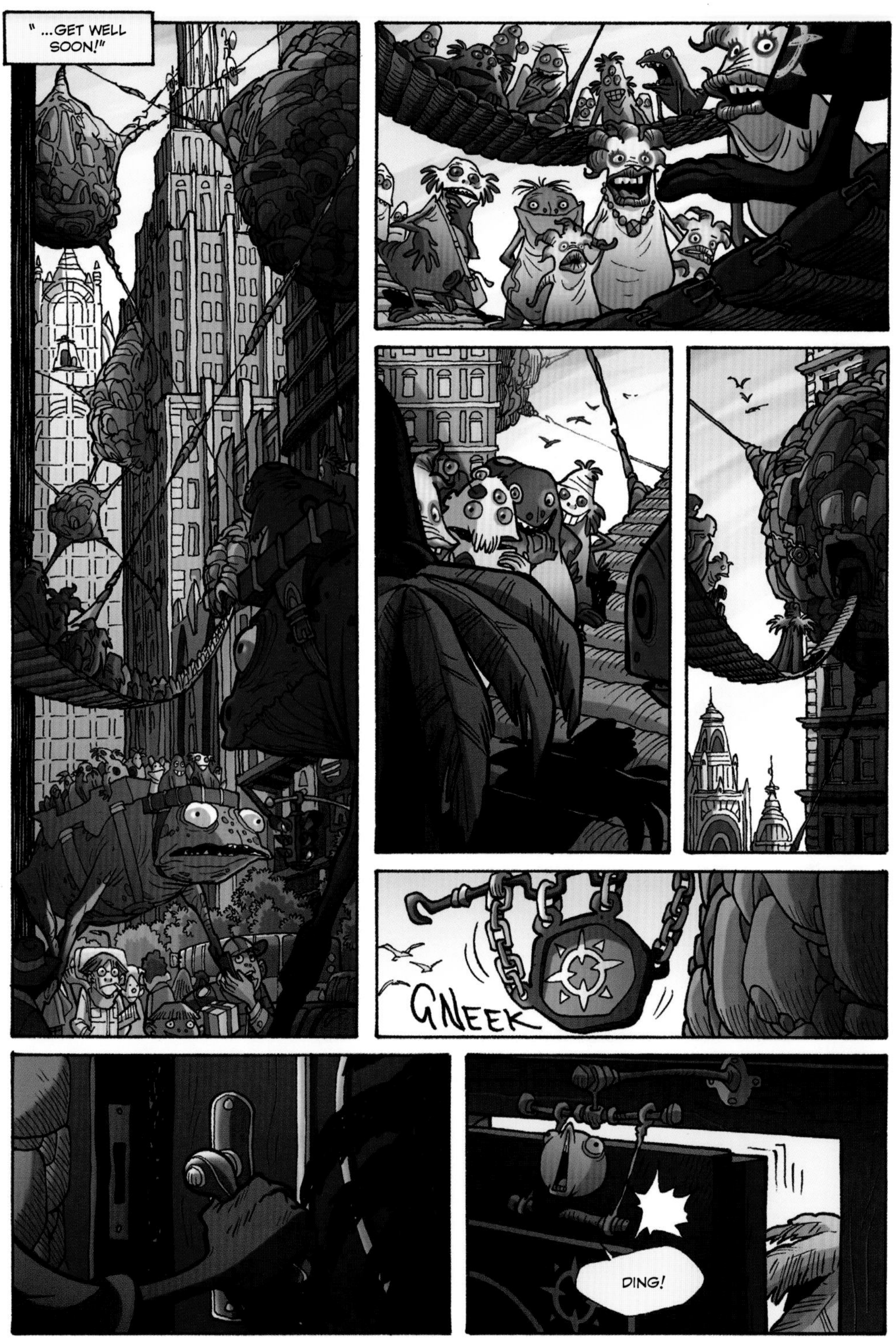

"...GET WELL SOON!"
GNEEK
DING!

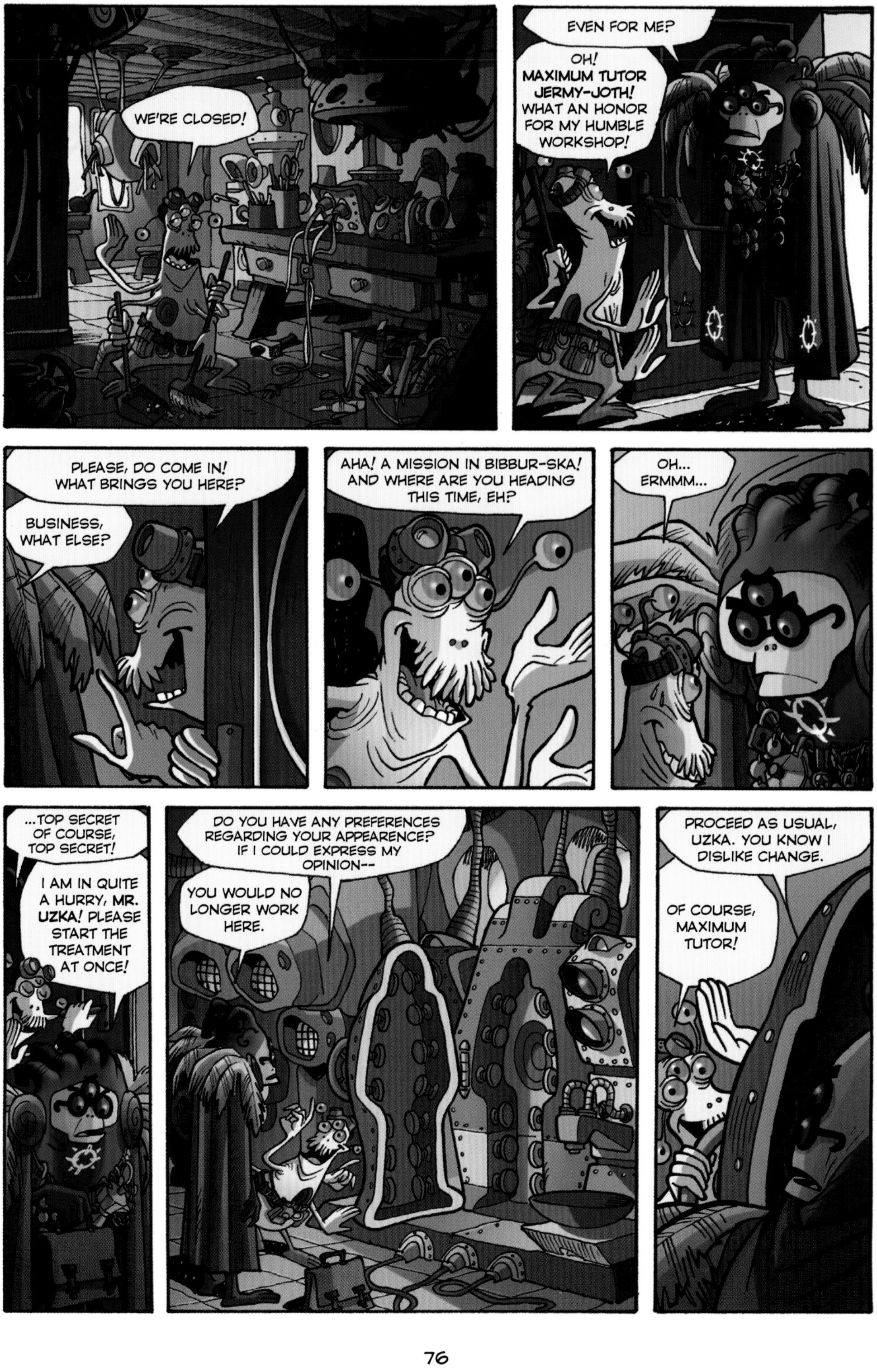

WE'RE CLOSED!
EVEN FOR ME?
OH! MAXIMUM TUTOR JERMY-JOTH! WHAT AN HONOR FOR MY HUMBLE WORKSHOP!
PLEASE, DO COME IN! WHAT BRINGS YOU HERE?
BUSINESS, WHAT ELSE?
AHA! A MISSION IN BIBBUR-SKA! AND WHERE ARE YOU HEADING THIS TIME, EH?
OH... ERMMM...
...TOP SECRET OF COURSE, TOP SECRET!
I AM IN QUITE A HURRY, MR. UZKA! PLEASE START THE TREATMENT AT ONCE!
DO YOU HAVE ANY PREFERENCES REGARDING YOUR APPEARENCE? IF I COULD EXPRESS MY OPINION--
YOU WOULD NO LONGER WORK HERE.
PROCEED AS USUAL, UZKA. YOU KNOW I DISLIKE CHANGE.
OF COURSE, MAXIMUM TUTOR!

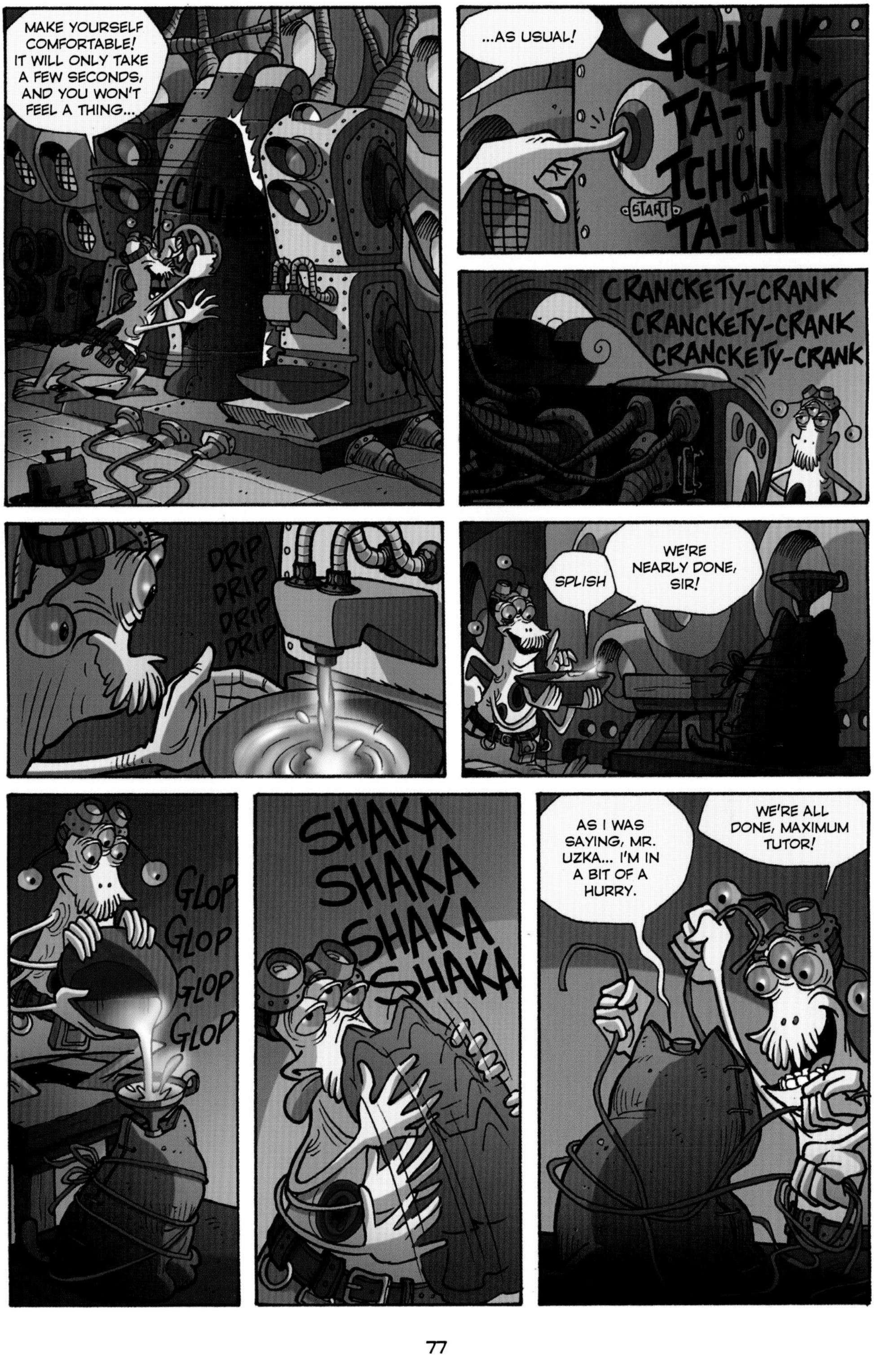
MAKE YOURSELF COMFORTABLE! IT WILL ONLY TAKE A FEW SECONDS, AND YOU WON'T FEEL A THING...
...AS USUAL!
TCHUNK
TA-TUNK
START
CRANCKETY-CRANK
CRANCKETY-CRANK
CRANCKETY-CRANK
DRIP DRIP DRIP DRIP
SPLISH
WE'RE NEARLY DONE, SIR!
GLOP GLOP GLOP GLOP
SHAKA SHAKA SHAKA SHAKA
AS I WAS SAYING, MR. UZKA... I'M IN A BIT OF A HURRY.
WE'RE ALL DONE, MAXIMUM TUTOR!

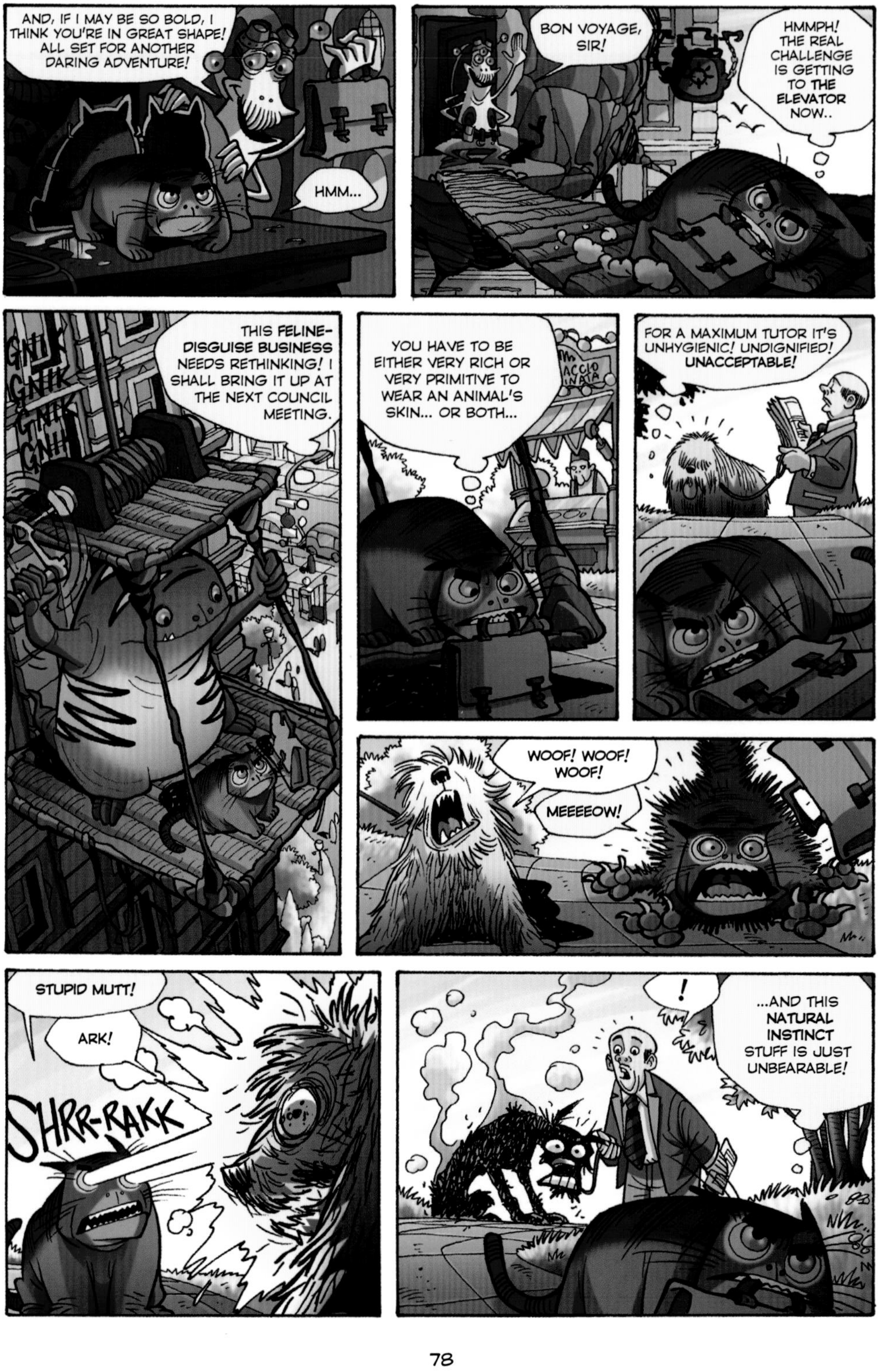
AND, IF I MAY BE SO BOLD, I THINK YOU'RE IN GREAT SHAPE! ALL SET FOR ANOTHER DARING ADVENTURE!
HMM...
BON VOYAGE, SIR!
HMMPH! THE REAL CHALLENGE IS GETTING TO THE ELEVATOR NOW..
GNIK GNIK GNIK GNIK
THIS FELINE-DISGUISE BUSINESS NEEDS RETHINKING! I SHALL BRING IT UP AT THE NEXT COUNCIL MEETING.
YOU HAVE TO BE EITHER VERY RICH OR VERY PRIMITIVE TO WEAR AN ANIMAL'S SKIN... OR BOTH...
FOR A MAXIMUM TUTOR IT'S UNHYGIENIC! UNDIGNIFIED! UNACCEPTABLE!
WOOF! WOOF! WOOF!
MEEEEOW!
STUPID MUTT!
ARK!
SHRR-RAKK
!
...AND THIS NATURAL INSTINCT STUFF IS JUST UNBEARABLE!

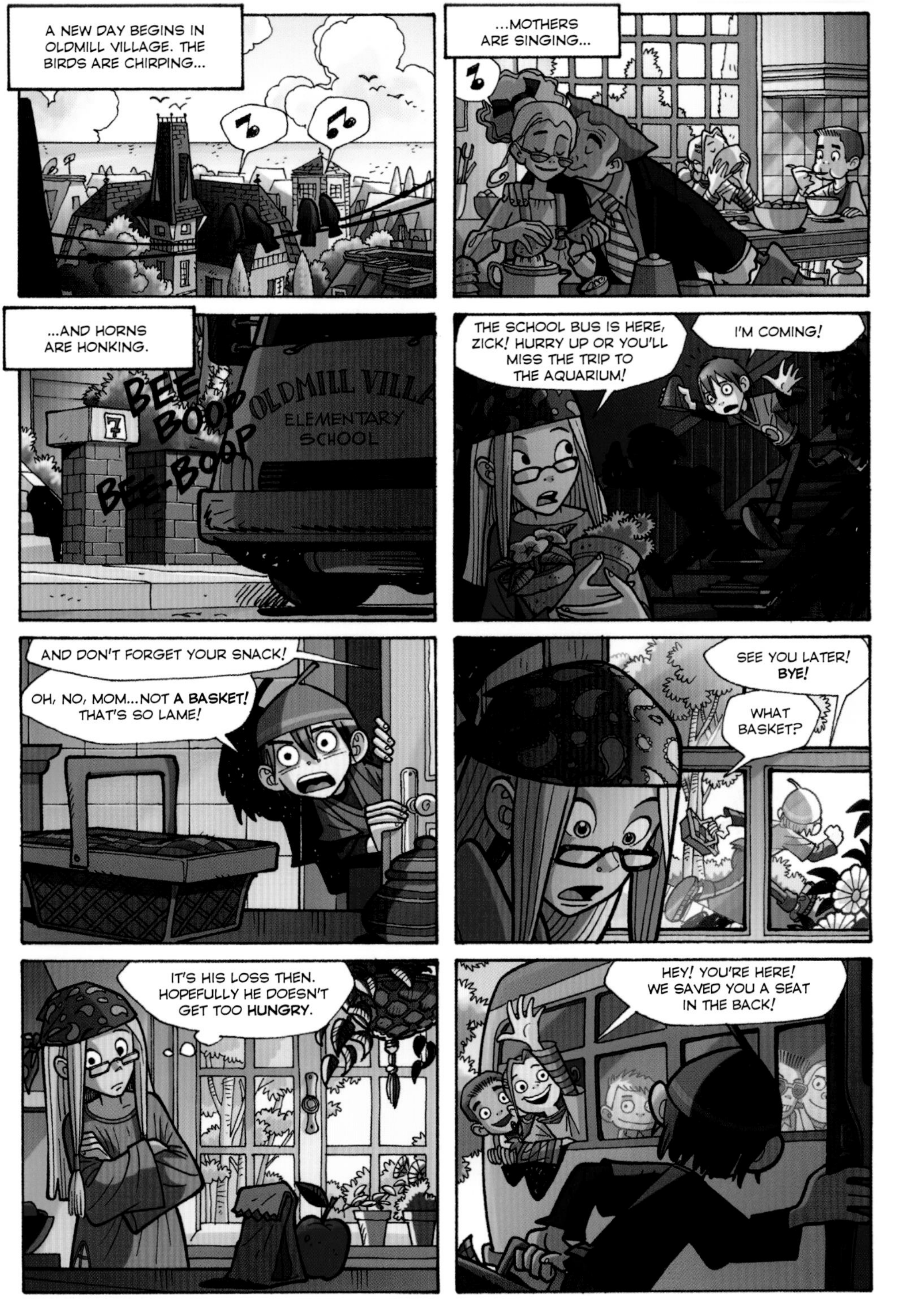
A NEW DAY BEGINS IN OLDMILL VILLAGE. THE BIRDS ARE CHIRPING...
...MOTHERS ARE SINGING...
...AND HORNS ARE HONKING.
BEE BOOP BEE-BOOP
OLDMILL VILLA
ELEMENTARY SCHOOL
THE SCHOOL BUS IS HERE, ZICK! HURRY UP OR YOU'LL MISS THE TRIP TO THE AQUARIUM!
I'M COMING!
AND DON'T FORGET YOUR SNACK!
OH, NO, MOM...NOT A BASKET! THAT'S SO LAME!
SEE YOU LATER! BYE!
WHAT BASKET?
IT'S HIS LOSS THEN. HOPEFULLY HE DOESN'T GET TOO HUNGRY.
HEY! YOU'RE HERE! WE SAVED YOU A SEAT IN THE BACK!

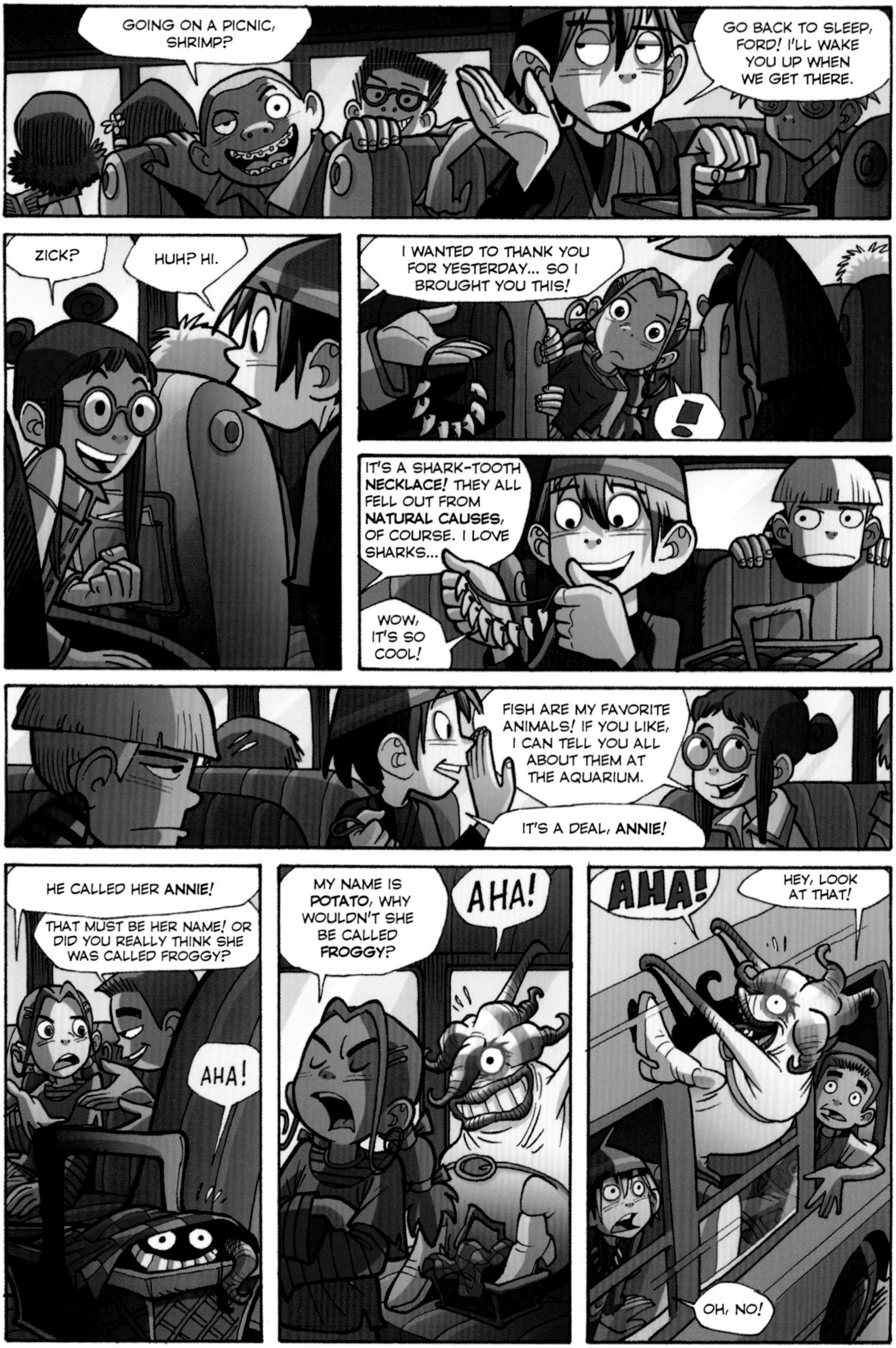
GOING ON A PICNIC, SHRIMP?
GO BACK TO SLEEP, FORD! I'LL WAKE YOU UP WHEN WE GET THERE.
ZICK?
HUH? HI.
I WANTED TO THANK YOU FOR YESTERDAY... SO I BROUGHT YOU THIS!
!
IT'S A SHARK-TOOTH NECKLACE! THEY ALL FELL OUT FROM NATURAL CAUSES, OF COURSE. I LOVE SHARKS...
WOW, IT'S SO COOL!
FISH ARE MY FAVORITE ANIMALS! IF YOU LIKE, I CAN TELL YOU ALL ABOUT THEM AT THE AQUARIUM.
IT'S A DEAL, ANNIE!
HE CALLED HER ANNIE!
THAT MUST BE HER NAME! OR DID YOU REALLY THINK SHE WAS CALLED FROGGY?
AHA!
MY NAME IS POTATO, WHY WOULDN'T SHE BE CALLED FROGGY?
AHA!
AHA!
HEY, LOOK AT THAT!
OH, NO!

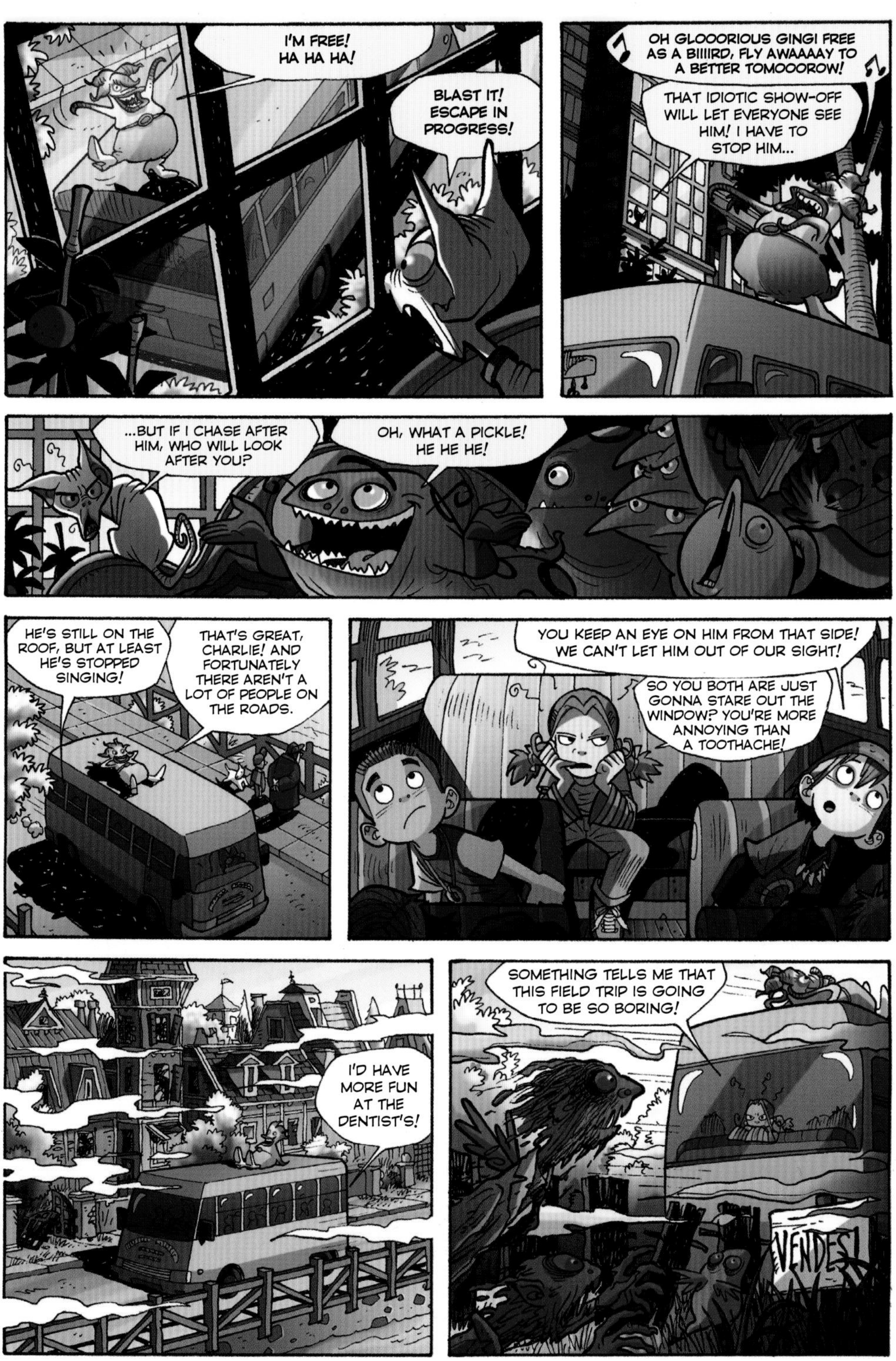
I'M FREE! HA HA HA!
BLAST IT! ESCAPE IN PROGRESS!
OH GLOOORIOUS GINGI FREE AS A BIIIRD, FLY AWAAAAY TO A BETTER TOMOOOROW!
THAT IDIOTIC SHOW-OFF WILL LET EVERYONE SEE HIM! I HAVE TO STOP HIM...
...BUT IF I CHASE AFTER HIM, WHO WILL LOOK AFTER YOU?
OH, WHAT A PICKLE! HE HE HE!
HE'S STILL ON THE ROOF, BUT AT LEAST HE'S STOPPED SINGING!
THAT'S GREAT, CHARLIE! AND FORTUNATELY THERE AREN'T A LOT OF PEOPLE ON THE ROADS.
YOU KEEP AN EYE ON HIM FROM THAT SIDE! WE CAN'T LET HIM OUT OF OUR SIGHT!
SO YOU BOTH ARE JUST GONNA STARE OUT THE WINDOW? YOU'RE MORE ANNOYING THAN A TOOTHACHE!
I'D HAVE MORE FUN AT THE DENTIST'S!
SOMETHING TELLS ME THAT THIS FIELD TRIP IS GOING TO BE SO BORING!
VENDESI

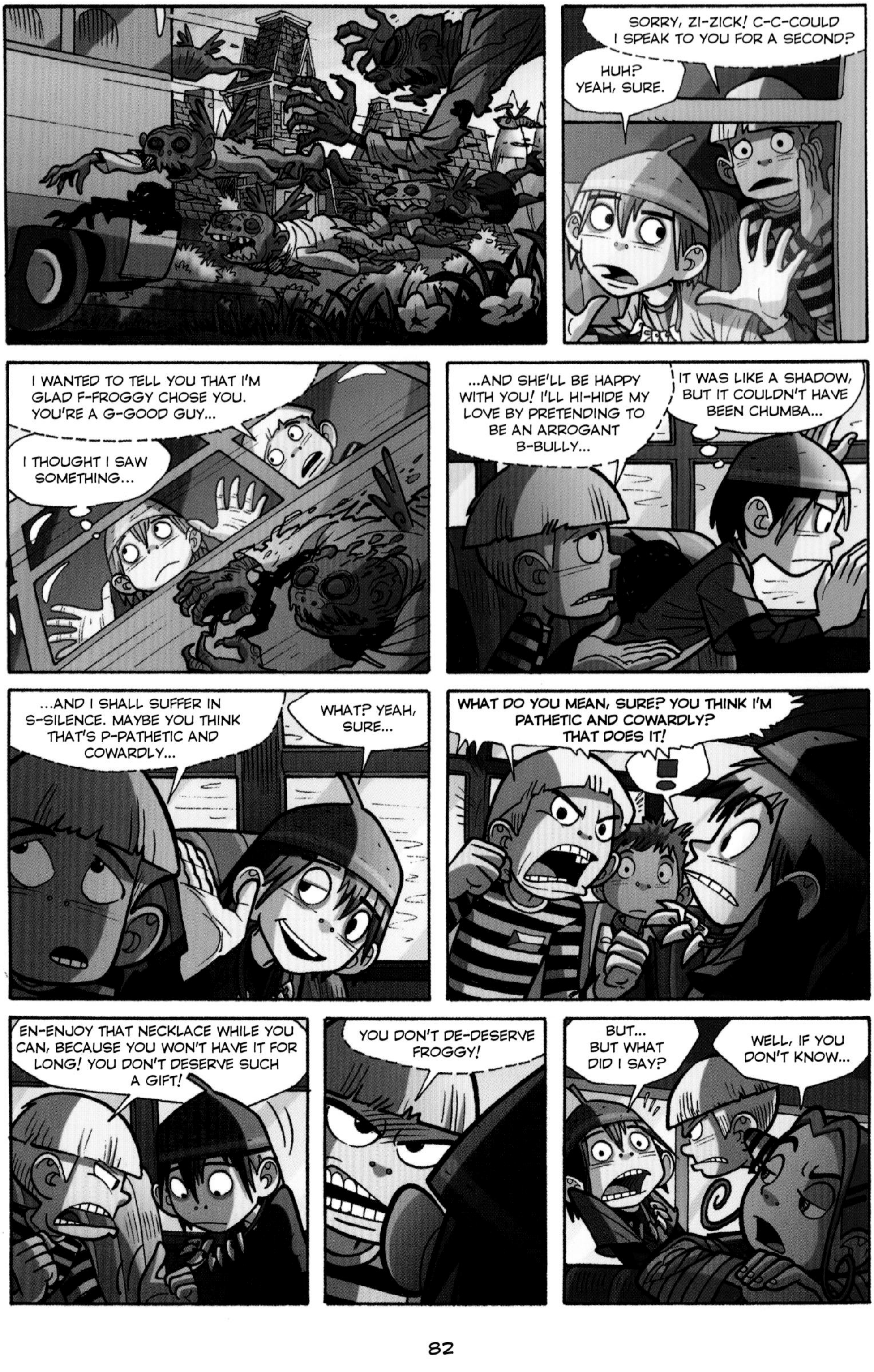
SORRY, ZI-ZICK! C-C-COULD I SPEAK TO YOU FOR A SECOND?
HUH? YEAH, SURE.
I WANTED TO TELL YOU THAT I'M GLAD F-FROGGY CHOSE YOU. YOU'RE A G-GOOD GUY...
I THOUGHT I SAW SOMETHING...
...AND SHE'LL BE HAPPY WITH YOU! I'LL HI-HIDE MY LOVE BY PRETENDING TO BE AN ARROGANT B-BULLY...
IT WAS LIKE A SHADOW, BUT IT COULDN'T HAVE BEEN CHUMBA...
...AND I SHALL SUFFER IN S-SILENCE. MAYBE YOU THINK THAT'S P-PATHETIC AND COWARDLY...
WHAT? YEAH, SURE...
WHAT DO YOU MEAN, SURE? YOU THINK I'M PATHETIC AND COWARDLY? THAT DOES IT!
!
EN-ENJOY THAT NECKLACE WHILE YOU CAN, BECAUSE YOU WON'T HAVE IT FOR LONG! YOU DON'T DESERVE SUCH A GIFT!
YOU DON'T DE-DESERVE FROGGY!
BUT... BUT WHAT DID I SAY?
WELL, IF YOU DON'T KNOW...

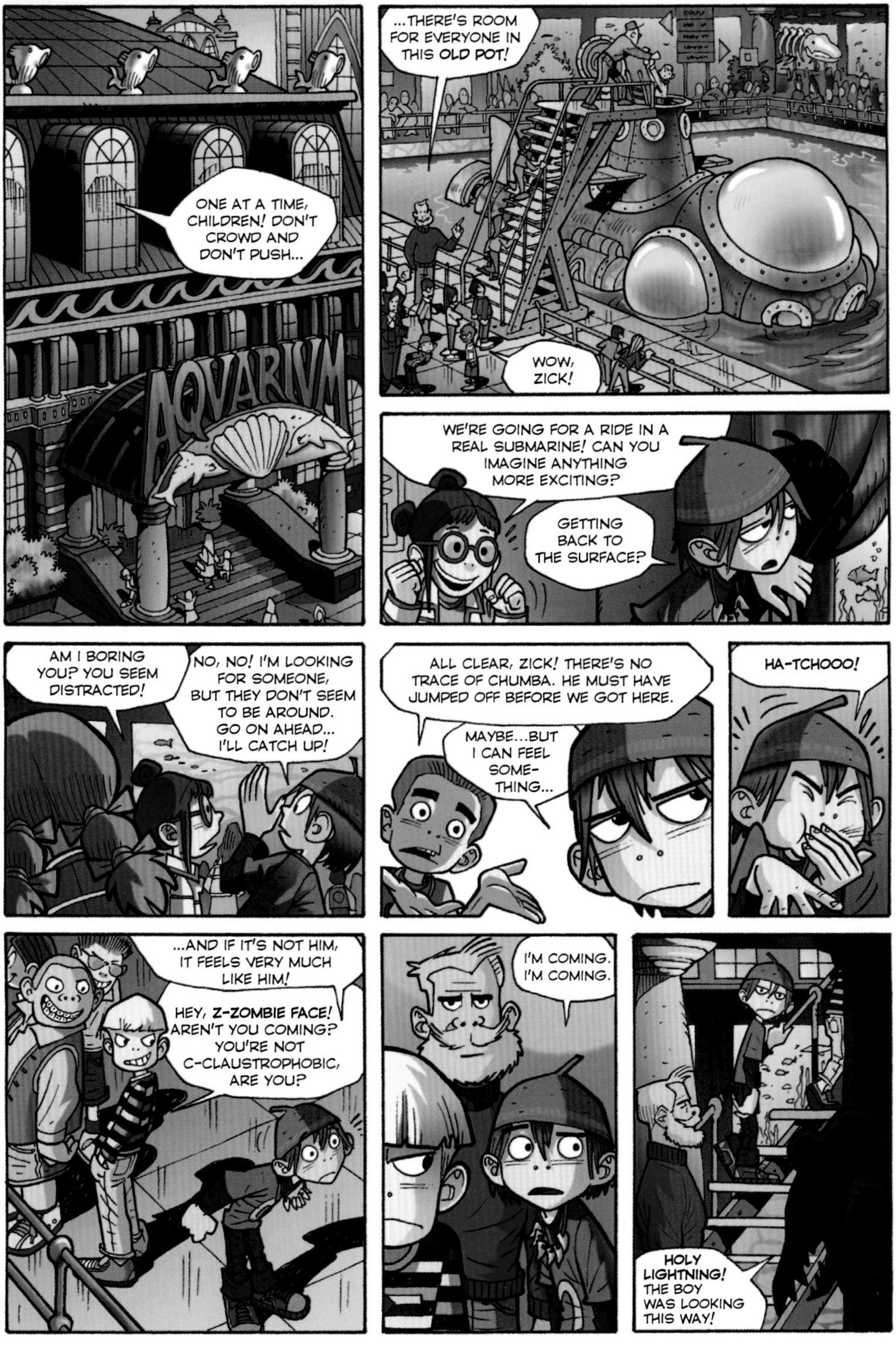

ONE AT A TIME, CHILDREN! DON'T CROWD AND DON'T PUSH...
AQVARIVM
...THERE'S ROOM FOR EVERYONE IN THIS OLD POT!
WOW, ZICK!
WE'RE GOING FOR A RIDE IN A REAL SUBMARINE! CAN YOU IMAGINE ANYTHING MORE EXCITING?
GETTING BACK TO THE SURFACE?
AM I BORING YOU? YOU SEEM DISTRACTED!
NO, NO! I'M LOOKING FOR SOMEONE, BUT THEY DON'T SEEM TO BE AROUND. GO ON AHEAD... I'LL CATCH UP!
ALL CLEAR, ZICK! THERE'S NO TRACE OF CHUMBA. HE MUST HAVE JUMPED OFF BEFORE WE GOT HERE.
MAYBE...BUT I CAN FEEL SOME-THING...
HA-TCHOOO!
...AND IF IT'S NOT HIM, IT FEELS VERY MUCH LIKE HIM!
HEY, Z-ZOMBIE FACE! AREN'T YOU COMING? YOU'RE NOT C-CLAUSTROPHOBIC, ARE YOU?
I'M COMING. I'M COMING.
HOLY LIGHTNING! THE BOY WAS LOOKING THIS WAY!

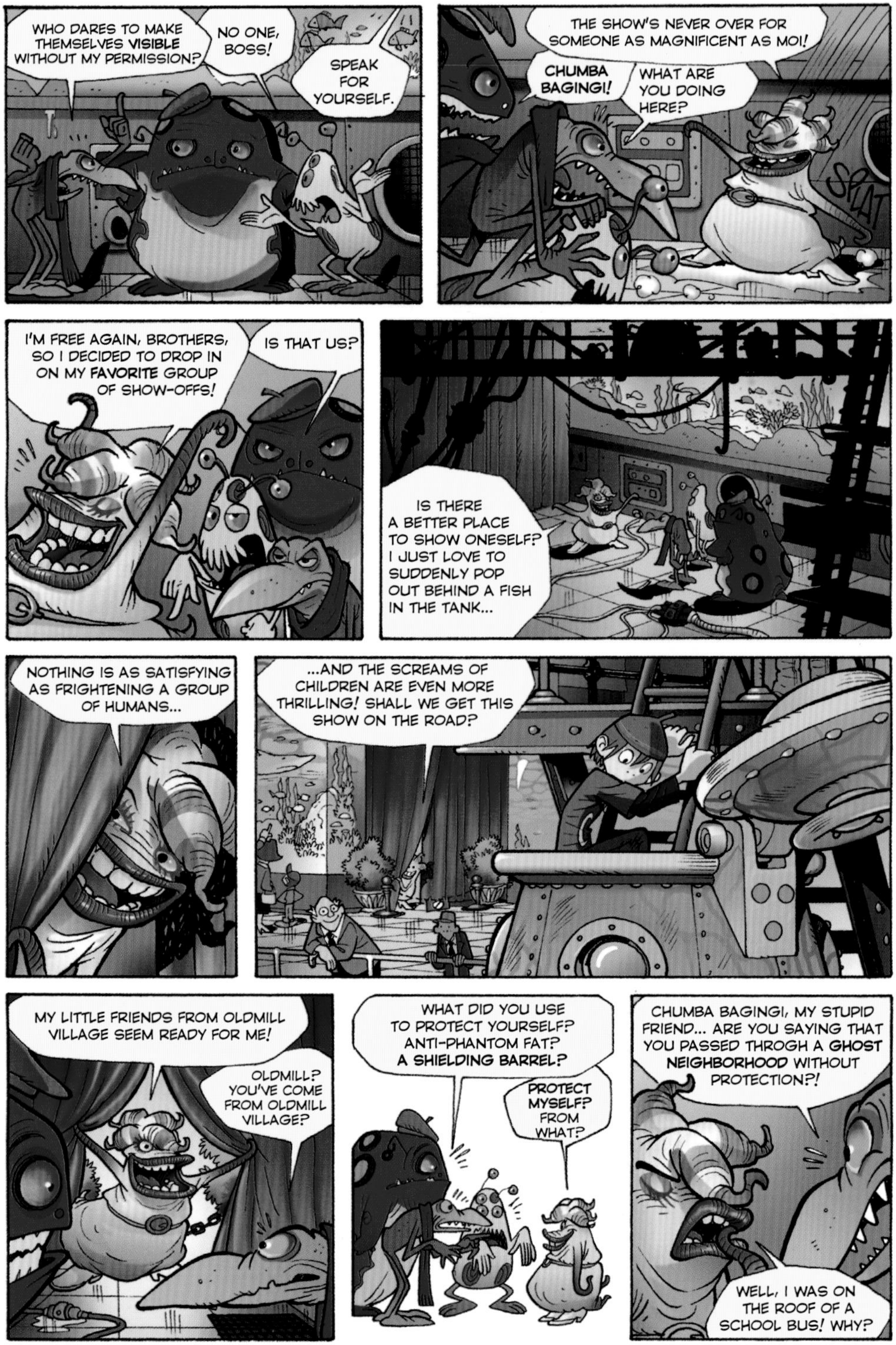
WHO DARES TO MAKE THEMSELVES VISIBLE WITHOUT MY PERMISSION?
NO ONE, BOSS!
SPEAK FOR YOURSELF.
THE SHOW'S NEVER OVER FOR SOMEONE AS MAGNIFICENT AS MOI!
CHUMBA BAGINGI!
WHAT ARE YOU DOING HERE?
SPLAT
I'M FREE AGAIN, BROTHERS, SO I DECIDED TO DROP IN ON MY FAVORITE GROUP OF SHOW-OFFS!
IS THAT US?
IS THERE A BETTER PLACE TO SHOW ONESELF? I JUST LOVE TO SUDDENLY POP OUT BEHIND A FISH IN THE TANK...
NOTHING IS AS SATISFYING AS FRIGHTENING A GROUP OF HUMANS...
...AND THE SCREAMS OF CHILDREN ARE EVEN MORE THRILLING! SHALL WE GET THIS SHOW ON THE ROAD?
MY LITTLE FRIENDS FROM OLDMILL VILLAGE SEEM READY FOR ME!
OLDMILL? YOU'VE COME FROM OLDMILL VILLAGE?
WHAT DID YOU USE TO PROTECT YOURSELF? ANTI-PHANTOM FAT? A SHIELDING BARREL?
PROTECT MYSELF? FROM WHAT?
CHUMBA BAGINGI, MY STUPID FRIEND... ARE YOU SAYING THAT YOU PASSED THROGH A GHOST NEIGHBORHOOD WITHOUT PROTECTION?!
WELL, I WAS ON THE ROOF OF A SCHOOL BUS! WHY?

BECAUSE THAT'S A GREAT WAY TO ATTRACT A BLACK PHANTOM!

GAAA AAARG!

TWO BLACK PHANTOMS, TO BE PRECISE.

QUICK, EVERYONE TURN INVISIBLE!

AAA AAAH!

TO THE SUBMARINE!

THEY WON'T FIND US IN THERE!

PROBLEMS, CAPTAIN?

JUST... GNNNN... A HINGE THAT NEEDS OILING! IN A SEC WE'LL BE WEIGHING ANCHOR!

COME ON! COME ON! INSIDE! ME NO HOLD MUCH LONGER!

CLUNK

GASP! PUF! HUF! HUF!

HEY! HERE'S CHUMBA! BUT WHO ARE THE OTHERS?

LOOK, ZICK! AN ANGEL FISH!

ITS SCIENTIFIC NAME IS HOLACANTUS CILIARIS! ISN'T IT MAGNIFICENT?

TH-THRILLING!

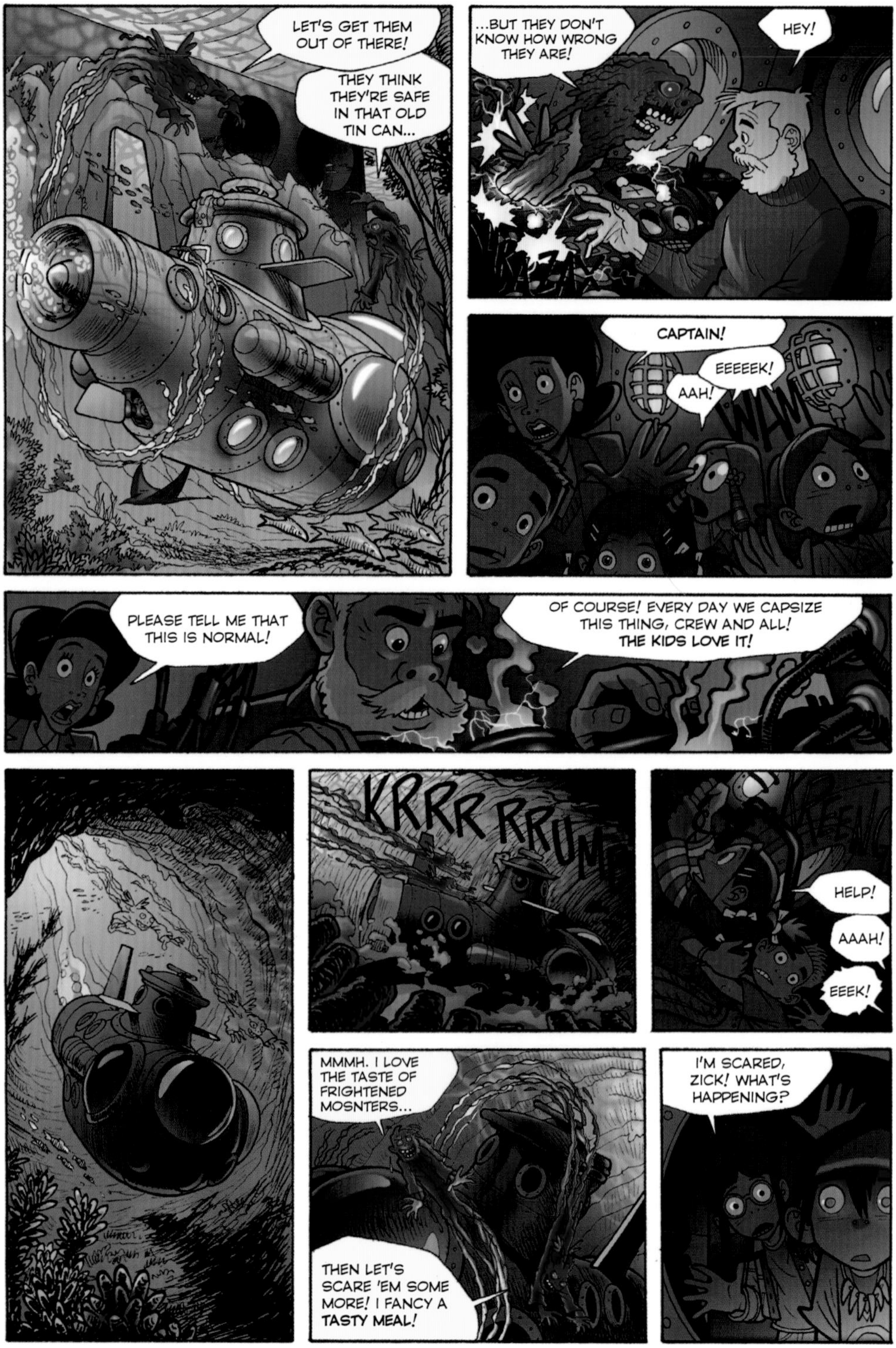
LET'S GET THEM OUT OF THERE!
THEY THINK THEY'RE SAFE IN THAT OLD TIN CAN...
...BUT THEY DON'T KNOW HOW WRONG THEY ARE!
HEY!
CAPTAIN!
EEEEEK!
AAH!
WAM
PLEASE TELL ME THAT THIS IS NORMAL!
OF COURSE! EVERY DAY WE CAPSIZE THIS THING, CREW AND ALL! THE KIDS LOVE IT!
KRRR RRRUMB
HELP!
AAAH!
EEEK!
MMMH. I LOVE THE TASTE OF FRIGHTENED MOSNTERS...
THEN LET'S SCARE 'EM SOME MORE! I FANCY A TASTY MEAL!
I'M SCARED, ZICK! WHAT'S HAPPENING?

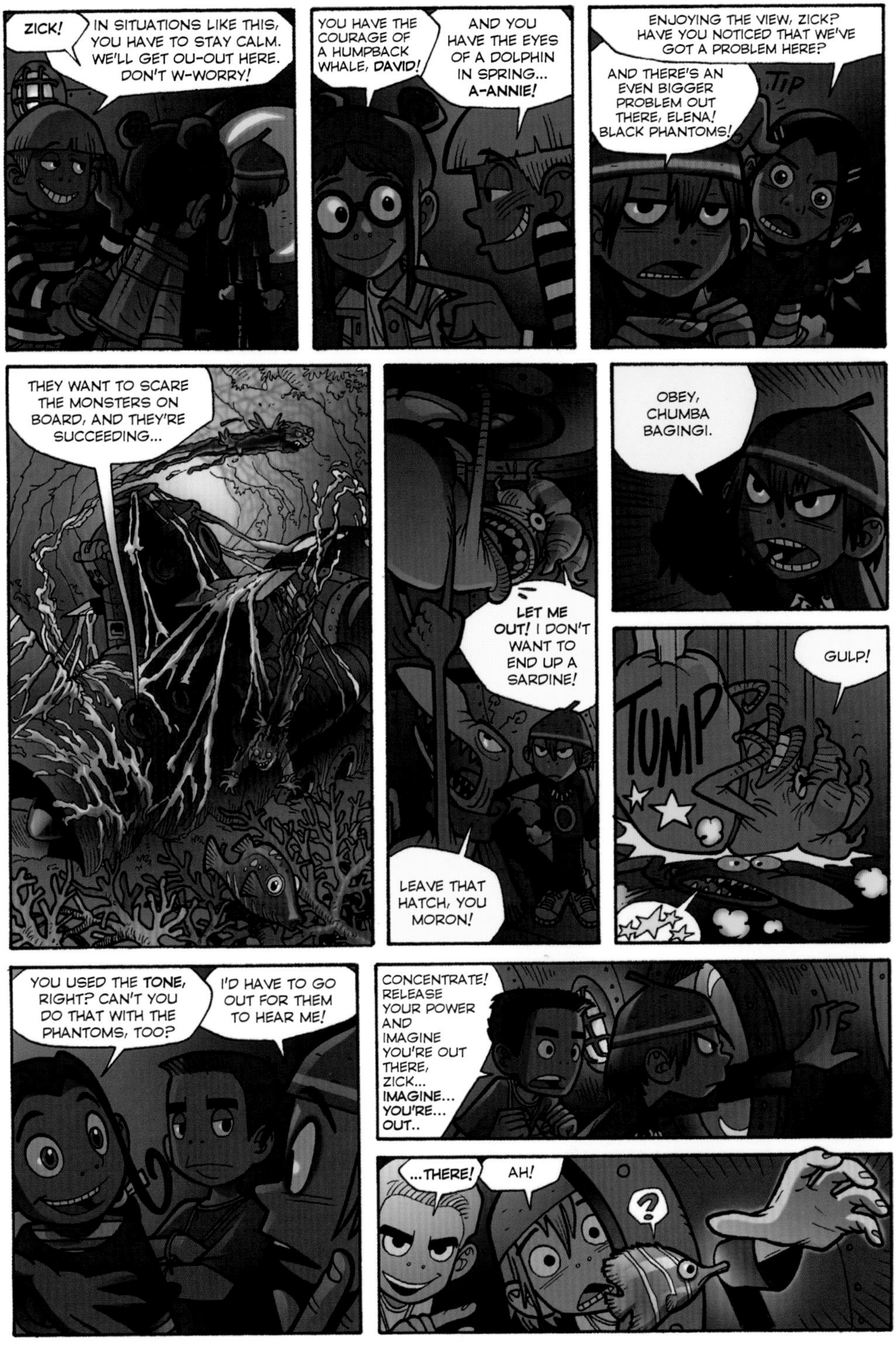
ZICK!
IN SITUATIONS LIKE THIS, YOU HAVE TO STAY CALM. WE'LL GET OU-OUT HERE. DON'T W-WORRY!
YOU HAVE THE COURAGE OF A HUMPBACK WHALE, DAVID!
AND YOU HAVE THE EYES OF A DOLPHIN IN SPRING... A-ANNIE!
ENJOYING THE VIEW, ZICK? HAVE YOU NOTICED THAT WE'VE GOT A PROBLEM HERE?
AND THERE'S AN EVEN BIGGER PROBLEM OUT THERE, ELENA! BLACK PHANTOMS!
TIP
THEY WANT TO SCARE THE MONSTERS ON BOARD, AND THEY'RE SUCCEEDING...
LET ME OUT! I DON'T WANT TO END UP A SARDINE!
LEAVE THAT HATCH, YOU MORON!
OBEY, CHUMBA BAGINGI.
GULP!
TUMP
YOU USED THE TONE, RIGHT? CAN'T YOU DO THAT WITH THE PHANTOMS, TOO?
I'D HAVE TO GO OUT FOR THEM TO HEAR ME!
CONCENTRATE! RELEASE YOUR POWER AND IMAGINE YOU'RE OUT THERE, ZICK... IMAGINE... YOU'RE... OUT..
...THERE!
AH!
?

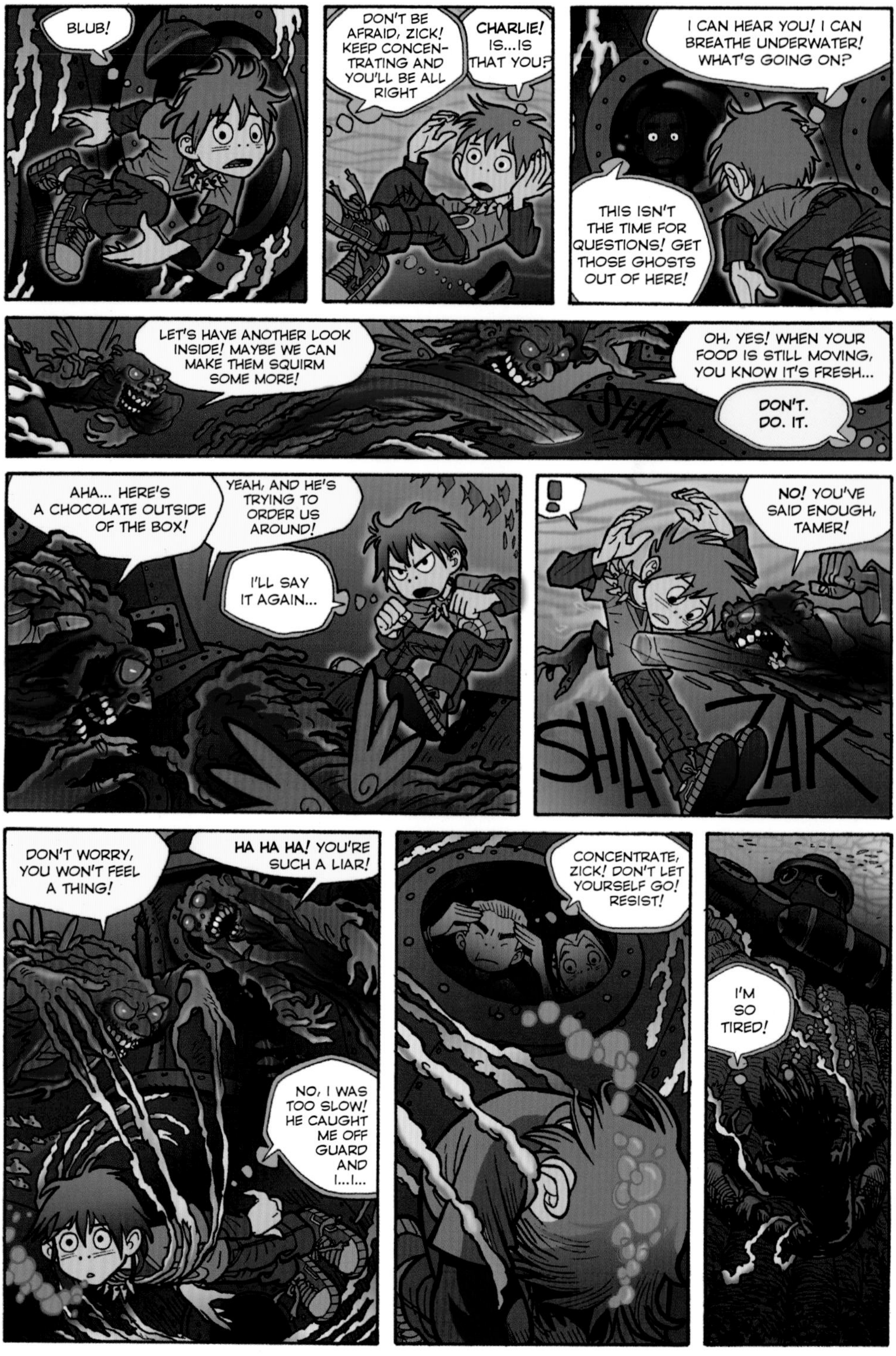
BLUB!
DON'T BE AFRAID, ZICK! KEEP CONCEN-TRATING AND YOU'LL BE ALL RIGHT
CHARLIE! IS...IS THAT YOU?
I CAN HEAR YOU! I CAN BREATHE UNDERWATER! WHAT'S GOING ON?
THIS ISN'T THE TIME FOR QUESTIONS! GET THOSE GHOSTS OUT OF HERE!
LET'S HAVE ANOTHER LOOK INSIDE! MAYBE WE CAN MAKE THEM SQUIRM SOME MORE!
OH, YES! WHEN YOUR FOOD IS STILL MOVING, YOU KNOW IT'S FRESH...
DON'T. DO. IT.
SHAK
AHA... HERE'S A CHOCOLATE OUTSIDE OF THE BOX!
YEAH, AND HE'S TRYING TO ORDER US AROUND!
I'LL SAY IT AGAIN...
!
NO! YOU'VE SAID ENOUGH, TAMER!
SHA-ZAK
DON'T WORRY, YOU WON'T FEEL A THING!
HA HA HA! YOU'RE SUCH A LIAR!
NO, I WAS TOO SLOW! HE CAUGHT ME OFF GUARD AND I...I...
CONCENTRATE, ZICK! DON'T LET YOURSELF GO! RESIST!
I'M SO TIRED!

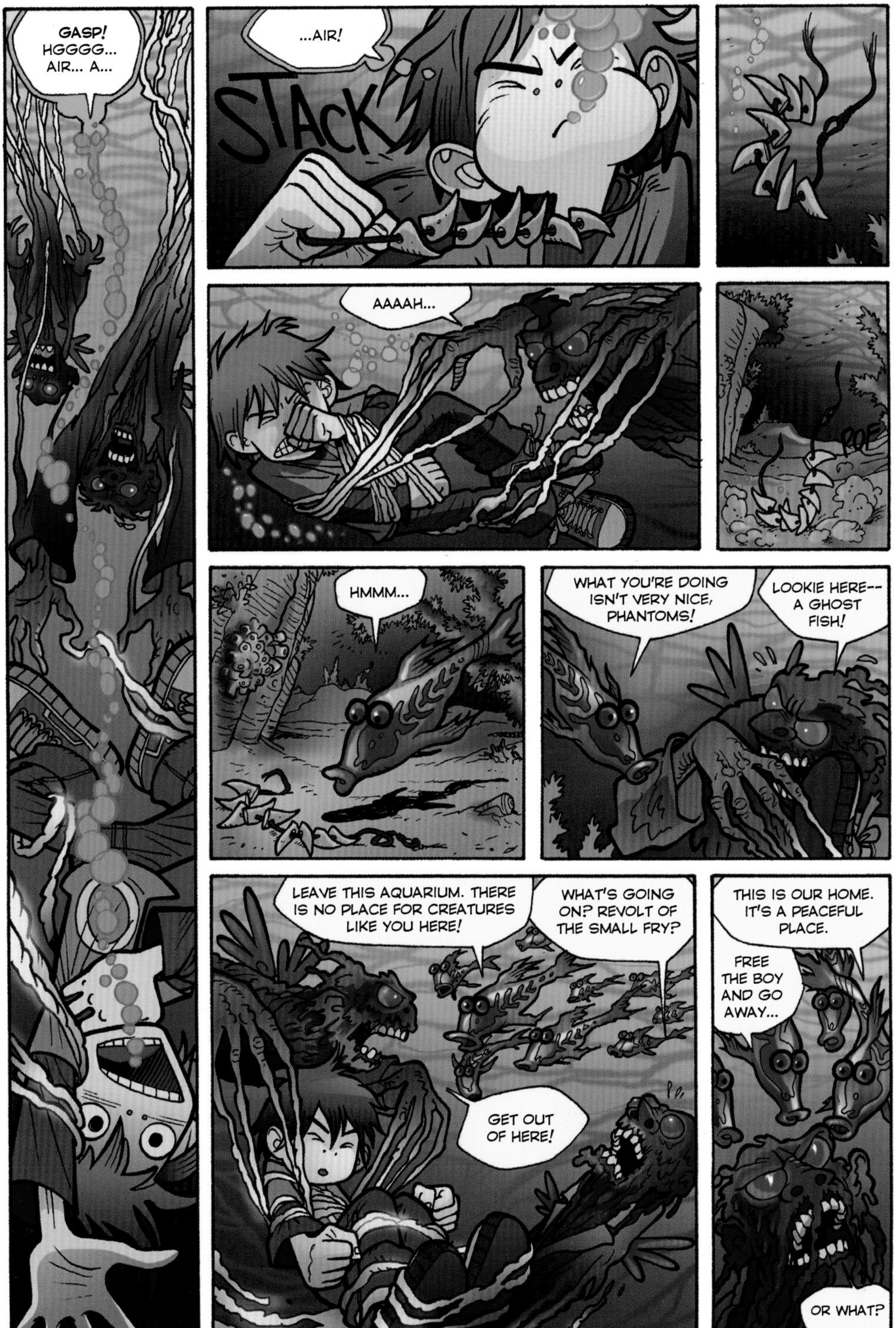
GASP! HGGGG... AIR... A...
...AIR!
STACK
AAAAH...
POF
HMMM...
WHAT YOU'RE DOING ISN'T VERY NICE, PHANTOMS!
LOOKIE HERE-- A GHOST FISH!
LEAVE THIS AQUARIUM. THERE IS NO PLACE FOR CREATURES LIKE YOU HERE!
WHAT'S GOING ON? REVOLT OF THE SMALL FRY?
GET OUT OF HERE!
THIS IS OUR HOME. IT'S A PEACEFUL PLACE.
FREE THE BOY AND GO AWAY...
OR WHAT?

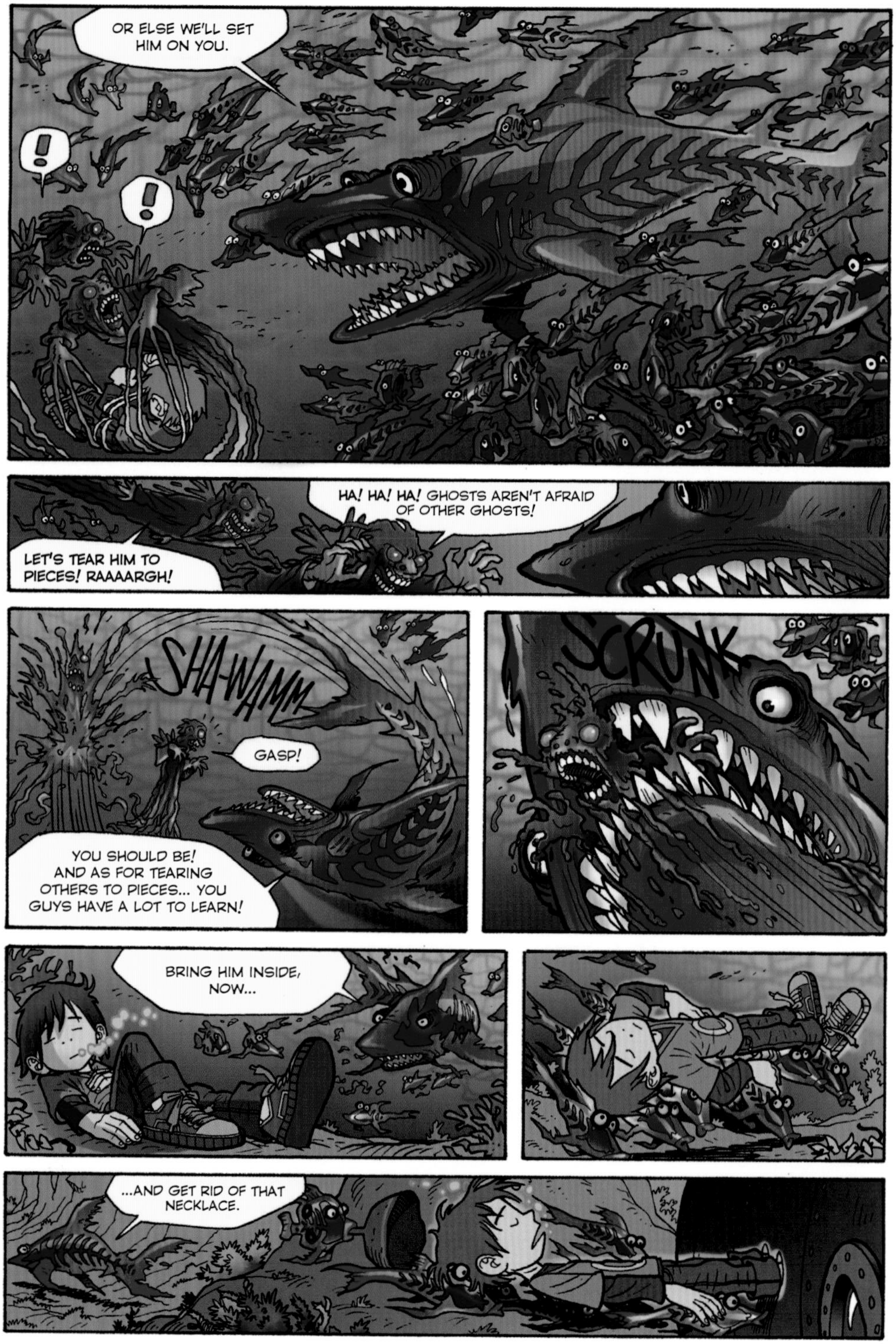
OR ELSE WE'LL SET HIM ON YOU.
!
!
HA! HA! HA! GHOSTS AREN'T AFRAID OF OTHER GHOSTS!
LET'S TEAR HIM TO PIECES! RAAAARGH!
SHA-WAMM
GASP!
YOU SHOULD BE! AND AS FOR TEARING OTHERS TO PIECES... YOU GUYS HAVE A LOT TO LEARN!
SCRUNK
BRING HIM INSIDE, NOW...
...AND GET RID OF THAT NECKLACE.

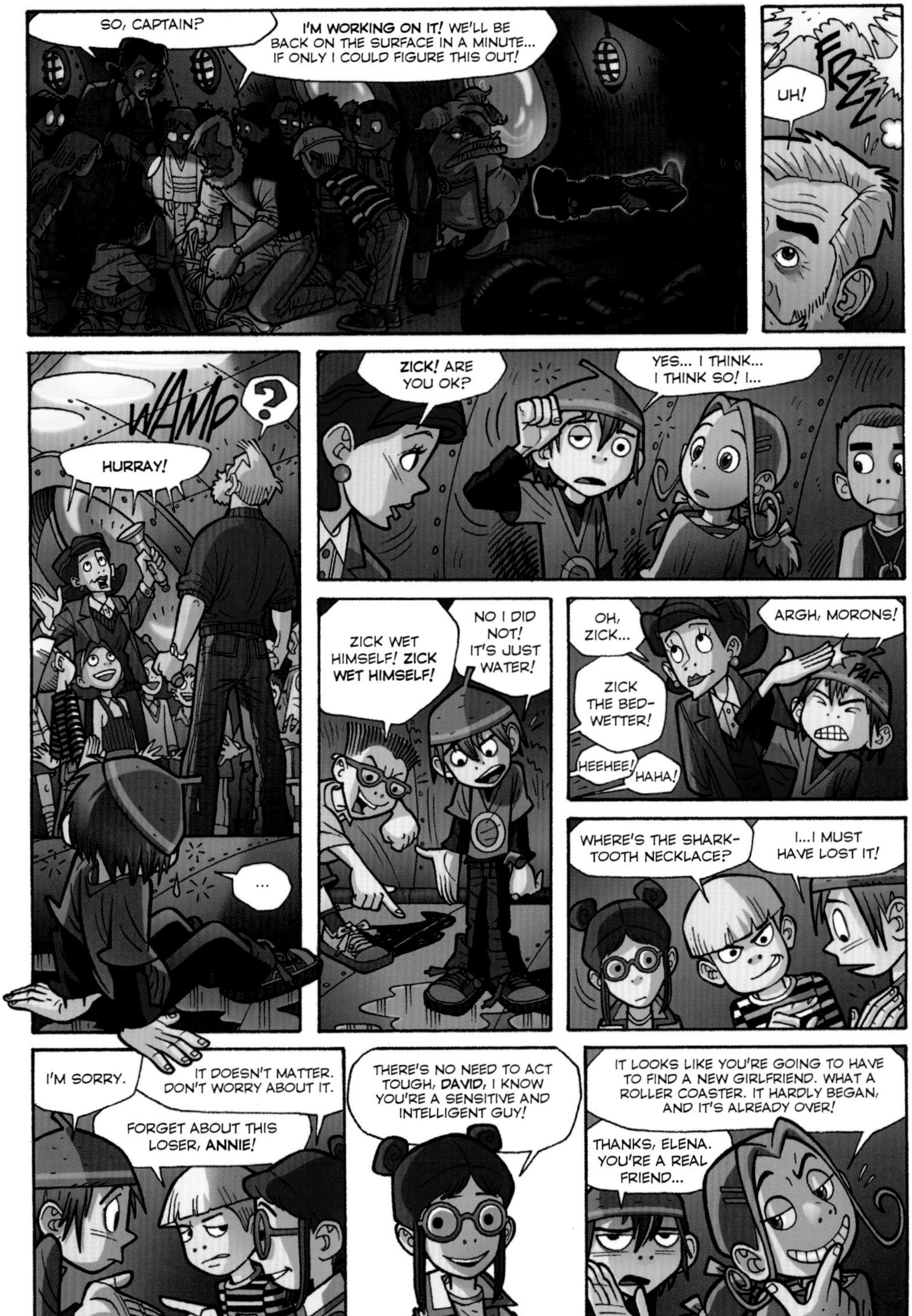
SO, CAPTAIN?
I'M WORKING ON IT! WE'LL BE BACK ON THE SURFACE IN A MINUTE... IF ONLY I COULD FIGURE THIS OUT!
FRZZ
UH!
WAMP
?
HURRAY!
...
ZICK! ARE YOU OK?
YES... I THINK... I THINK SO! I...
ZICK WET HIMSELF! ZICK WET HIMSELF!
NO I DID NOT! IT'S JUST WATER!
OH, ZICK...
ARGH, MORONS!
ZICK THE BED-WETTER!
PAF
HEEHEE!
HAHA!
WHERE'S THE SHARK-TOOTH NECKLACE?
I...I MUST HAVE LOST IT!
I'M SORRY.
IT DOESN'T MATTER. DON'T WORRY ABOUT IT.
FORGET ABOUT THIS LOSER, ANNIE!
THERE'S NO NEED TO ACT TOUGH, DAVID, I KNOW YOU'RE A SENSITIVE AND INTELLIGENT GUY!
IT LOOKS LIKE YOU'RE GOING TO HAVE TO FIND A NEW GIRLFRIEND. WHAT A ROLLER COASTER. IT HARDLY BEGAN, AND IT'S ALREADY OVER!
THANKS, ELENA. YOU'RE A REAL FRIEND...

WHAT A CRAZY DAY! SO MANY THINGS HAVE HAPPENED... **TOO MANY NOW!** ALL I WANT TO DO IS GO HOME.

BUT WHAT ABOUT CHUMBA BAGING!?

I'LL SEE TO HIM. I SEE YOU'VE MANAGED VERY WELL ON YOUR OWN...ALMOST.

TIMOTHY!

AS USUAL, TONS OF WEIRD THINGS HAPPENED TO ME, BUT CHARLIE HELPED A LOT!

CHARLIE WHO?

CHARLIE...

WHERE'D HE GO?

EPILOGUE #1: THE BARRYMORES' HOUSE.

I PROTEST MOST HEARTILY! YOU CANNOT TREAT ME THIS WAY! IT IS MY **RIGHT** TO ATTEMPT ESCAPE!

SURE...

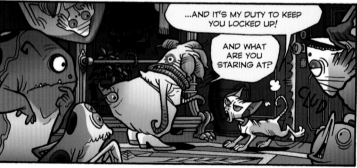

...AND IT'S MY DUTY TO KEEP YOU LOCKED UP!

AND WHAT ARE YOU STARING AT?

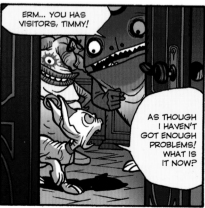

ERM... YOU HAS VISITORS, TIMMY!

AS THOUGH I HAVEN'T GOT ENOUGH PROBLEMS! WHAT IS IT NOW?

AM I DISTURBING YOU, TUTOR TIMOTHY-MOTH?

92

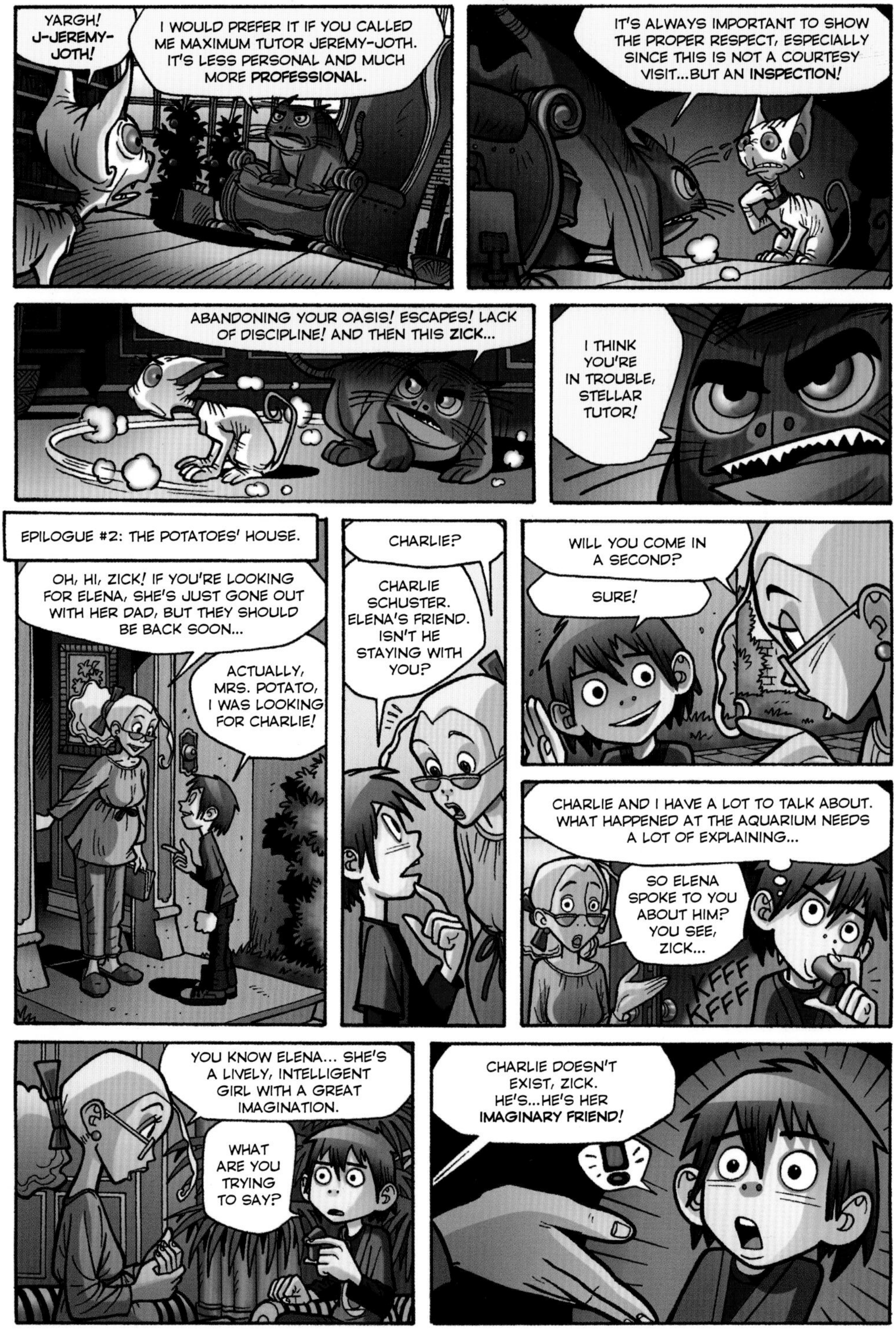
YARGH! J-JEREMY-JOTH!
I WOULD PREFER IT IF YOU CALLED ME MAXIMUM TUTOR JEREMY-JOTH. IT'S LESS PERSONAL AND MUCH MORE PROFESSIONAL.
IT'S ALWAYS IMPORTANT TO SHOW THE PROPER RESPECT, ESPECIALLY SINCE THIS IS NOT A COURTESY VISIT...BUT AN INSPECTION!
ABANDONING YOUR OASIS! ESCAPES! LACK OF DISCIPLINE! AND THEN THIS ZICK...
I THINK YOU'RE IN TROUBLE, STELLAR TUTOR!
EPILOGUE #2: THE POTATOES' HOUSE.
OH, HI, ZICK! IF YOU'RE LOOKING FOR ELENA, SHE'S JUST GONE OUT WITH HER DAD, BUT THEY SHOULD BE BACK SOON...
ACTUALLY, MRS. POTATO, I WAS LOOKING FOR CHARLIE!
CHARLIE?
CHARLIE SCHUSTER. ELENA'S FRIEND. ISN'T HE STAYING WITH YOU?
WILL YOU COME IN A SECOND?
SURE!
CHARLIE AND I HAVE A LOT TO TALK ABOUT. WHAT HAPPENED AT THE AQUARIUM NEEDS A LOT OF EXPLAINING...
SO ELENA SPOKE TO YOU ABOUT HIM? YOU SEE, ZICK...
KFFF KFFF
YOU KNOW ELENA... SHE'S A LIVELY, INTELLIGENT GIRL WITH A GREAT IMAGINATION.
WHAT ARE YOU TRYING TO SAY?
CHARLIE DOESN'T EXIST, ZICK. HE'S...HE'S HER IMAGINARY FRIEND!

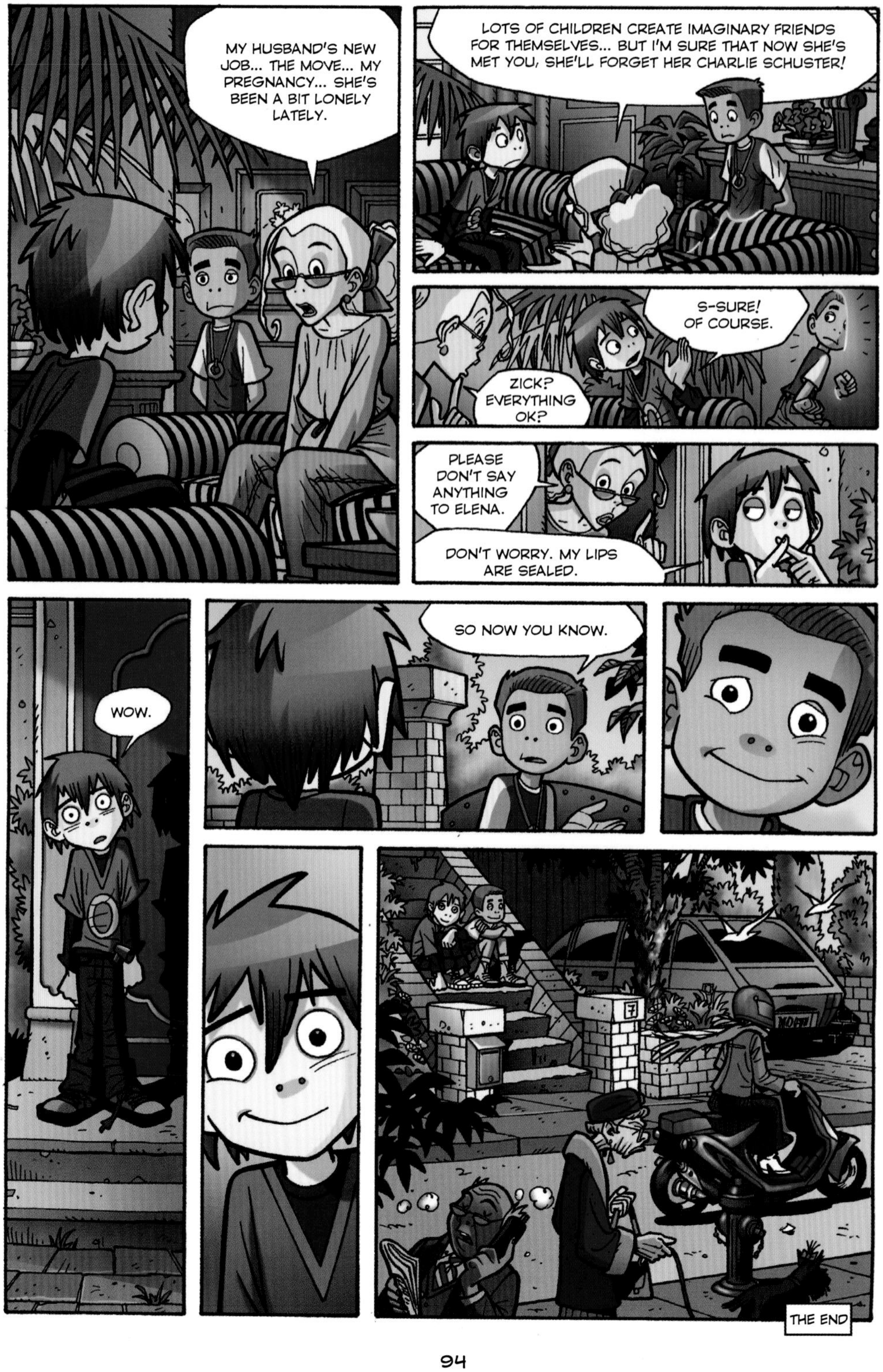
MY HUSBAND'S NEW JOB... THE MOVE... MY PREGNANCY... SHE'S BEEN A BIT LONELY LATELY.
LOTS OF CHILDREN CREATE IMAGINARY FRIENDS FOR THEMSELVES... BUT I'M SURE THAT NOW SHE'S MET YOU, SHE'LL FORGET HER CHARLIE SCHUSTER!
ZICK? EVERYTHING OK?
S-SURE! OF COURSE.
PLEASE DON'T SAY ANYTHING TO ELENA.
DON'T WORRY. MY LIPS ARE SEALED.
WOW.
SO NOW YOU KNOW.
7
THE END

An Imprint of Insight Editions
PO Box 3088
San Rafael, CA 94912
www.insightcomics.com

Find us on Facebook:
www.facebook.com/InsightEditionsComics

Follow us on Twitter:
@InsightComics

Follow us on Instagram:
Insight_Comics

Published in the United States in 2020 by Insight Editions. Originally published in Italian in two parts as *Monster Allergy Collection Vol. 5* and *Monster Allergy Collection Vol. 6* by Tunué, Italy, in 2017.

Library of Congress Cataloging-in-Publication Data available.

ISBN: 978-1-68383-718-3

Publisher: Raoul Goff
President: Kate Jerome
Associate Publisher: Vanessa Lopez
Design Support: Brooke McCullum
Executive Editor: Mark Irwin
Associate Editor: Holly Fisher
Senior Production Editor: Elaine Ou
Production Coordinator: Eden Orlesky

ROOTS of PEACE   REPLANTED PAPER

Insight Editions, in association with Roots of Peace, will plant two trees for each tree used in the manufacturing of this book. Roots of Peace is an internationally renowned humanitarian organization dedicated to eradicating land mines worldwide and converting war-torn lands into productive farms and wildlife habitats. Roots of Peace will plant two million fruit and nut trees in Afghanistan and provide farmers there with the skills and support necessary for sustainable land use.

Manufactured in China by Insight Editions

10 9 8 7 6 5 4 3 2 1